LOCH NESS

A NOVEL

MATT KUNZ

Dear Dave,
Keep Believing!
your Friend,
Matt Kunz

LOCH NESS
Copyright 2017 Matt Kunz

Twitter: @MattKunz59
www.facebook.com/mattkunzauthor
mattkunz59.wordpress.com

Print ISBN 978-0-9976298-4-2

Library of Congress Control Number - 2017908435

This is a work of **fiction**. Names, characters, businesses, places, events and incidents are either the products of the author's imagination or used in a fictitious manner. Any resemblance to actual persons, living or dead, or actual events is purely coincidental, and that includes the Loch Ness monster!

DEDICATION

To Jack, who made every day an adventure.

CHAPTER 1

"I'm na' off tae die t'night." Sean Paterson ducked his head under the hood of his raincoat. The rain fell steady under the black clouds. Sunset came early, darkening the Highland hills with stormy shadows. The weather had driven the other evening boaters home, but Sean had to press on. He owed it to Marella.

He piled his equipment onto the dock next to his small rowboat. Coolers, fishing poles, nets, flashlights, life jacket, fishing hat. The rain and the shadows blurred their contours. These were tools for a fisherman, not for a scientist. He sighed as the rain continued to fall.

"Nothin's easy," he said. He grabbed the plastic handle on the cooler. Next to him, the swaying from the waves rocked the boat, splashing water into the air. The dock rolled up and down, and he felt his shoe slip. Steadying himself, he lifted the cooler, but he dropped it as the wet plastic handle slipped from his fingers.

I'm na' made fur this!

He stood up, spun around, and threw his hands into the air. The dock bounced and he lost his balance. He fell to a knee. The rain increased.

Sean gathered himself. He remembered that James O'Neil had drowned when he tried to go fishing in weather like this.

Don' think abou' tha'!

He scanned the dock. Was anyone around? Several boats cast moving shadows as they rocked in the waves. He smelled the ozone in the mist. Rain fell in front of the glow from the electric security lights.

But the dock was empty.

No one had heard his frustration. All he heard was the sound the rain made as it splatted upon his raincoat.

Sean decided to get on both his hands and knees. Balancing himself, he grabbed the cooler's handle once more, and brought it to the edge of the unsteady dock. He gripped the boat, but the rolling waves made it hard for him to hold it. He gritted his teeth, and he jerked the cooler towards the boat. The cooler spun around and tumbled in the boat.

Still on his knees, Sean raised his hands and shouted "Ah, ha!" but a sudden move by the dock frightened him and he quickly brought his hands back to the wood. Though he was unbalanced, he was encouraged that he managed to get his cooler in the boat. The rain splashed off the wood onto his face.

Maybe after t'night, Marella, ye'll believe me. Maybe after t'night.

Sean loaded the wet equipment. Next, he put on his life jacket, and he buckled the straps. The rowboat clanged as a violent wave knocked it against the dock. Sean moved his legs and sat on the edge of the wood. The boat moved constantly, held to the dock by two heavy ropes. The wood creaked and groaned with each surge of the water. How would he get into the boat? He imagined what would happen if he slipped from the dock and fell into the water. He might hit his head on the wood, the boat, or both. He might lose consciousness. With no one around, he would drown. Moments passed as he examined his plan. He watched for a rhythm, but he couldn't identify a pattern.

"Damn it all!"

He shifted closer to the edge, and lowered himself so he was on his belly. He moved his right leg then his left over the sides of the dock and over the edge of the tiny rowboat. He felt nervous, straining his leg muscles to find something steady, but everything moved. He grabbed the rail of the boat to steady himself, worrying that the rain might cause him to slip. He shifted his weight.

Suddenly, he lost his grip, and gravity took over. He yelled and felt the scrape of the wood on his belly. He raised his arms to grasp something, but his head hit the edge of the boat, and he felt his teeth knock together.

He had fallen into the boat.

Though dizzy, he was relieved he wasn't in the water. As the boat rocked, Sean gathered himself and sat down on the wooden bench. "Waves are pure tough t'night," he said, and he untied the ropes. He grasped his oars, and he rowed away from the dock.

"Hang on, Sean. Keep rowin'!" His muscles ached as he rowed. He couldn't steer. The waves were in control. He noticed he had travelled almost thirty meters away from where he had launched. Under one of the lights, he thought a shadow moved.

Was it th' ghost o' O'Neil?

He rowed, and prayed that he'd return alive.

* * *

Thirty minutes later, the clouds had moved east and, though the waves subsided, Sean's heart raced. The first quarter moon and the stars shone their light upon him. The frost of his breath reflected hints of the moon's light.

When he had reached his destination, he stopped rowing. His grip remained tight upon the oar handles. The nearby landmarks cast dark shadows. As he had done on every attempt, he took a few moments to reflect. He was in the same place he was thirty years before, near St. Michael's Catholic Church, where he saw the monster. He had been to this spot several times, and each time he tried a different experiment to bring the monster back. Of course, no one believed him, except for Marella. Well, at least she used to. She had grown up, and she no longer believed. But he continued to search. He had seen it before. He believed he would again.

The Church's silhouette stood strong like a castle, its cross imposing in the night sky. The priests lived in the rectory next to it, and many of their windows reflected soft electric glows. He imagined the priests as they counseled volunteers, prepared couples for the sacrament of marriage, or studied the word of God. Sean felt an affinity to their study of mystery. He had his own mystery to solve, and it belonged somewhere in the waters below.

The fishing rods lay at Sean's feet. They were long and cumbersome. They swayed with the movement of the waves, but Sean's scientific mind knew these rods were the best he could buy.

They were strong, made to catch deep sea fish. At least that's what he had told the salesman. He wouldn't dare mention he was trying to catch a plesiosaur.

Sean grabbed the first fishing rod and stuck its handle in its holster. He laughed. Over the years, he had spent his life's savings on technical scientific equipment to find the monster. Back at his home he had sonar and heat sensor equipment, all attached to powerful computers. They collected dust locked up in his garage. He had tried the scientific approach over and over again throughout the years with no success of finding the Loch Ness monster. Tonight, Sean humbled himself to the skills of a fisherman.

Except he knew nothing about fishing. He considered himself a scientist, not an outdoorsman. He remembered a conversation he had with a local fisherman. The fisherman had explained to Sean how it was they who had found the wonders of the world. It was fishermen who explored beyond the horizons. It was fishermen who stumbled upon the unexplained. It was fishermen who…

A wave rocked the boat, and Sean bounced on the small bench. His stomach swayed by the sudden move. He had to let go of the oar and grab the rail to keep from falling overboard.

"Hell, I'm na fisherman!" shouted Sean. Amidst the rocking, he set the remaining fishing rods in their holsters along the rails. He opened the cooler, and smelled the bait. He coughed at the fleshy scent, like ancient sailors did when they baited there hooks during whaling expeditions.

Of course, those sailors were on large vessels. He was on a rowboat.

At night.

He had found that during daylight, baiting a line on a rowboat was hard enough. Trying to do it in darkness was impossible.

To his right, a large and dangerous three-barbed hook swung in the misty air. He grabbed the line, careful to keep from getting pierced. He pulled his fingers down along the line to control the hook, and one of the pointed tips of the hook barely punctured his skin. He jerked his hand back, letting go of the line. The hook swung again.

"Canny, Sean!" he said, reminding himself to be careful.

He reached for the line a second time. This time he grasped it. The wet line slipped between his soaked fingers, and he controlled the hook.

Holding the hook with one hand, he reached inside the cooler with the other. He smelled the odor of the flesh as his fingers touched several large pieces of meat. Steak, mostly, but others were pork and fish. He grabbed a steak and baited it on the hook, sliding the flesh over the barbs.

He dropped the steak overboard, and he listened to the reel as the bait fell deep into the water. He felt relieved. It was his first successful baited hook. Last week, he had made an attempt. Instead of baiting a hook, however, he had managed to hook his forearm. He had to end his search early, and he had rowed his boat back to the dock. He never even thought to cut the wire, and he drove to the medic with the entire fishing rod still attached to his arm. The nurses had laughed he walked in holding the rod. Though the doctor was patient, Sean had felt embarrassed when they cut the line for him. He felt more embarrassed when they jabbed him with the needle to give him a tetanus shot.

But things were going his way tonight. In half an hour his five lines were cast and his baits were in the water.

I'm a fas' learner, he thought. *I guess now all I have tae do is wait.*

* * *

Several hours passed. A mist hovered over the water, and Sean made out St. Michael's silhouette. The surface of the water calmed below the night sky. Sean's back stiffened. The air felt cool and damp, but the raincoat and the life jacket kept him warm. He grabbed his fishing net in his hands and, standing it up between his legs, leaned on it for support. Swaying with the gentle rocking of the boat upon the water, he worried he might doze off to sleep.

He shook his head. "Got tae stay awake."

He hummed a song, then another. The black shadows of the church caught his attention. He noticed a light in one of the rectory windows.

Would a priest be up at this hour?

A song came to his memory, one he hadn't remembered in some time. He hummed it. The rhythm of the tune brought back visions from his youth. Where had he heard it before? He couldn't remember. As he swayed in the boat, he thumped the base of the net on the boat's hull, creating a slow rhythmic beat that echoed from the small rowboat. He thought other songs, and he thumped his net with each song's rhythm.

Two hours passed. The rectory was dark, and he remembered another song. Was it the same one he hummed before? He lifted his wrist and pulled back his coat sleeve. His watch said two-seventeen. "One more hour," he said. "Fur Marella." He hummed the song making the rhythmic beats on the boat's hull.

Suddenly, a sound startled him. One of the reels of his rod to whirred. He dropped the net, and reached over to grab the rod. "Wha' do I do?" he said. He grabbed the rod and lifted it from its holster. The reel whirred in front of him. He made a quick decision, and he locked the reel.

The rod jerked out of his hands and plunked into the water. Sean lost his balance at the force with which the rod leapt from his grasp, and he grabbed the rails to keep from falling overboard.

Another reel spun. Sean felt his heart leap. He jumped upon the rod. He wrapped his left arm around it, putting his body weight on top of it and pressed it to the edge of the boat. The line cut through his raincoat as it sped into the water.

He locked the reel.

The boat tipped. Cold water rushed over the rail and into the boat. He gasped, and water entered his mouth. He spat it out, but more water poured over the rails. Whatever had the line was too strong. It was pulling the boat!

He knew he couldn't hold the rod. He agonized over letting the rod go, but a moment later he watched as it jerked from his grasp and disappeared into the water. He grabbed the railing and held tight as the unsteady boat swayed from side to side, sloshing the water around his legs.

Silence.

"Wha' in th' world…?" He scanned the remaining rods. They stood in their places, untouched. He held his breath and listened.

Nothing.

He listened more.

Just his heart beat. His veins pulsed.

A thump! The boat lifted out of the water, and Sean screamed as it tipped to the port side. His stomach lurched. He smelled a strong odor, like rotting fish. Gravity leaned him over the waters, and he shifted his weight starboard, trying to keep the boat from capsizing. His grip on the rails failed. He panicked.

Then the boat fell, splashing its hull on the surface.

There was silence.

Sean's heart pounded inside his chest. He tried to hold his breath, but he couldn't control it. Everything closed in on him. He felt trapped. He listened, watching. He sensed something was hunting him. He twisted in the boat. What was in the water? The mist covered everything. That smell! What was it? Something had lifted the boat.

Could it be…?

He heard a noise, and the hairs on his neck and arms stiffened. He had never heard a sound like that before. It sounded ancient, prehistoric. He felt himself shaking. Would he die? Would he drown? Would he be eaten?

He peered over the edge of the port rail. Fear and excitement gripped him. Nothing appeared in the dark waters. The church silhouette loomed in the darkness. Should he pray?

Water splashed behind him.

"Wha' was tha'!"

A large, black fin and a muscular back crested the water. It moved gracefully as it broke through the surface, spreading fast dark ripples that radiated outward from its black leathery skin. The body dipped into the water, and then it was gone.

Sean's heart beat like a locomotive. His eyes widened, and he lost his breath. *Wha' tae do, wha' tae do?* He slid off the bench and crouched in the water behind the railing. *Would they attack? Wha' then?*

"Gaaaa!"

Sean heard a thump under the hull. The boat rocked. Sean's fingers dug into the railing. Large ripples reflected the moonlight. They rocked the small boat back and forth. Sean didn't dare to move.

A few moments passed. Sean froze as he crouched in the flooded rowboat. He noticed his clothes were soaked. His breath came under control. *Wha' next, wha' next?* The other rods remained in their holsters. None of the other reels had spun. The water was calm again, and except for the mist, nothing else was out of the ordinary.

Was it still under him? Would it come up suddenly, knock him over, and drag him down to the bottom of Loch Ness?

He sat motionless.

Waiting.

After several minutes, he mustered some courage, and he managed to peer over the rail into the Loch. The water glimmered in the moonlight, and the shadow of the church continued to dominate the landscape upon the shore.

He decided to stand and survey the area. His knees wobbled, but he steadied himself upon the boat as his feet sloshed in the water. There was no sign of the creature, just the moon reflecting in the water and the soft glow of Thurwick's lights. Next to Thurwick stood the towering presence of St. Michael's Catholic Church, resting like a monument upon the shores.

He raised his triumphant arms and yelled. His fear had turned to excitement. He had found it. After thirty years, he had finally found it.

I have tae call Marella and tell her!

Then he sat down in the rowboat, and he passed out.

CHAPTER 2

Tom wayne sat at the small table outside the Dixie Café in Buckhead, the popular area north of Atlanta. Evening had set in, and the weather was much warmer than he'd expect for March. His roommate, Bob, sat next to him. Tom enjoyed this table. They watched the people as they walked around Lenox Mall and Peachtree Street.

"You know," Bob said. "It was just a softball game. You didn't have to run over the catcher."

"Yes I did," Tom said. "We won, didn't we?"

"Remember Sun Tzu? To win without fighting is best."

"That's your problem. You're too philosophical."

"You know, life's about more than winning and losing."

Tom lifted his glass. "Given the choice, I'd rather win."

"Okay, tough guy. What about her?"

"Don't start." Tom blushed.

Bob scanned the restaurant. "I'm not seeing her."

"You always were an instigator."

"Wait," Bob said. "Did you run over that guy today to brag to her?"

"Don't be ridiculous," Tom said.

"Oh, man, you did." Bob laughed. "Why don't you just have a conversation with her?"

"Shoot. There she is." Tom's face flushed. Marella waited tables inside the restaurant, taking orders from guys from a competing softball team. Tom held his breath.

"You don't have to stare."

"Knock it off!"

Marella talked with the other team. She was so graceful, so natural. The team laughed. She talked with them pleasantly, but she rolled her eyes. She frowned, then backed away. As she walked away from their table to the patio, her shoulders tensed.

"She's coming!" said Tom.

"Maybe third time's a charm," Bob said.

Marella entered the patio. "Ye're back," she said. Tom loved her Scottish accent. Her skin was pure white. Her hair had the feel of autumn amidst her curls.

"Yes. Yes, we are," said Bob.

Tom tried to act cool. "Hi." No other words came to him.

"Did ye two win t'day?" Marella asked.

Bob nudged Tom with his fist.

"We did," said Tom. "I ran over the catcher at the end of the game and earned the winning score."

"Ye did? Did ye break his shank, tae?" Marella asked.

Tom check with Bob. *Shank?*

Bob pointed to his leg.

Tom lowered his eyes. *I'm not winning.*

"What'll ye two have?"

Bob placed his order. Marella waited for Tom. "I'll pass," he said.

"Suit yerself." Marella went inside.

Tom admired the small of her back as she walked away.

"Not so eager, my friend," Bob said.

"What was I thinking? I mean, really. What kind of chance does a guy like me have with a girl like her?"

"Well, look on the bright side. I think you actually did break that guy's leg."

"What am I doing?" He buried his head in his hands. It had always been this way for him. Fight for everything. Overcome the obstacles. Win in dramatic fashion. If he didn't win, he didn't eat. Nor did he experience love.

Except Marella threw all of that upside down. He imagined impressing her, but any attempts to do so only drove her away.

If only there was a way to recognize an opportunity.

He heard laughing inside. Through the window, standing near the other team, Marella appeared upset. One of the men reached out to grab her clothes, and she backed away. Tom rose, and rushed inside.

As he moved towards the action, Marella said, "Don' touch me."

One of the men replied, "Come on. It doesn't have to be that way."

Tom stepped between Marella and the men. There had to have been twelve of them. "Hey, have respect for the lady." He expected one of them to punch him in the stomach.

One of the men stood up. He was six inches taller than Tom, with broad shoulders. "Don't you get in the way of our business," he said.

Tom glared at the man, and then he noticed his muscles. He could get pummeled, but it didn't matter. Marella deserved respect, and he was going to make sure they understood that.

Tom clenched his jaw. "What are you going to do? Break my leg?" He winked at Marella.

The giant pointed at Tom's shirt. "So you play softball, too? Well, when we play your team, I'd watch your back."

"Grow up." Tom turned to Marella. "Are you ok?"

Marella nodded.

"If they treat you bad again, you let me know, and I'll help your management team escort them out."

Tom faced the giant. His legs stiffened, and he clenched his fist. The giant frowned. Tom nodded. Facing such a large man, he knew a neutral outcome would be a victory. Tom backed up. The giant, realizing others were watching him, sat in his seat. Tom grinned, knowing he had won.

He returned to his table in the patio. As he sat down, Bob said, "Now that's how to impress a lady."

Tom gave a thumbs-up. He didn't want to admit to him that his knees were shaking. He was concerned about Marella. The other team talked in hushed tones. Every now and then one of them glared at him. He wouldn't let them affect him.

He watched Marella. She was making drinks. Her simple movements captured his attention even as she wore her restaurant outfit. He imagined getting to know her more, her thoughts, her personality. If he could just find the right moment.

"Hey, hero," Bob said. "When she comes back, you have to ask her out."

"What, with you here?"

"You just faced down a six-foot-four monster. I'm a nobody."

"You know…"

"I have tae thank ye." Marella said. She stood next to Tom. She placed a drink in front of him. "I know ye said ye didn' wan' anythin', but this is compliments o' th' house."

Tom blushed again. He admired her green eyes as they shimmered in afternoon light.

Oh, hell, he thought.

"Marella," Tom said. "Would you do the honor of going out with me tomorrow night?" He grimaced. *She's going to say no. I just know she's going to say no.*

"T'morrow's Sunday, and I don' work t'morrow," she said. "I do attend evening Mass, bu' maybe somethin' after."

She didn't say no.

Tom grinned. "Could I pick you up at your place?"

"I'm at th' Buckhead Apartments off Peachtree Street," she said. "My lest name's Paterson. When ye get tae th' box, just find my lest name, and I'll let ye in."

"What time?"

"Seven?"

"I'll be there."

"Aye, I'll look forward tae it." Marella's eyes sparkled at Tom before she went back inside.

"Did you hear that? She said she'll look forward to it!"

"You are the man!" Bob said.

Tom grinned, the feeling of victory rushing through his veins. He decided, no matter what happened next, he'd never forget this moment. He raised his triumphant arms and closed his eyes. Then he let out a satisfied "Yes!"

CHAPTER 3

"**D**on't blow this." Tom felt nervous and excited at the same time. Was he too prepared? Was he trying too hard? Could he do more? Would it be too much? *How in the world does one make a date perfect?*

He stood in a t-shirt and his boxers. Several clothing items were set out on his bed: four different colored shirts, three different style pants, and three different pairs of shoes.

"Hey, which ones should I go with?" he yelled.

Bob appeared in the doorway. "Just go with what feels right."

"You're no help. I can't screw this up."

"If you don't get a grip, you will screw it up." He disappeared down the hallway.

"I'm going to go with the golf shirt and the slacks."

"On a Sunday?" shouted Bob. "Dude, the workweek is tomorrow. Don't make her think of work on a Sunday night."

"You're right. Jeans it is."

"Do you have flowers? Is your car washed?"

Tom stepped into the hallway. Bob's door was closed, but the apartment walls were so thin that sound traveled right through them. "Man, don't put so much pressure on me," he said. "Yes, the car's washed, and I'm going to get flowers on the way."

Bob didn't answer.

Tom slid on the golf shirt and pulled on his nicest pair of jeans. Then, for the third time that afternoon, he flossed and brushed his teeth. He sprayed some cologne in the air, and he walked through it. The whole time, he felt like an idiot, but the excitement of Marella waiting for him in an hour focused his efforts. He examined himself in the mirror one more time before he knocked on Bob's door.

"You ready?" Bob opened the door. His room was a mess, with clothes hanging from the back of an office chair. His bed was a mattress in the corner, and Bob believed the sheets hadn't been made or washed in a month, about what he'd expect from a twenty-something year old bachelor.

"How do I look?"

"Good," Bob said.

"If this works, you'll have to find another roommate."

"Just don't be overeager."

"Wish me luck."

"You'll do fine."

Tom walked through den, and opened the front door.

"Hey, if you're going to be out past eleven, be sure to call."

"Thanks, Dad!" Tom shut the front door behind him, and he hummed as he trotted to his car.

As Tom turned the key in the ignition, he imagined the night in his mind. He wanted to ask her about her accent, and how she came to America. What was she was doing in Atlanta when she could have chosen to go anywhere? He pictured her green eyes and her curly hair, and how everything about her glowed, making the world more beautiful.

His mind circled on these thoughts as he picked up her flowers from the Kroger floral department. Funny, he had never noticed flowers much before. The colors all around him had brightened as he drove through Buckhead, and the afternoon was perfect as he arrived at her apartment complex.

He pulled up to the gate and rolled down his window. A shiny metallic box faced him, and he pressed some buttons and found Paterson on the screen. He pressed another button, and he heard the dial tone on the sound box.

Be confident.

He couldn't believe how nervous he was.

How does a woman make a man feel this way?

After three rings, a woman's voice answered. He didn't recognize it.

"Hi, I'm here for Marella Paterson," he said.

"I'm sorry," said the woman. "She's not here."

Tom paused. "Are you sure? We had a date tonight. I brought flowers and everything."

"Oh, she mentioned that. I'm sorry. She had to leave suddenly. Her father called last night, and she flew back home this morning."

Tom paused.

"Who are you?"

"I'm her roommate."

"Oh." The metal box shimmered under the spring Atlanta sun. "Are you sure? She's not standing there behind you, is she? I can promise I'm not a bad guy."

"Yes, I'm sorry. It was an emergency."

"Is everything alright?"

"She didn't say, just that her father needed her."

Tom thought a moment. His heart sank.

"Where did she go?"

"She's from Scotland. I believe she went back to Thurwick, her hometown."

"She left the country?"

"I'm sorry."

"Is she coming back?"

"I don't know."

Marella's flowers rested on the seat next to Tom. They still had their colors, but they weren't as bright as they had been.

"I'll tell her you were here," the roommate said.

"Thanks," Tom said, and he hung up the line.

Scotland. I finally get a date with the girl of my dreams and she leaves the country.

Tom pulled his car around and drove slowly along the winding Atlanta streets. Couples held hands as they walked through the quiet neighborhoods. The flowers sat in the passenger seat next to him. An elderly woman, out for a late afternoon walk, strolled along the sidewalk. He parked his car near her. He got out of his car and he handed her the flowers.

The woman took them, puzzled. "Thanks," she said.

"Have a good night, ma'am," Tom said.

Then he climbed into his car and he drove home.

CHAPTER 4

Under the lights, the basketball bounced off the rim, echoing the common sound of rubber on metal often heard on an outdoor court. Tom jogged to pick up the bouncing ball. It was eleven at night, and Tom couldn't sleep. He and Bob had talked briefly in their apartment. Rather than sulk about it, Bob suggested they hit the court and shoot some hoops. Feeling some exercise would vent some frustration, Tom agreed.

"That's an 'H' for me," Bob said.

"You know I'm not focused enough to win tonight," Tom said. Tom often won when he and Bob played HORSE, so whenever Bob took a lead, Bob would repeat the score just to get in Tom's head.

"I'll take all I can get," Bob answered. He dribbled the ball again, and then he shot a two-pointer from the edge of the free-throw line. The ball arched in the air, then dropped through the hoop, making a metallic whishing sound as it fell through the chained net. "You better pull yourself together, or else this could get ugly."

Tom shrugged and moved to the spot where Bob shot the ball. He dribbled a couple of times, then stopped and grabbed his basketball with both hands.

"I should be out with the girl of my dreams right now, but, no, I'm stuck here with you."

"Hey, it happens to the best of us." Bob dribbled and shot a quick layup into the net.

"Really? When's the last time the girl of your dreams fled the country to avoid going on a date with you?"

"All the time," Bob said. "The girl of my dreams is a Sports Illustrated swimsuit model. She's probably in Morocco right now posing on some nude beach. Just turns out she's got to do that to avoid going out with me."

Tom laughed. He lifted his ball and shot it towards the basket. It bounced off the backboard, hit the hoop, and bounced away from him onto the pavement. Bob punched the ball back to Tom. "That's an 'O'."

"The sad part is I don't even know if she's coming back, or if everything's alright. Not even her roommate knows anything. She just left."

"Is her roommate available?"

"I'm serious, man."

"So am I," Bob said. "If she is, maybe I'll ask her out."

"You'll have to clean your room, first," Tom said. "If she's anything like Marella, she's too proper for someone who doesn't pick his clothes up off the floor."

"For the right girl, I can change." Bob made another easy layup. "Here's a shot you can make."

"Give me a break," Tom said. He dribbled the basketball and jogged to the hoop. He shot the ball, and watched as it rolled off the back rim and fell to the pavement, missing the net. "Unbelievable."

"R," said Bob.

Tom picked up the basketball and tucked it under his arm. He stood still as he watched for Bob's next move.

"So why don't you ask out another girl?" Bob said. "Wasn't it you who always told me that there are plenty of fish in the sea?"

"That was until I saw Marella," Tom said. "I don't know what there is about her."

"Ok," Bob said. "What about another option." Bob dribbled the ball then shot a bank shot from the three point line. Neither he nor Tom reacted when the ball whished through the metallic chain-link net. "Why don't you go to Scotland and find her?"

"Are you serious?"

"Yes. That'll be an 'S' if you don't make that shot."

Tom dribbled his basketball a few moments. The thought of going to Scotland hadn't crossed his mind, but for some reason Bob's suggestion lit a spark. "You know, that's a crazy idea, but you might be onto something."

"Of course I am," said Bob. "I'm on fire tonight. It's that whole mind-body connection thing."

"She'll think I'm a stalker if I show up at her door."

"No she won't."

"How do you know?"

Bob stopped dribbling his basketball and walked over to Tom. "Think about it. It's the Hallmark movie. Girl is saved by hero in American restaurant. Girl has to go across the ocean to save her father. Girl is in trouble across the ocean. Hero in love travels half-way across the world to find girl. Hero rescues girl. They get married and live happily ever after. Then hero sets up best friend Bob with hot Scottish bridesmaid. It's the perfect love story."

"You're not right. I mean, something about you is off."

"Maybe so," said Bob. "But I'm right about this."

Bob was a nut, which was why he was fun to be around. But sometimes Bob would come up with a crazy idea that pressed Tom's boundaries. Most of Bob's ideas were so ridiculous that he would frequently endure being the butt of jokes amongst friends. This idea, however, got Tom thinking. Tom had a job, and some time off due to him. That would give him about a week. His passport hadn't been used since he visited the Bahamas a few years back, but it was still valid. What would he do if he found her? What if his idea worked and they began a relationship? Could he stay in Scotland? Would he have the courage to resign from his sales position and start anew overseas? Or, maybe she'd come back with him and he'd find another job in Atlanta. Most of his family remained in Arizona, where he grew up, so it wasn't as though being across the ocean would be that much different. He'd work some agreement with Bob on the rent. Logistically, he'd make it work.

It was the romance part that struck him. Yes, Tom wanted to see Marella again. However, romance didn't drive him. Deep down, he felt concern for Marella. Something told him he needed to go there to help her, but he couldn't put his finger on what that was. Was her father in danger?

Was she?

He had to go, if only to be sure.

"You going to shoot?" Bob said.

Tom blinked. Bob pointed to the hoop. Tom raised the basketball from the three-point line, and sunk a perfect shot through the hoop.

"Hey, great shot," said Bob. "Too bad you were standing in the wrong place."

"You're right. I do need to move," Tom said. "I'm going to go to Scotland."

"You are? I mean, really?" Bob said.

"Yeah, something tells me I need to go," Tom said.

"I love it. Just so you know I wasn't kidding about that hot Scottish bridesmaid."

"You can count on it." Tom picked up his basketball and, holding it with both his hands, jogged towards their apartment.

"What about the rest of our game?" Bob asked.

"I've got to run," Tom said. "It's time I took a game winning shot."

"Make it count," Bob said.

Tom left Bob on the court and hurried toward their apartment. There wouldn't be much time to find a flight to Scotland for tomorrow.

And, until he arrived, there'd be no way to know if Marella was safe.

CHAPTER 5

"**D**on't tell me I forgot my cell phone!" Tom kneeled outside the terminal at Hartsfield Jackson International Airport. He opened his backpack and found the few essentials he had remembered to pack: shirts, jeans, toothbrush, comb, map of Scotland.

But no phone.

He stood and padded his leather coat pockets.

Nothing.

It had to be at the apartment, or in his car. There was no time to go back to check his car.

What the hell am I doing?

As he stood in line at the ticket counter, sunlight shone through the glass windows. *Should I forget this whole thing?* People surrounded him with luggage and strollers. A couple and their three children stood in line. The kids behaved well, reflecting their calm parents. The four of them watched Tom. Why was he nervous? Tom checked his clothes. He had rushed getting dressed before he left. Did he remember to comb his hair?

LOCH NESS

He stepped up to the ticket counter and told the lady he was going to Dublin. She told him his flight schedule, flying first to Boston, then to Dublin, and finally to Inverness. He thanked her and went to his gate. He patted his pockets once more for his cell phone, but his pockets were empty. He went into a restroom. Yes, he had combed his hair. He bought a cup of coffee.

Relax.

When he boarded the plane, he sat in his seat but he fidgeted. Eventually, he gave up, he shut his eyes, and he imagined what he'd do in Thurwick without a phone.

* * *

Twenty-Three hours had passed when his plane landed in Inverness. Tom peered out the window. Fog covered the airport, dimming the lights in the distance.

He rubbed the stubble on his face. His eyes were heavy, but the adventure pumped his adrenaline. He reached into his backpack and pulled out his map of Scotland. Thurwick was a town on the southern edge of Loch Ness, right in the middle of the area known as the Highlands. He hoisted his backpack over his shoulder and walked past the baggage claim. He'd catch the Line Sixteen bus from Inverness, which travelled the country roads through the town of Foyers and then to Thurwick.

Tom boarded his bus and sat near the front, ready to observe the Highland countryside. He planned to take mental notes so he could make pleasant small talk with Marella. It was his last thought before sleep overtook him.

* * *

Tom opened his eyes. They felt dry as he blinked. Someone had a hand on his shoulder. The hand shook him. It was the bus driver.

"Wake up, laddie," the driver said. The Scottish accent confused Tom. "Ye don' want tae ride th' bus yer whole life, do ye?"

Tom peered through the window. Several grey buildings stood like large boulders through the thick fog.

"Where am I?"

"Thurwick," said the driver.

"Geez, I must've dozed off."

"Aye, ye slept th' whole trip."

Tom grabbed his backpack. He felt awkward as he stood and flung it around his shoulder. His muscles were stiff. He thanked the bus driver and made his way off the bus.

The mist surrounded him when his feet touched the ground. He breathed in the heavy moisture. The fog covered the buildings, causing shadows in the distance. Above him, the sun reflected a halo as its rays penetrated the fog. The sunlight disappeared and reappeared through the flowing mist. The scent of fresh ozone filled his nostrils.

Shadows moved like ghosts through the fog. Headlights flashed their dim lights along the misty roadways, and the wet air muffled the sounds of the square. Was he behind a commercial district? Were there people on the other side, people with information where he could find Marella?

He was about to ask the bus driver where he'd find the town square, but the door had closed and Tom heard the bus engine rev as it pulled away. Tom squinted from the sunlight. Even in the mist, the light irritated his blue eyes.

The distant landscape remained hidden, but shadows of movement told him Thurwick bustled with activity. People walked in the shadows, holding onto umbrellas. With the threat of rain looming, he decided to find a nearby store to ask for directions. A side street went through an alley, and he stepped through it. What was on the other end?

He stumbled upon the cobblestones. *Cobblestones? How old is this place.* They were hard for him to walk on, at least until his legs recovered.

He neared the other end of the alley. He stopped to admire the commotion. He was on the edge of a foggy square, busy with people, cars, and bicycles. He stepped onto a nearby sidewalk, excited to partake in a new adventure.

"Thurwick. I'm here," Tom said. He grabbed his backpack shoulder harness and hoisted it up near his neck. Through the fog, Thurwick was a busy place. The people walked amongst the square, as cars drove along the wavy roads that curved around buildings, buildings that had been built centuries ago.

Where should I go first? And why did I rush out without my phone?

He had also forgotten to arrange sleeping quarters, as his focus was acquiring a plane ticket and getting to the airport. He decided sleeping arrangements had to be at the top of his list. He didn't want to impose on Marella, asking for a couch on a first date. *Yeah, that could be bad,* he thought. *Especially if her father wasn't pleased.*

Okay, sleeping arrangements. He surveyed the buildings. They appeared old and worn out, but many of them had signs on them written in English. As he stood on the cobblestones, a woman walked toward him, holding a cell phone to her ear.

"Excuse me, ma'am," Tom said, but the woman walked past, keeping her eyes forward.

"Friendly folks." Should he be more assertive? A man in a business suit walked towards him. This man didn't have a cell phone. "Sir, excuse me."

The man stopped.

"I just got off the bus, and it's my first time in Thurwick," Tom said. "Could you direct me to a hotel?"

"There's Annabel's Bed and Breakfast down near th' church. If ye'll donder down tha' road a wee bit, ye'll see their sign. Tis a white house wi' green shutters."

Tom thanked the man and took a few steps into the square. The shops appeared normal, about what any small town would have. But it was old. Only a few of the stores had lighted signs. Most of the signs were worn, as though they had all been carved out of shipwrecked wood.

He walked past a window. Posters and books about the Loch Ness monster caught his attention. In his trek to find Marella, he had forgotten he was next to Loch Ness. He noticed a post office next to a place called Dorlan Hall. He walked further, saying hello to people as they passed by.

Most didn't respond.

Others looked the other way.

He was a stranger in Thurwick. He'd have to find a friend somewhere.

His eyes widened when he noticed a sign in the fog. It read, "Guthrie's Pub." Tom nodded. *Where else than a pub to get information from the locals,* he thought. *After all, one can discover many things if he just sits amongst people and listens.*

Tom entered the Guthrie's. Much of the inside had the feel of the thirteenth century. It reminded him just how young the pubs in America were. It was hard for him to get used to. Scotland had been populated for centuries before America was even an idea. It had a long history, stories and legends of heroes from ages ago. Everything was thicker and solid. The rooms were smaller. The tables were closer together. The walls were made of stone. Not much had changed inside this building for at least three hundred years.

He found a stool near the bar. He lowered his backpack. His back was relieved to remove the weight. A finely dressed bartender in a vest cleaned a glass. Tom ordered a lager from the bartender and surveyed the scene. Some of the locals gathered in one of the rooms. Back in America, the manager at the Brookhaven Olde Blind Dog Pub had once referred to these sorts of rooms as 'snugs', and Tom figured they'd be called the same in Scotland. Inside one of the snugs, four men sat at a table. A couple of them talked. They paid Tom little attention.

"Bartender," Tom said. "You know any Paterson here in Thurwick?"

The bartender raised his head. "Aye, we have a few. Which one are ye lookin' fur?"

"Do you know one with a daughter named Marella?"

The bartender stopped cleaning the glass. "Marella Paterson? Sean Paterson's daughter? Why, lest we knew she skipped out o'er th' Atlantic. I think she went tae th' States."

"I'm here to find her. She came back a few days ago."

One of the men in the snug stood up from his seat. He was tall, and though his hair was gray, the man had a strong appearance. He walked up to Tom. "Did I hear ye say Marella Paterson came back?"

"I did."

The man was silent for a moment. Then, he and his friends laughed at once, slapping the table. "Wouldn' ye know it," the large man said. "Maybe th' scientist captured th' beast!" They laughed some more.

The bartender chuckled, put the glass down, and shook his head. He poured a drink into it and pushed it in front of Tom.

"That's fur th' joke."

"I must be missing something," Tom said.

The bartender put his hands on the bar. "Sean Paterson calls his-sel' a scientist," the bartender said. "We just call him doolally." He circled his index finger near his ear, representing someone who is crazy. "He's claimed he saw Nessie thirty years ago. Poor lad's been lookin' fur him e'er since. He was so obsessed wi' finding th' monster that his wife left him when Marella was a wee child. Th' girl stayed wi' him. We all supposed she wanted tae believe. Then she grew up. Couldn' take it anymore, and left fur America."

"Aye!" said the tall man in the snug. "When she left, th' fool's been takin' his rowboat out on th' water several times a week. Seems her leaving's made him more determined tae find th' beast!" The men in the snug laughed some more.

"Wha' we heard," said the bartender, "was tha' Sean made Marella promise him if he e'er did find th' monster, he would call her, and she'd take th' next flight back tae Scotland."

"So that's what happened?" asked Tom.

"I'm sure he ne'er found th' monster," said the bartender. He grinned. "We're all certain th' man's doolally. Poor lass, though. Marella was a good kid. Hate fur her tae suffer."

Tom sat on the stool, and took a few swigs of his lager. Still tired from his trip, he felt confused. Did he really follow a girl all the way to Scotland? And did she come to Scotland because of a myth? Bob is never going to believe this.

But something inside him told him there was more. He needed to check on Marella.

He paid the bartender. "If you don't mind, I traveled a long way to find her, and I just want to make sure she's alright. Where does Sean Paterson live?"

"He's in a cottage outside o' town. Ye go past Annabel's and Saint Michael's church, and ye'll find a dirt road called Mackay Road. Go tha' way a kilometer or so. Th' cottage will be on yer right. Ye can' miss it, wha' wi' all his trinkets and windmills."

"Annabel's Bed and Breakfast is on the way?"

"Aye. When ye find th' church, ye'll find Annabel's."

A second idea came to Tom. "Do you know where I can pick up a map of Thurwick?"

"Convenience Store is around th' neuk," the bartender said.

Tom thanked the bartender, paid him, and stepped outside. He went around the corner and found the store. He went inside, bought his map, and stepped back into the square. The dark clouds opened up, and rain fell. He squinted from the rain that hit his face. To his right, the shadows of a steeple and cross arose above the fog. *That had to be the church,* he thought. He lifted his coat collar and jogged into the rain towards the cross.

* * *

Several hundred yards later, he came to the church. It stood large and imposing on the edge of town. Its cross towered over the street atop stone walls.

Across the street was a two-story house with green shutters. Next to the front door was a freshly painted green sign which read "Annabel's Bed and Breakfast" written in white stencil. He opened the front door and walked inside. His clothes had soaked through and his hair was wet and dark and falling over his eyes. He brushed his hands through his hair. An elderly woman sat in a chair reading a book.

"Are you Annabel?"

She said, "Aye."

"Do you have a room?"

"Howfur long?"

"A week?"

She had him fill out a form, took his credit card information, and gave him his key. He went to his room, used the shower, and changed his clothes. He sat on the bed, and his bare feet hung above the floor. He was still tired from the trip, but he was also confused by what he heard at Guthrie's Pub. He didn't believe in fantasies.

Was Marella's father really searching for the Loch Ness monster? No wonder they thought he was crazy. If Sean Paterson was mentally unstable, though, Marella could very well be in some sort of danger.

As Tom sat on the bed, he decided not to rest. He stood up. The weather on the other side of the window was changing. The rain had passed, but a new dark cloud threatened another storm. He went downstairs and asked Annabel if he could rent an umbrella. She handed him one. Then he opened his map and pinpointed Mackay Road.

CHAPTER 6

That's one impressive church!

Across the street from Annabel's, Saint Michael's Catholic Church towered before him. Its stone structure rose from the ground as a testament to time. Though he grew up Catholic, he hadn't been inside a church in years. The castle-like features made him want to go in and tour the premises at least once while he was in Thurwick.

He walked along the road. He hoped Mackay was up ahead. The weather blew the cold mist into his face, and he shrugged to lift his collar up to cover his neck. How far would he have to walk to find Marella? He opened Annabel's umbrella, lowered it into the mist, and trudged forward.

The road lost its hint of civilization and became dirt and mud. He noticed some buds on the tip of a nearby bush, though he imagined blooms were rare in the early spring as the passing winter left its mark on the countryside. To his right was the Loch. Its width stretched out a mile to the other shore. The width of Loch Ness was five times that of the Mississippi River in some places.

Ten minutes passed when he came to a street sign. It was old and weathered, but he made out the name Mackay Road. It was another dirt road, and it was full of mud and rain puddles. In the distance, the road curved through the countryside and the trees, but it disappeared through the thickening fog. He gripped his umbrella for the onset of rain.

He remembered the bartender said to go a kilometer. Was a kilometer longer or shorter than a mile? He couldn't remember. But he knew walking a mile took the average person approximately twenty minutes. The time on his watch said 11:42 a.m. *That's not right,* he thought. *What am I, five hours ahead of Eastern Standard Time?* His lack of sleep wasn't doing him any good. He counted five hours on his fingers. It was four forty-two local time.

The sun hovered above the gray hills. If he managed to find Marella, he'd have little time to make an impression. Evening was fast approaching. He decided he'd make a quick announcement of his arrival. Then, if that went well, he'd ask if he could see her tomorrow. Since she broke her date with him on Sunday, his request wasn't all that unreasonable.

He walked another twenty minutes until he came to a small cottage. A single small blue car sat parked in the driveway. The car needed a paint job. Around the cottage there were some rusting metallic items. They were windmills, spinning and squeaking with all their contraptions in the gentle evening breeze.

This had to be the house the bartender mentioned. *Marella could be on the other side of the door,* he thought. His heart raced. *Don't be nervous.* He had spent the past forty hours planning and making the trip.

But what if she recognizes me? What if she thinks I'm a stalker? What if she has me arrested? I could wind up in jail in a foreign country!

Tom took a deep breath. "Take the shot," he said. Then he remembered. "Flowers. Damn it!" *Improvise. Improvise.* Everything was wet and cold. *What about...*

Wildflowers! He searched the brush for something, anything. He couldn't find any. It was too early in the season. Then he thought of an early bloom. One of the trees a few yards back had some blooms on them. He went to the tree and pulled off a few branches. The white blooms were tiny, but noticeable. In another week or two they'd be beautiful. *They'd have to do.* He shrugged, tapped his umbrella on a stone, and went to the door.

"You only live once."

He listened outside the door. He heard muffled voices, but the thumps inside his chest drowned them out. "Ok. Here goes." He raised his hand, and rapped on door with his right hand. He stood back. Trying to be suave, he put his umbrella behind him, and he held the blooms in front.

A short, stocky man with glasses opened the door. "Aye, can I help ye?"

Tom stuttered, raised his blooms and said, "Hi. I'm Tom Wayne, from America. I'm here to see Marella."

The man frowned. His eyes scanned Tom from his feet to his head. "Marella. Ye have a visitor."

"Wha' is it?" It was Marella's voice. Tom melted when he heard it. He hoped he didn't appear too tired, or too eager, or too anything. He hoped she'd be pleased. He hoped his hair wasn't a mess.

The man said, "Someone named Tom. Says he's from America."

She appeared behind the man. When her eyes met his, she put her hands to her mouth. Tom's heart skipped a beat. He handed her the bouquet of white blooms. "These are for you."

The man went back inside. "Make sure ye'r done in fifteen minutes."

"Tom? From th' restaurant?" Marella said. "I can' believe ye came all this way."

"Well, when I missed you Sunday night, I got worried about you," Tom said.

"Did Kathy tell ye where I was?"

"Your roommate? Yes, but she was a little confused, if you ask me"

The man inside said, "Should I wear my bunnet? It might make me look more professional."

Marella said, "Nothin's goin' tae help wi' tha' t'night."

"Is that your father," Tom said. "Sean Paterson?"

"How do ye-?" She shook her head. "Look, Tom. Thanks fur comin', but ye shouldn' have. Tis best if we catch up another night."

"Are you alright? There's no trouble, is there?" Tom said.

"Tis best if ye just go."

The man reappeared behind the doorway, wearing a brown vest, a tie, and a fedora. "Are ye invitin' yer friend? Why na' bring him along? Th' more we ha' on our side, th' better."

"That's a bad idea," Marella said.

"Where are you going?" Tom asked.

"Oh, tis a big night," the man said. "One fur th' history books. Ye should come along so ye can be a part of it."

"Please don' invite him," Marella said. "We don' want tae make this worse than it already is."

"If it's any consolation, I don't mind," Tom said. "I'm still on Atlanta time. I won't be able to sleep for a few hours, so I'd be glad to be a third set of eyes."

Marella stepped out of the house and closed the door behind her. As she moved closer towards Tom, his heart moved. Her green eyes flashed wildness yet tenderness under her curly hair. Her aroma reminded him of spring. He imagined Bob telling him to calm down. He politely took a step back.

"Ye canno' come," she said. "I'm worried tha' my father may be goin' doolally. I fear he'll harm himself t'night. I don' mean physically, but economically, professionally, socially. Tis all so embarrassing. There's nothin' I can do tae stop him."

"Then let me help. I promise I won't judge."

The man swung the door open. Tom thought Sean Paterson was G.K. Chesterton. "Well, ye two. Shall we ge' goin'?"

Tom shrugged and raised his eyebrows, hoping she'd agree. Marella shook her head. "Na' again," she said.

Sean pushed between Marella and Tom, shutting the door behind him. "Come on, ye two. Let's go change the world!"

CHAPTER 7

The three of them climbed into Sean's blue car, and they drove into town. Sean asked Tom a few questions, such as where he was from and what his family was like, but the conversation quickly turned to strategy.

"We need tae be positive, and optimistic," Sean said. "We know they are goin' tae have trouble believing me, but if we use reason wi' them, they should agree tae th' funding."

"I just hope there's na crowd," Marella said.

"There shouldn' be," said Sean. "Chairman Briggs promised me a fair hearin'."

They pulled into the square. A large crowd had gathered near one of the buildings. Also near the buildings parked several brightly painted vans. Next to them were news crews. Reporters spoke into cameras under artificial lights.

"This isn' good," said Marella. "We need tae go back."

"My dear, we didn' get dressed up fur nothin'."

Sean parked the car, climbed out, and shut the door behind him. He strode towards the crowd and the news cameras.

Marella put her hands on the top of head. "How did e'eryone find out abou' this? It was supposed tae be a secret. A special called meeting wi' wee fanfare."

Tom thought back to his conversation in Guthrie's Pub. Had the large man or the bartender spread word? "Are these meetings advertised ahead of time?"

"Aye, but special called meetings don' draw crowds like this."

Tom opened the door. "Well, let's go help your father." He climbed out of the car, shut his door, and opened Marella's. She pulled herself from her seat, straightened her outfit, and walked toward the crowd. Tom shut the door behind her and followed.

Sean was being interviewed by one of the news reporters. Several cameras pointed at him as he spoke into the microphone. Tom overheard some of the reporters' questions, and he heard Sean repeat that he was saving his comments for the Council.

Tom's eyes caught those of a man holding a sign that read, "KEEP NESSIE FREE!" The man was shabbily dressed, but his face was young. His hair was white, and his skin was pale. *An albino, maybe?* Tom shivered. He moved his eyes toward Sean just in time to hear a ridiculing voice. Others chimed in, exclaiming that Sean had lost his mind, his sanity, and his reputation.

It was painful to watch.

Marella acted embarrassed. She was trying to keep her composure. She'd lose it at any moment.

"Where are we going?" asked Tom.

She pointed to the large stone building. "In there. Dorlan Hall. Tis where th' Local Council has their meetings. Let's hurry and ge' this o'er wi'."

Tom, Sean, and Marella worked their way through into Dorlan Hall. Inside, a long hall with rows of benches faced a raised wooden podium at the far end. The wooden fixtures were as ancient as the aged walls, adding to the signs of the long Scottish history.

Tom imagined what history had happened inside these walls. What scenes had played out between them? What had been argued? Were people sentenced to death? Were any executed inside these walls? *Time sees many things,* he thought.

"We have seats reserved in th' front," Sean said. He pushed his way down the aisle, making a path through the people. Marella followed. Onlookers gave curious glances at the three of them as they passed.

One man in particular, a short but athletic character, watched Marella with less inhibition than the others. His expression, though, was purposeful, plotting.

"Don't you know it's impolite to stare?" Tom said as he bumped into him. The man glared at Tom. He had a reddish beard, and his eyes flashed a hint of violence. Tom returned the glare and moved past him.

The three of them found their seats on the front row. Sean and Marella sat down. A cast of characters gathered in the room. They appeared like ordinary people. *Not too different than Americans,* he thought. As he heard them talk, however, the Scottish accent continued to remind him he was in a faraway land.

A man in a brown leather coat and a fedora walked next to the stone walls near the front and approached Tom. The man had a sincere countenance.

Tom liked him instantly.

The man extended his hand. "I hadn' seen ye before."

"It's my first time to Scotland," Tom said. "I'm just learning my way around."

"My name's Caleb," he said. He tipped his hat to Marella. "I don' know what's goin' tae happen t'night, but when 'tis all o'er, make sure ye find me."

"Why?" asked Marella.

"Let's just say I'm rooting fur ye. Come find me after," Caleb said, and he disappeared into the crowd.

Tom said, "That was interesting."

"I just wan' this to be o'er wi'," she said.

Sean was about to say something when several men and women appeared from the sides behind the wooden dais and sat down. As they took their seats, the room quieted. A balding man in his late fifties sat in the middle, took the gavel, and banged it several times on the desk. "If e'eryone would be quiet and take their seats, th' meeting will now begin."

"Who's that?" Tom asked.

"That's Chairman Gordon Briggs," Marella said. "Th' eight people up there are members of Thurwick's Local Council. They are all elected, bu' Chairman Briggs runs th' meeting."

"Is he like a mayor?"

"Sort o'," she said. "Th' Local Council doesn' have a lo' o' authority, bu' they do have influence tae get help from th'

Highland Unitary Council. That's wha' my father's hoping tae get t'night, some funding tae further his research."

The room hushed. Tom twisted in his seat to see the crowd behind them. There had to be over two hundred people packed within the wooden benches. Many stood along the stone walls along the sides. In the back, reporters and camera crews flashed lights to the front.

If Marella had hoped this meeting would be unnoticed, it didn't turn out that way.

"We wan' tae thank all o' ye fur coming, and I'll go ahead and call this special called meeting tae order." Chairman Briggs leaned forward. "I also want tae say tha' th' subject matter here is o' an unusual nature. We would appreciate all o' ye refraining from talking or applauding during th' discussion." Chuckles echoed off the stone walls.

"Would th' clerk please read th' item on th' agenda?"

A lady with a soft voice spoke, and it was the first time Tom noticed the desk near the side. The lady said, "Th' foremost item on th' agenda is th' approval o' th' meetin' agenda."

"I'll make a motion tae approve th' meetin' agenda," said a woman on the Council.

"Second," said a man sitting next to her.

"We ha'e a motion tae approve th' meetin' agenda from Councilwoman Harris, and a second from Councilman MacGillivray. All in favor?"

All eight of the members said, "Aye," in unison.

"The 'ayes' have it. Would th' clerk please read th' next item?"

"Th' next item on th' agenda is a consideration tae request funding from th' Highland Council fur Loch Ness monster research."

Laughter.

Chairman Briggs banged his gavel three times, and the laughter subsided.

Marella buried her head in her hands.

"Do we have any public comment?" Briggs asked.

"We do have three," she answered. "Th' foremonst public comment comes from Mr. Scott Mincey."

An older man walked toward the podium. He leaned into the microphone. "My name is Mr. Scott Mincey. I just wan' tae say tha' this whole meeting is a waste o' money. We don' nee' tae look fur some mythological monster in th' Loch, and all o' ye should be voted out fur e'en allowing this meeting tae take place. I wouldn' be surprised if some of ye are gettin' money from special interests in th' film industry or somethin' like tha'. That's all I have tae say." The old man went to his seat, and a few people in the audience applauded.

"Th' next speaker is Mrs. Johansen."

A lady walked to the podium. She had gray hair, which she wore in a bonnet. She wore glasses, and her face was stern. "My name is Patti Johansen. Wha' I want tae know is when ye are going tae forget abou' fake creatures and send someone tae fix my water runoff. I mean, tis been three weeks now, and nothin's been done." Some laughter in the audience, but it died quickly. "Please stop this nonsense, and do yer jobs." She left the podium, walked into the audience, and took her seat.

"Thank ye, Patti. We'll get someone out there tae look at it t'morrow," said Chairman Briggs.

"Th' third and final speaker is a Ms. O'Hara."

An attractive middle-aged woman walked up to the podium. The room quieted as she approached. "Hello Councilmembers. My name is Marissa O'Hara. My request is simple. I'm na' in favor o' askin' fur funding fur monster research. My hope is tha' ye will show mercy tae th' requester, because I'm convinced he's na' in his right mind, and he's going tae need some type o' substance abuse help."

Someone in the crowd shouted, "Here! Here!" Marella stood up. She clenched her fists and her her jaw, ready to fight, but Sean grabbed her by the arm. He gently pulled her down to her to her seat. Murmurs ran through the room. Tom felt the tension in the room. Briggs picked up his gavel and hammered once, demanding silence. O'Hara left the podium and walked back into the crowd. Marella glared as she walked past.

"Alright, then." Briggs nodded to the three of them in the front row. "Will Sean Paterson please come tae th' podium?" Sean stood, his mustache displaying an honest dignity. Marella frowned. As Sean walked to the podium, the packed room grew silent.

"Ladies and gentlemen o' th' Council," Sean said. "I want tae thank ye fur taking th' time tae hear my request, and I must say I'm honored tha' so many o' Thurwick's finest residents have come tae support this idea I bring before ye t'night." A couple in the crowd laughed. Tom admired his courage to stand and speak before such a large crowd.

Was it courage, or was he just crazy? Did he really discover something unusual in the Loch.

"Lest Saturday e'ening, I decided tae try tae find Nessie again. Aye, we all know him tae be th' Loch Ness monster. Many o' ye have heard tha' I found th' beast almost thirty years ago, right ou' there on our shoreline. Well, I have tried many scientific methods tae brin' proof tha' th' beast exists. I've tried sonar, radar, water displacement, heat sensors, and all sorts o' contraptions. I know some o' ye remember my unusual permit requests."

"Aye, Mr. Paterson," interrupted a councilwoman on the far right of the podium. "Th' yellow deep sea diving suit brought a lot o' attention tae Thurwick in th' European press, and na' in a good way."

The comment brought murmurs and chuckles, but Sean kept his cool. "Aye, I can appreciate tha', Councilwoman. And tha' experiment, tae, provided na proof. But I would say it did brin' tourism tae our lovely town o' Thurwick."

"I'd say it made a mockery o' us." The councilwoman folded her hands and sat back in her seat, frowning.

Sean said, "My dear Loretta. Ye and I were in school together. Why, I remember when ye used tae believe in fairies and Irish leprechauns, as well as Nessie. Wha' changed in ye?"

The councilwoman leaned forward. "I grew up."

"Aye!" Sean said. He slapped the podium. "She grew up. I agree. Tis time fur us tae all grow up!" His raised voice caused some in the crowd to chatter.

Mayor Briggs hammered his gavel again. "Get tae yer point, Sean Paterson."

"Thank ye, Chairman Briggs," Sean continued. "I apologize fur my outburst, bu' I was so excited tae hear tis time fur all o' us tae grow up. Ye see, I decided tae grow up, too. I decided tha' all my scientific experiments were just toys. None o' them worked. So I decided I needed tae grow up if I e'er was goin' tae find th' beast again."

"Go on," Briggs said.

"Aye. Well, th' real discoverers o' nature's wonders weren' scientists. They were fishermen. They were seamen. They were explorers. They were men o' action. Aye, sir. I decided if I would e'er find Nessie, I would have tae grow up and return tae my roots. I would have tae do somethin' real men have done fur generations. I would have tae do somethin' I hadn' done since my father tried tae teach me when I was a boy. I would have tae go fishin'."

An eruption of laughter burst within the room. Marella buried her head in her hands and shook it, her curly hair flowing back and forth over her shoulders. Tom put his hand on her shoulder. It was the first time he had touched her.

Chairman Briggs hammered the gavel, and the room quieted. "Please, Mr. Paterson. We don' need ye tae waste our time."

"Ah, Chairman Briggs. I would na' have asked fur this meetin' if I though' it would be a waste o' time. Let me explain. I loaded my boat lest Saturday e'ening, and hooked several large pieces o' meat tae hooks. Some o' them were pork, but most were steaks."

"Could've had a cook out!" said a voice in the back, but the voice was hushed.

"I was out late, near Saint Michael's in fact, when one o' my lines ran. I grabbed it, but wha'ever was on th' other end o' th' line pulled it wi' so much force it slipped right out o' my hands and fell intae th' water. Then I noticed a second line run, and I jumped on it, grabbed it, and tried tae use my weight tae keep it from also disappearin' intae th' water. It wasn' enough. Th' line pulled so hard I had tae let it go, else my boat would've capsized."

"This sounds like a 'ye should've seen th' one tha' go' away' story." Laughter filled the room. Then everyone heard the sound of Brigg's gavel.

"I'd laugh, tae," said Sean, "except that's when I saw it. I smelled it. It moved so gracefully. Th' lest thing I remember was a large fin and th' creature's back crest out o' th' water. It was larger than my boat. It dipped intae th' water. And then it was gone."

After a few moments of silence, Councilwoman Harris asked, "Mr. Briggs, ye don' expect us tae believe this, do ye?"

"Aye, I do."

"Tis likely a caber floating in th' Loch."

"Wi' all due respect, Councilwoman, 'twas no caber. I know wha' it was. I would na be here if I hadn' seen it myself."

"Then wha' do ye want?"

"Wha' I'm asking fur is funding, maybe fur better fishin' and camera equipment, hooks, and a boat. Somethin' more sturdy and reliable. If I'm goin' tae catch a prehistoric creature, I can' do it in a dinghy!" Several chuckles echoed between the walls. Briggs picked up the gavel, but the voices dissipated and he lowered the gavel without using its force.

Councilwoman Loretta leaned forward. "And, Mr. Paterson, just wha' would ye do wi' this prehistoric creature once ye've caught it?"

Sean paused. He took a deep breath and said, "Well, Loretta, I mean, members o' th' Council, I just wan' tae prove it exists, and then le' it go."

The councilmembers looked at each other, and then at Sean. "That's it?" asked Chairman Briggs. "Just go fur a wee fishin' trip, catch a monster, and then le' it go?"

"Aye."

There were moments of silence.

Briggs leaned into his microphone, and he asked Sean if there would be anything else he'd like to add. Sean said "Na," and he sat down next to Marella.

Marella frowned.

Councilwoman Loretta leaned forward into the microphone. "Wi' all due respect tae th' requester o' this agenda item, I fur one am na' in favor o' makin' a resolution tae th' Highland Unitary Council tae request funds tae find proof o' a Loch Ness monster. Th' idea is preposterous, and we need tae get back tae serving th' people o' Thurwick."

Councilwoman Harris then spoke. "If we approve this, people na' only in Scotland but throughout th' entire globe will laugh at us. Why, Chairman Briggs, yer picture might be posted on th' leadin' magazines wi' th' headline, 'We're goin' tae find Nessie!' Tha' would ruin yer credibility and ours as a Council. I'm na' about tae let th' reputation o' th' people o' Thurwick flounder in th' press."

"But wha' if he's right?" Councilman McCulloch rubbed his gray beard. The audience murmured. "That Loch is o'er two hundred meters deep. Have any o' ye been down there? I doubt it. There are a couple o' benefits here. Foremost, it shows th' world tha' th' people o' Thurwick have an adventurous spirit. We are a brave lot who admire nature's mysteries. That's a positive thing. But, what's more, imagine th' economic boom we'd get. Imagine all th' tourism it would bring. Why, we've all witnessed th' people who've come tae Thurwick just fur th' idea o' a creature in th' Loch. Whether or na' one exists, a small expense by th' Highland Unitary Council would boost our tourism economy by a' least a million pounds. I'm na' sayin' I'll vote fur this or na', bu' this should, at th' very least, be somethin' we ought tae consider."

"If Nessie exists, he belongs tae th' people o' Thurwick." Councilman MacGillivray shuffled his hands as he spoke. "There are two issues wi' tha'. If Nessie is tae be found, it should be done by government officials. People who provide professional services and are involved in th' plannin'. It should be a far more precise operation. We don' need civilians like Mr. Paterson puttin' their lives a' risk. Who would pay fur th' emergency medical services? If we do any funding a' all, it should be fur a better plan. Na' fur a civilian who thinks if he puts steak in th' water he'll find a prehistoric monster."

There were murmurs in the crowd, and MacGillivray hesitated before he raised his voice and said, "But if Nessie is tae be found, we should na' let it go. It should be killed and hung from a trellis. Photographed fur th' whole world tae see. Then na one would doubt its existence."

The noise from the audience grew, and Briggs hammered his gavel. Sean winced at the idea of killing Nessie. Before the crowd quieted, MacGillivray leaned forward and said, "Chairman Briggs, I'd like tae make a motion tha' we deny this agenda item as read."

Loretta leaned into her microphone, her face stern. "I'll gladly second tha'."

Briggs said, "We have a motion tae deny and a second. Do we have any discussion?" None of the councilmembers spoke, and there was an uneasy silence in the room. After a few tense moments, Briggs said, "Hearin' na discussion, all in favor please say, 'Aye'."

All eight councilpersons said, "Aye." Five of them raised their hand as they said it. None were opposed to the motion.

"Very well. Th' 'ayes' have it," Chairman Briggs said. The council made another motion to adjourn the meeting, and after the vote, Briggs hammered the gavel and declared the meeting over.

Sean said, "Well, tis on tae plan B."

"Please, can we le' this go?" Marella said. Her voice sounded desperate.

Before Sean answered, a reporter interrupted him. A light flashed from the camera into their eyes. "Sean Paterson. Can we ask ye a couple o' questions about wha' happened tae ye lest weekend?"

Sean rose and spoke with the reporter. Marella reached for Tom and pulled him aside. "Help me ge' my father home safely."

Tom nodded. "I'm here for you," he said.

A few people filtered out of Dorlan Hall, but most grouped together and chatted amongst themselves. Tom observed how they would talk in small circles, yet their eyes shifted to study Sean and Marella. He hated how others liked to gossip. It made him feel like an outcast.

Marella said, "This is aff tae hurt him."

"You don't know that," Tom said.

"How's he going tae keep his customers? They'll all laugh a' him. He'll go bankrupt!"

Tom shrugged. He watched from the short distance how Sean gave his interview with the reporter, so calmly and confidently. Marella, on the other hand, was giving way to worry.

Tom said, "He thinks he saw something. You can't deny that."

"Just ge' us out o' here."

Tom went to Sean and put his hand on his shoulder. "Marella says we should go."

"Aye," Sean said. He stood in front of the camera and said to the reporter, "I'm na' quittin'. I'll prove th' monster exists."

"Mr. Paterson. Please," Tom said.

"I will!"

"Mr. Paterson, we need to go."

Sean said, "Oh," and he followed Tom over to Marella, where the three of them made their way along the stone wall towards the door.

That's when Caleb appeared and blocked their path. He had been talking with a small group of people, but he suddenly left them to make contact with Tom. Caleb's blue eyes were covered under the shadow of his fedora, and his leather coat blended into the coloring of stone walls. Tom was taken aback at the passion and wildness in Caleb's eyes. They possessed knowledge of some truth, some mystery, that Tom had not understood.

Caleb stuck out his hand to Sean and leaned close. He spoke softly, directing his comments to Sean. "We knew this would happen. Don' be discouraged."

What did he mean by "we"?

Caleb whispered, "I was sent tae tell ye tha' ye're na' alone."

CHAPTER 8

"Wha' do ye mean we're na' alone?" Marella asked.

Caleb paused, observed the audience, and then maneuvered next to the wall. Caleb was stealthy, and Tom deduced that Caleb did not want to be noticed.

"There are people in Thurwick who are familiar wha' ye are seekin'," Caleb said. "Tis history goes back longer than ye know."

Sean's face beamed, and he was about to shout, "I knew it!" when Caleb hushed him.

"We mustn' brin' attention tae oursel'es," Caleb said.

"What exactly is going on?" asked Tom. "The local government just ridiculed us, and the audience laughed at us. Now you're telling us there's more going on. You need to answer the question. What did you mean when you said we're not alone?"

Caleb scanned the crowd, careful of others who would be watching their conversation. He tipped his hat so as to cover his eyes and remain anonymous. "I canno' tell ye everythin' now," he said. "Bu' there are se'eral groups ye need tae be aware o'."

"Groups?" Sean said. "Like who?"

"Foremost, this Council. Their vote t'night was purely political. None o' them want tae appear foolish. Make sure yer search doesn' give them a public black eye."

"Wait," Tom said. "We'd only make them look foolish if Nessie actually existed."

Caleb's eyes flashed, but he pursed his lips.

"Wha' other groups should we be aware o'?" asked Sean.

Caleb paused and hushed his voice again. "There's a second group out there tha' believes Nessie exists, but tha' he should na' be found."

"What do you mean?" asked Tom.

"They're a strange group, but they would do wha' they can tae keep th' secret o' Nessie hidden."

"Why?" asked Marella.

Caleb again scanned the audience. The room dissipated, but he continued his suspicious behavior. "Tis hard tae explain," he said. "Some believe findin' Nessie is a blessin'. Others say he's a curse, and they'll resort tae violence tae keep him from bein' found."

"Well, that's comforting," Tom said.

"Wha' do ye mean 'violence'?" asked Marella.

"There's na tellin'," said Caleb. "I only know they would use any means necessary tae keep Nessie a secret. If somethin' bad happened tae th' one who was about tae find him, it would be na accident."

"Are you threatening us?" asked Tom.

"Tis na' me ye have tae worry about," Caleb said.

"Is there anybody else?" Tom said.

"Aye. Th' closer ye get tae th' monster, th' more people notice."

"Who?"

"Trust me. This meetin' has made ye targets."

"Who is targeting us?"

"I must be goin'."

"Wait, you can't just leave us hanging. Who sent you?"

"I canno' say. Na th' now, anyway. Tae many are watchin'. Ye should keep lookin'. Just be canny." Caleb tipped his fedora and gestured good day, then he turned and left the three of them alone.

"What was that all about?" Tom said.

"Da', we need tae go," Marella said. "The monster is a fairy tale. I think tha' man is full o' lies."

"Wha' if he's tellin' th' truth?" Sean said.

"Let's na' lose our minds," Marella said.

"That guy believes there's a monster in the lake," said Tom. "Do you think others do as well?"

"Don' be ridiculous."

Sean said, "I believe th' man is right. Th' idea o' th' Loch Ness monster is grand, and there's na telling how people would react when their reality is challenged."

"Who is Caleb, anyway?" asked Marella. "Da', have ye e'er seen him before?"

"Na."

"He's good at blending in," said Tom. "His coat and his hat almost matched these stone walls. Was that by design?"

Sean shrugged. He turned to Marella. "My dear, let's ge' ye home."

They walked out the door into the Thurwick night. Cool air hit Tom's face. He was exhausted, and he imagined he had circles under his eyes with going so long without sleep. As they left the stone structure of Dorlan Hall, Marella said, "Da', I know ye're going tae want tae go forward. Ye always do. Bu' who's going tae watch out fur us?"

Tom tapped Marella on the shoulder. "Leave that to me."

Marella observed him, unbelieving, as they followed Sean back to the car.

CHAPTER 9

As they walked to the car, Tom thought about all that had just happened. The pressures of drowsiness weighed on him, but he fought it off, focusing on the adrenaline rush he experienced being around Marella.

But this whole Loch Ness monster thing confused him. Marella had obviously come back to Scotland, but why had she left in the first place? Her father believed he discovered a legendary creature, and it appeared he was willing to take whatever steps he needed to prove its existence, even if that meant public ridicule.

And who was Caleb? What he had said made no sense. Were there others in the area who believed in the monster and that it was more than a tourist attraction? Were there others who believed there was a real live remnant from the time of the dinosaurs? Tom admitted he was unfamiliar with Scottish marine life, but was there a scientific explanation? Perhaps the monster had been mistaken for some type of large fish already known to man. Why couldn't Sean Paterson tell the difference?

Caleb, however, indicated that the monster was real. He suspected some would use violence to keep it a secret, while others wanted to find it first. Was everyone in Thurwick playing charades?

They walked over the cobblestones. Then Tom admired the way Marella walked. Even in darkness she had elegance. His heart ached, as though he felt her disappointment in her father's beliefs. He also felt her concern for her father's well-being. Tom gathered she did not believe in the monster. It was just as the men in Guthrie's Pub had said. He understood their story. Marella loved her father, but she could no longer handle his obsession. That's why she left for America.

Tom remembered the men in Guthrie's. They had laughed when they told the story. Tom doubted that he had to be concerned about them. But Caleb said there were others he had to watch.

So who were they?

"Why does th' car look different?" Sean said. He quickened his pace toward his blue car. The reflection of the street lights cast shadows around the parking space. Tom noticed something different, too. Something was …

Then he saw it. It was lower. Several inches lower.

"Oh, no. Someone slashed th' tires!" Sean said. Two tires on the passenger side were flat. Someone hadn't just released the air. There were deep knife punctures. "Looks like they go' all four," Sean said.

Marella threw her hands in the air. "Tis terrific. Just wha' are we goin' tae do now?"

Tom said, "Let me find help. I'll see if anybody back at the hall can help us." Before Sean or Marella responded, he jogged across the darkened cobblestones to Dorlan Hall. The lights inside the building were still bright, so he figured someone would be around to help. From outside the door, he heard people talking. He opened the door, where he found himself face to face with Chairman Gordon Briggs, the man who just voted "No" against Sean Paterson.

CHAPTER 10

"Sorry to interrupt," Tom said. "My friends and I ran into some trouble. Someone slashed our tires, and now I need help to get them home. Would any of you be able to give us a hand?"

The men paused before Chairman Briggs left the group and walked over to him. He introduced himself and then said, "I hadn' seen ye in town before."

"It's my first day in Thurwick," Tom said.

"Sorry yer first day wasn' a better one."

Tom hesitated.

Briggs stood, patient.

"I'm Tom Wayne, from Atlanta, Georgia."

"Aye. From th' States, then."

"Yes."

Briggs said, "Any relation tae John Wayne, th' actor?"

"I get asked that a lot," Tom said. "But, no."

"Tae bad," Briggs said. "I loved him in 'Th' Quiet Man'." Briggs put his hand on Tom's shoulder and led him outside. "So ye're havin' car trouble?"

"I'm with Sean and Marella Paterson," Tom said. "While we were inside, someone vandalized their vehicle. There are knife punctures in all four tires."

"We canno' have tha'," Briggs said. "Being Chairman, I'll notify th' authorities. How abou' I arrange fur a ride home fur th' three o' ye?"

"That would help."

"Good. Then, in th' morning, th' police will come and fill out a report."

"Wouldn't the police have been around to stop them?"

"Unfortunately, they were both inside."

"Both? This town has two policemen?"

"Aye, bu' we manage tae get by."

But four tires are slashed. That's getting by?

Briggs said, "Don' worry. We'll make sure ye get home safe."

Tom nodded. Then, a question popped into his mind. "If you don't mind my asking, why'd you vote 'No' on that funding?"

Briggs said, "I'm rootin' fur Sean. I am. But I canno' justify askin' th' Highland Council tae distribute taxpayer funds fur a mythical creature."

"But couldn't you have helped some other way?"

"Oh, I did. Lad, some o' th' other councilpersons wanted tae request a law be passed tha' would have prevented *any* sort o' search fur Nessie. By voting 'No' on Sean's request, we at least allowed Mr. Paterson tae keep lookin'."

"Do you believe there's a Loch Ness monster?" Tom said.

Briggs said, "Ye three have had a long day, and it can be stressful goin' through a meetin' like tha'. Now ye're stranded. Le' me get ye yer help."

Tom was awake enough to gather that Briggs didn't want to answer the question, but he suddenly remembered how tired he was. As he stepped into the shadows outside Dorlan Hall, he heard Briggs say, "This is Alex. Alex Vaas. I've arranged fur him tae take ye home."

There was a man in the shadows. Tom noticed the beard, but his eyes were heavy and he didn't study the man's face. Tom extended his hand.

"Nice tae meet ye," Vaas said.

Tom pointed to the car. "They are over there. I'll head over that way and let them know you're coming."

They separated and Tom walked to the car on the cobblestones. He staggered a time or two as he lost his balance. He reunited with Sean and Marella. "Good news. I have help coming. There's a ride that's going to take us home. I spoke with the Chairman himself. He's going to have law enforcement look at your car, and then they'll come to your house in the morning and fill out a report."

"Would've been more help if th' Chairman voted 'Aye'," Sean said.

"I talked to him about that," Tom said. "Sounded like his vote was political."

"All votes are political," Sean said.

"Well, he might be someone we should talk with later. Maybe he can help in other ways."

"Don' encourage him," Marella said. "I don' want anythin' else tae go wrong."

A pair of headlights approached, and seconds later a black SUV pulled up alongside them. Tom heard Vaas say through his window that he was sent by Chairman Briggs to take them home. Tom opened the driver's passenger door, and helped Marella climb inside. He circled around to the other side, jumped in, and clicked on his seat belt. He rested his eyes a moment, then he opened them again and studied the driver.

That's when he remembered the red beard. Vaas was the same man he bumped into in Dorlan Hall.

CHAPTER 11

Alex Vaas turned off the radio. Sean told Vaas where they lived, and the SUV's engine hummed as it moved, its shocks bouncing over the cobblestone road.

Tom grew suspicious.

Chairman Briggs appeared helpful. He probably had to be since he was elected to his position. Tom thought it ironic that Briggs, though, would send Vaas to take them home. First, why was it not a member of the local law enforcement? Were there only two of them? Perhaps Tom didn't understand how the governments worked in Scotland. In America, law enforcement is handled by municipalities, counties, or states. *Maybe it was different here.*

Vaas leaned over to Sean. "I was in th' meetin'. Tell me more about how ye found Nessie."

"Ye think he's real?" Sean said.

"Ye tell me."

"Okay, then. It was like I explained. I had tae use five fishin' rods wi' pounds o' meat hooked tae th' lines. I used pork and steak. Maybe Nessie go' tired o' eating fish all th' time." Sean laughed, and Vaas laughed with him.

"Where exactly did ye find him?"

"Same place he was thirty years ago. O'er by Saint Michael's," Sean said.

"Ye sure God didn' send him tae ye?" Vaas said.

"I didn' pray fur him if that's wha' ye mean."

As they bounced along the road, Vaas said, "Others tried tae find Nessie o'er th' years, and I'd bet some used th' same methods. Why ye? Why were ye successful?"

Sean paused for a moment. "Perhaps thirty years o' persistence pays off."

Vaas proceeded to ask Sean many questions. Tom, his eyes longing for sleep, put all his effort into staying awake. What was Vaas doing? Was he prodding for information, or was he simply curious.

The SUV stopped. Marella got out of the car. Were they back at the cabin? Outside the window, there was brown sign for Annabel's.

"I guess this is where I get off."

He thanked Vaas, but he didn't trust him. Tom then tapped Sean on the shoulder. They shook hands, and he got out of the car. He walked to the rear, where he met Marella. Her green eyes were large under her curly hair.

"Please come o'er as soon as ye wake t'morrow morning." She handed Tom a piece of paper. "Dial this number from yer phone."

"I'm embarrassed to say I left my cell phone across the ocean."

"Then use th' phone in yer room. If ye have trouble, Annabel should help ye. Let us know ye're on yer way."

Tom couldn't pull his eyes from hers. Her face was worried, but she had an air of hope. Tom was glad he helped her. He didn't want to let her down.

"How early is too early to call?"

"Be o'er by nine, if ye can. Call before then."

Tom nodded. Then, to his surprise, Marella leaned forward and hugged him. "Ye were an angel sent by God," she said. "I couldn' have handled this situation t'night without help."

"I'm not through helping. You two get home safe. And watch out for that driver. He's asking a lot of questions."

Marella nodded, and she climbed into the SUV. He stood with his hands in his pockets, watching the SUV drive away and disappear into the darkness. He walked into Annabel's Bed and Breakfast, climbed up the steps, and found his way into his room.

Could Alex Vaas be trusted? Chairman Briggs was very personable. How were the two of them connected? Maybe it was just coincidence that Vaas had been assigned to help. Then again, maybe he had misread Vaas, and they got off on the wrong foot.

Tom sat on the edge of the bed. Thurwick was a strange place. He imagined the subject of this whole mess, the Loch Ness monster. As he pictured the aquatic dinosaur swimming beneath the deep blue waters in between sloping Scottish hills along the shores of Thurwick, he thought how it all felt so surreal. Then, before he fell asleep, he pictured an image of himself on a large boat. He had a harpoon gun in his possession, and he was aiming it at a sea creature before everything went dark.

CHAPTER 12

Tom jumped up in his bed. Loud ringing echoed in his head. "What in God's name—!"

Church bells.

Saint Michael's church bells. He covered his ears until the bells stopped. "That's one way to wake up in the morning!" he said.

The rest had done him well. He had called Marella, and told her he was on his way. He couldn't tell if she was happy to hear from him or not. Maybe she hadn't had enough sleep. Maybe she wasn't a morning person? He didn't know. He just knew he wanted to be with her again.

He dressed, and went downstairs for breakfast. The Annabel was there, and she offered to feed him, and the aroma smelled good, but he decided he'd pass, hoping, just maybe, he'd have breakfast with Marella. He had to get going right away. The church was across the street. Had God Himself awoken him?

As he walked along Mackay Rd, he appreciated the cool nature around him. Then there was the Loch. To his right, a few hundred yards through the brush, was a body of water harboring a mystery. He felt uncertain whether he believed or not.

Sean had given no hesitation about his experience. *Was he right? Was the creature real? No. He had probably been mistaken.* Tom sympathized with Sean. It would be exciting to believe a monster like the one in the Loch actually existed.

But, really?

The man was probably losing his mind, Tom thought. If he had to choose, he decided he'd take Marella's side on the issue.

So how would he help? Tom knew he had no experience with delusion. This would all be new to him. He decided simply being there would be enough. He'd help in little ways, and then see where that took them.

He arrived at the cottage. Outside some of the windmills squeaked as they spun in the cool morning breeze. His coat was barely enough to protect him from the cold, but as the sun rose he felt the warmth of its rays.

Marella opened the door. She was dressed warmly, her curly hair draped over her shoulders. She stepped outside and shut the door.

"Hi," she said. "Let's go fur a walk." She stepped along the dirt road. Tom's stomach grumbled, but he told himself breakfast would have to wait. He heard the crunch of the dirt under their feet as they moved away from the cottage.

"I want tae thank ye fur comin'," Marella said. "Twas a surprise."

Tom said, "Well, the night of our date, when I missed you at the apartment, I wanted to make sure I kept up my end of the bargain. A man's got to keep his promises, you know." Tom grinned.

"Ye shouldn' have come."

"I'm glad I did."

"Ye should leave and go back tae America. Things are tae dangerous."

"What do you mean?"

"Look," Marella said. Her voice rose. "My father is doolally. He's insane, actually. He believes in this fairy tale, and he won' stop pursuin' it."

"He believes he saw something."

"Ye don' understand," she said. "He's been chasin' this monster my whole life. I stayed wi' my father fur years, believin' my father was right about th' monster. It was a quirk, but he was havin' success as a scientist, so we didn' mind. My mother and I thought 'twas just a hobby. Then one day he disappeared. He had gone lookin' fur th' monster one mornin'. Said he'd be back tha' evenin'. But when he didn' come home, my mother was beside herself. She was worried sick. Well, he came home two days later as though no'ing had happened. He even tried tae convince her he was only gone a few hours, but two whole nights had passed. Tha' was the last straw. My mother couldn' take it anymore, and decided tae leave. She disappeared and ne'er came back."

"I'm so sorry to hear that. I didn't know."

"She ne'er would have left if he hadn' driven her away."

"Well, a lot of couples have problems."

"Ye don' understand. After tha', he wasn' well anymore. And more bad things happened, just odd things we couldn' explain. Da's money dried up. We go' by, bu' we had tae struggle. I missed my mother terribly, but I had nowhere tae go. And e'en wi' all that, he still kept lookin' fur th' monster. He'd become obsessed about it. One day, I had had enough. I wanted more, and I left fur America."

There was pain in Marella's face. "That's a lot for someone to go through," Tom said. "But maybe that's why we met."

Marella's shook her head. "I'm sorry I skipped out on ye. I should have let ye know. Tis just tha' things were so hectic…"

"Oh, it's ok," he said. "You would have appreciated the flowers, though."

"I'm sure they were beautiful." She grew serious. "Still, I think ye should leave. Things are getting' dangerous. Tis enough fur me tae try tae protect my father. I don' want tae also be responsible fur ye."

"I'm a grown man," he said. "And so's your father. We'll be alright."

Marella frowned.

Tom kicked a rock with his shoe. "Who slashed the tires?"

"Don' know," she said. "But 'twas a threat. Someone wants tae stop us from findin' somethin' tha' doesn' exist. If people in Thurwick believe there's a Loch Ness monster, why, this whole town is goin crazy. I don' know who tae trust."

"You're not alone, Marella. I came here because I thought you'd need help. I intend to help."

"Ye need tae go back."

"I have an idea. I met with Chairman Briggs, and he told me that he was rooting for your father."

"He's a politician. Ye canno' trust him."

"Maybe not, but I believe he doesn't want anybody to get hurt. I think we can go to him for protection."

Marella paused. "This whole thing would be easier if Da' would just stop. Bu' he won'. I'm afraid fur his safety. Foremost, they damaged his reputation and his livelihood. Now they are vandalizin' his car with knives. Na tellin' wha' will come next. He just needs tae stop."

"He's been around a long time. I'm sure he knows how to take care of himself."

"But things are heatin' up, Tom. Somethin' is brewing. I can just sense it."

"Sense what?"

"After speakin' wi' Caleb, my father is even more inspired. He said tae me this mornin', 'If others are trying tae stop us it means they believe Nessie exists, tae. Tha' means they've seen him.' I tell ye, all o' Thurwick's gone mad."

"I thought about that, too."

"He doesn' even care about th' vandalism report. He asked me tae take care o' that fur him. He's already said he's getting' his tires fixed. Then he's gettin' more bait and he's goin' back on th' water t'night."

"Tonight?" Tom asked.

"Aye. T'night."

"Then I'll go with him," Tom said.

Marella raised her arms. "I don' believe this. Has everyone around me gone mad?"

"No," Tom said. "Hear me out. If I go with him, and we find the monster, he'll have a witness."

"Ye're insane."

"I didn't say I believe there's a monster," Tom said. "But I do believe your father loves you. He wants to prove himself to you. Maybe what he needs is for someone to give him a chance. Every man needs someone to give him a chance. If I go with him, he'll have that chance. Then, maybe I can talk with him on the boat about his priorities. Maybe I could help him change course."

"Ye mean get him tae change his mind?"

"Yes."

"Will it work?"

"It's worth a try."

Marella paused. "He's stopped listenin' tae me years ago. Maybe ye'll have more luck."

Tom nodded.

Marella smiled. "I still think ye're doolally."

Tom winked. Then he gave her a warm grin before they turned around and walked the dirt path to the cottage.

CHAPTER 13

The blue car, with four shiny new tires, sat in the driveway. "See how determined he is?" Marella said. She led Tom into the house. The den was a pure bachelor's pad, without much real cleanup over the years. Marella apologized for the mess, but Tom said he didn't mind.

They heard some clanking in the kitchen. "Da', Tom came back."

Sean appeared around the corner. His glasses were dusty. "Oh. Wonderful!" he said. He disappeared behind the wall. Tom heard the sink running, and then Sean reappeared with a dish towel to dry his hands. "I ne'er thanked ye fur yer assistance lest evenin'." He stuck out his hand. "Thank ye fur comin'."

Tom said, "I have to admit, I didn't expect to attend a meeting like that when the bus dropped me off."

"Aye, I'll bet." Sean said. "Marella, come see what I've put together this evenin'." They followed him into the kitchen. Several large packs of meet wrapped in cellophane, enough to feed a family for a week, sat on the kitchen table. Underneath the table, intermixed between the chairs, were several coolers with their lids open. Inside each one were bags of ice. Standing against the walls in the corner were two brand new fishing poles. Each had their marketing cards still attached.

"I had tae get two new fishing rods fur th' ones I lost lest weekend," Sean said. "I made a mistake. Th' poles I used lest time were freshwater poles. I must have lost my mind usin' those. There was na way they'd hold up tae a plesiosaur. This time, though, I picked up some saltwater poles. Th' line is stronger, and they might hold up enough tae give me time tae take a picture and ge' proof."

"Mr. Paterson," Tom asked. "You said you saw the Loch Ness monster thirty years ago. Did you use all this stuff to find him the first time?"

Sean stopped his preparations. "Na. Actually, th' foremost time was quite coincidental."

"Why don't you tell me about it?"

Sean hesitated. "Do ye really want tae know?"

"Please."

Sean hesitated, his eyes pleading with Marella. Then he motioned both of them to sit in the den. The sofa and chairs were old and dusty, and Tom figured the furniture hadn't moved since they first were placed in their positions several decades ago.

"Have a seat," Sean said. They sat down. The worn pillows sank, worn from thirty years of use. "Ye know, it happened when I wasn' much younger than th' two o' ye. Oh, I was pretty sure o' myself, like most young people are. I was apprenticin' fur another scientist in Thurwick, Dr. Elroy. He had studied at Oxford. I'd say he was more o' an engineer than a scientist. He put out some great gadgets.

"One day, he asked me tae deliver one o' his inventions tae th' priests at Saint Michaels. It was some kind o' speaker. It kind o' surprised me tha' a two-thousand year old church had ministers who were interested in speakers, but somehow he sold one tae them. All I remember was it was in a small box.

"In any case, I made th' delivery. When th' attendant opened th' door, I remember I heard them singin' inside. Well, chanting, really. That's when I figured they wanted th' speaker tae project sound. Their music was beautiful, and I wanted tae hear more, but I had tae get goin'. So I left. The day was bright. It had a magical feeling. Instead o' goin' right back, I decided tae steal a few moments and walk by th' Loch.

"Now, I'm na' a prayin' man by any stretch o' th' imagination. But as I stood outside th' Church and heard th' singin' comin' through th' windows, I thought they had hooked up th' invention, because th' music became a little clearer. I felt at peace at th' nature scene around th' Loch.

"And that's when I saw him. Near th' shore, a dark bulge rose out o' the' water. It surprised me foremost. In fact, I thought it was just a rogue wave or somethin' o' th' sort. But then it surfaced several feet abo'e th' water, and it lifted its neck and head. Oh, ye should have seen it!

"Needless tae say I was shocked. My eyes widened. Its head was about th' size of a rugby ball. Then its neck twisted, and its snout pointed right at me. The creature and I made eye contact. I have tae tell ye th' hairs on th' back o' my neck stood straight up. I'll ne'er forget tha' moment. I still get chills... Anyway, I took some steps backward and fell on my ass. My stumblin' must have scared it, because it dipped its head intae th' water, and with a splash it was gone. It moved so quickly. I'll ne'er get o'er how fast it was."

Sean paused, as one does when they relive a moment from the past. Tom caught Marella's eyes, and she shrugged.

"What happened next?" Tom asked.

Sean shook his head, returning to the present. "I wondered if anybody else had seen it. Sadly, na one was around. I still heard th' chants from inside, but I figured th' priests would have stopped singin' if they had seen it. I ran back tae th' front o' th' Church, and towards th' square. E'erybody was mindin' their own business. I didn' know what tae do. I felt I had tae tell somebody, but how do ye announce th' presence o' th' Loch Ness monster?

"Well, my knees weakened, and I fell tae th' ground in front o' th' Church. As people ran up tae me tae check on me, I just started yellin', 'I saw th' Loch Ness monster! I saw th' Loch Ness monster!' Some people said I was doolally, but others asked me where. 'In th' Loch!' I said. I confess I was hysterical. I was a young scientist. Wha' I witnessed disrupted everythin' I thought I knew up tae tha' point in my life."

"What did everyone do?"

"A group o' people took me tae th' doctor. They gave me water and checked all my vitals, but I was fine. I kept asking, though, fur a report o' any sightings. They declared me delirious, tha' I had been working tae hard fur Dr. Elroy, and they prescribed me tae go home and get some sleep."

Sean chuckled. "O' course, tha' was impossible. I went home and tried tae follow th' doctor's orders, but my heart and my mind raced tha' entire day. I couldn' take it anymore. I had tae go back tae th' Loch. Well, when I went back, there had tae have been three hundred people out there. And I arrived just as a news truck had come in from Inverness. They stuck a camera in my face, and they interviewed me. I missed th' broadcast, but someone told me later I appeared disheveled. I'd imagine most people would, though, after just havin' seen th' Loch Ness monster.

"But th' news created a firestorm," Sean said. "O'er th' next several weeks, thousands o' people came from all o'er. I was a celebrity fur a short while, but it wasn' that I wanted tae be. However, it turned out tae be a good thing, because one o' those people who came tae look fur Nessie was Marella's mother."

"What," Marella said. "Ye told me ye both met at Church!"

"We did," Sean said. "We met on th' Church property. Oh, she didn' believe in th' monster. She was just there fur th' excitement. Bu' she was beautiful, and she captured my heart. In fact, I had been thinkin' about Nessie fur so long, meeting Marella's mother was th' first time anyone took my mind off it."

Sean paused, watching the weather outside the window. Then he scratched his head as he relived the memory. "All th' people went away. Yer mother and I go' married, and I had some success wi' a few o' my inventions…"

"Bu' ye were obsessed," Marella said. "It was all th' time…"

"I know wha' I saw!" Sean's face became stern. "And na one will tell me differently." He stood up and paced. Sean's intensity rose. "Changin' th' world involves great sacrifice. I didn' ask tae discover th' Loch Ness monster. I didn' ask tae get all th' attention, tae have people believe I'm doolally th' past thirty years. Bu' often moments in life come when a man realizes his purpose, why he's here. Mine hit me thirty years ago, and 'tis my mission in life tae prove tha' th' Loch Ness monster does exist."

Marella tensed. "Tis hopeless."

Tom said, "Mr. Paterson. What have you tried in order to find him?"

"Oh, lots o' things," Sean said. "Radar technology. Heat technology. Shoreline cameras. Underwater cameras. Water displacement technology. Sonar technology. I've got th' equipment in th' spare room. None o' them proved useful, though we did learn a lot about th' Loch because o' them. Later, other efforts were led by other teams. They tried tae drag th' Loch wi' nets, and use many o' th' same technologies as I did. But they, tae, failed."

Sean sat back on his sofa. "Imagine na success fur thirty years. It wasn' until I decided tae go fishin' fur him that I had success. I'd been overthinkin' him all this time."

"Da', maybe 'twas somethin' else…"

"Mr. Paterson," Tom interrupted. "I want to go with you tonight to help you look."

Sean paused. "I can handle it myself, thank ye."

"Mr. Paterson, you have a lot of equipment, and I can help you on the boat. Plus, when he comes back, you'll have a second set of eyes to help verify your story."

"Na. Ye might scare him off."

"So might you."

"I don' want tae be responsible fur ye if somethin' happens."

"And I feel the same way about you, so that makes us even."

"And if I don' find him…?" Sean asked. "What if I am supposed tae` see him only once every thirty years?"

"Then my being there won't change a thing," Tom said. "And I can help you load the equipment back in the car when you're ready to go home."

Sean paused.

Marella nodded.

"Okay," Sean said. "We'll leave here just before sunset. Ge' some rest. It will be a late night."

Tom stood up and shook Sean's hand. "Alright, then. Let's do it."

CHAPTER 14

Tom sat in the passenger seat as Sean pulled into the parking lot. Sean said, "We're goin' tae unload and take everythin' o'er there." He pointed to a wooden dock that led out onto the blue waters of Loch Ness. Through the windshield, several boats swayed above the water, tied to their sections on the dock.

"Which one is yours?" Tom said.

"Th' silver one. Near th' end."

"The pontoon boat?"

"Na. Th' one just in front o' it."

Tom squinted. "The speedboat?"

"Na, th' one just after tha'." Sean opened the car door and stepped out of the car. There nothing obvious floating between the speedboat and the pontoon boat. "Are ye goin' tae just sit there, or are ye goin' tae help me unload?" Sean had opened the rear door and removed the fishing gear.

"Sorry. I just don't see it."

Sean didn't reply.

Tom examined his side of the back seat. A net and some towels leaned against the coolers. He unloaded the coolers. He was surprised at how heavy they were. The meat and the ice together had to weigh forty pounds each. "Is your boat big enough to carry all this weight?" Tom asked.

"Hope so."

It was not the answer he expected. Sean hadn't been on a boat since he was out with friends on a lake back in Arizona. It was the summer before he went to college.

Sean picked up the cooler and carried it to the end of the dock. He set it down, and Tom did likewise. He lifted the cooler and carried it toward the rowboat. The dock's swaying made him uneasy, and he stopped a time or two while trying to regain his balance.

Sean didn't acknowledge him as they passed each other. Was he up to this?

He sat the cooler down next to Sean's. Between the pontoon boat and the speed boat floated a small rowboat. It was miniscule compared to the others.

"You can't be serious!"

"Wha' do ye mean?" Sean answered.

"That thing won't hold both of us and the coolers. We'll drown!" Tom said.

"Ye might. I've go' a life preserver."

"You didn't bring another one?"

"Don' have one," Sean said. "I've ne'er had company before."

"Great," Tom said. "I'm going after the Loch Ness monster without a life preserver."

"What was tha'?" Sean had his head in the car and was removing the fishing poles.

"I said, 'Save some of that gear for me."

Tom returned to the car. There was a net and a flashlight in the trunk. He grabbed them as Sean stood on the dock next to the rowboat. Sean strapped on his life preserver and he placed the coolers in the boat.

Tom stepped in the boat. His feet felt unsteady as the small rowboat rocked in the water. He set the fishing poles in the sockets. The oars rose and fell with the ripples in the water. The boat creaked as the waves rocked it up and down. Sean, standing on the dock, handed equipment to Tom.

"Would you like me to row?" Tom said.

"Tha' wasn' part o' th' deal," Sean said. "All I needed ye fur was tae help load th' boat, and tae be a second set o' eyes. Other than tha', ye are tae sit and be quiet. Oh, and don' scare anythin' away."

Tom nodded, but he didn't plan to comply. He had promised Marella he'd talk with Sean about his priorities. Once they were on the open water away from the shoreline, Sean wouldn't be able to keep Tom from saying anything.

"I know ye're just doin' this tae get a chance at my daughter," Sean said.

Tom paused. "What makes you say that?"

"I may be thirty years older than ye, but I'm na fool."

Tom didn't answer.

"Why else would ye travel from America all th' way tae Scotland and show up at my door? Tae look fur th' Loch Ness monster? Na one's done tha' in thirty years."

"I'm helping you now, aren't I?"

"I've got eyes. I know she's a looker. I've had tae fend off creeps half her life. So tell me, was this your idea, or did Marella put ye up tae this?"

"Mr. Paterson…"

"Own up tae it, laddie."

"It was my idea."

"So what's th' plan? When we sit out there all night and not'ing comes, ye're goin' tae tell everybody tha' I'm insane? Tha' I've lost my mind? Then ye're goin' tae whisk her away and leave me here alone tae fend fur myself?"

Don't get defensive.

"It won' work. I know yer game." Sean locked eyes with Tom, glaring down on him from the raised dock elevation.

"What if something does come?" Tom asked, unsteady in the rowboat.

Sean didn't answer. After a few moments, he shrugged and went back to his preparations.

"I'm not here to judge," Tom said. "I admire your passion, and your belief. Yes, Marella is beautiful. I hope to get to know her more. But, first and foremost, I'm here to help. You let me do that, and whatever happens, we'll make the most of it."

Sean stepped down from the dock into the boat. He sat between the oars.

Tom, already in the boat, sat down on the opposite bench. He grabbed the rails, and he steadied himself as he felt the boat rock back and forth. He zipped up his coat remembering again that it would not suffice as a life preserver.

Sean, wearing his life jacket, untied the rope connecting his rowboat to the dock. He then grabbed the oars, stroked the water gently, and the boat drifted away from the dock into the open Loch.

Here we go. Am I ready for this?

"Thirty minutes," Sean said. "We row until we get tae Saint Michael's. That's where we'll hook our bait. Then we wait."

Tom watched the shore. Thurwick was very quaint from the water. The buildings were alive with people, all of them oblivious to Tom and Sean and their search for the Loch Ness monster.

"Here." Sean tossed Tom a rope. "Tie a bowline knot around yer waist. Then we'll be hooked together. If anythin' happens, I won' lose ye in the water."

"What's a bowline knot?"

"Have ye e'er been on th' water?"

"Not since…"

"Ne'er mind," Sean interrupted. "Let me show ye."

Sean demonstrated by pulling his end of the long rope around his waist and, holding the end of the rope with his right hand, maneuvered his wrists in such a way around the taught line that it formed a knot, lassoing the rope around him. As Tom attempted to do the same, Sean said, "Practice is all it takes. Keep tryin' and I'll let ye know when ye've go' it."

Tom nodded. He practiced over and over again with the rope around his waist. It didn't appear complicated, but the more he tried, the more he felt out of place.

Sean rowed the small boat toward the destination. The boat bounced along the choppy waves. *Either Sean was crazy,* Tom thought, *or he was right.* The depths of the dark waters surged underneath them. Could he swim if it mattered?

I hope I won't have to find out.

CHAPTER 15

"Is that storm going to hit us?"

Dark clouds appeared in the west. Shadows stretched and covered the land in darkness as the last light from the sun disappeared over the horizon.

"Likely," Sean said. "Looks only tae be rain, though. So long as we don' hear thunder, we're okay." Sean had rowed the boat to the spot in front of Saint Michael's Church.

"I think I got this bowline knot," Tom said. As he practiced, he understood the mechanics. He was without a life jacket. However, knowing he was tied to Sean and his life jacket gave him a slight hope from drowning. He tied the bowline one more time and pulled it tight around his waist.

"Alright," Tom said. "You'd better stay safe. If something happens to you, I'm fish food."

"Aye, tha' means we'll have tae have each other's back," Sean said.

Tom nodded.

Sean was far more practical than everyone believed. Though he was somewhat clumsy in and around his boat, he learned quickly, and applied common sense to most problems.

Except then there was the issue with the Loch Ness monster. That one claim, that he had found it not once but twice, caused a ripple of commotion amongst the population. The people attacked his reputation. They had destroyed his marriage, hurt his income, and now strained his relationship with his daughter.

And yet he persisted. Why?

Sean stopped rowing. "Looks like th' priests are up again t'night."

As the church shadows covered the stone details, several windows were lit in the building next it.

"That's where the priests live?" Tom asked.

"Aye. 'Tis their rectory. There are five priests there t'day. There used tae be more, but wi' th' Church losing influence, there are more empty rooms."

"Have you ever been inside?"

"A few times when I was a boy."

Tom admired the dark church silhouette, its ancient walls rising from the earth. When was the last time he was in church? Also not since he was a boy.

"You ever wonder if the church has anything to do with the monster?"

"Wha' do ye mean?"

"Well, both times you saw him you were in front of the church. Does that have anything to do with it?"

"Wha', like th' priests feed it or somethin'?"

"Just wondering."

"Th' only ones out here throwin' steaks in th' water t'night will be ye and me," Sean said. "And we'd better ge' goin' if we don' want tae be out here all night."

He opened the cooler. Inside, large steaks were wrapped in plastic grocery bags, buried in ice. Sean had grabbed one of the fishing poles, and found the hook at the end. "Grab a pole and hook some steak tae th' end o' th' line," Sean said.

Tom grabbed the pole next to him. The hook was large, about the length of his finger. The line was strong. "You sure this line will hold a dinosaur?"

"Plesiosaur."

"Yeah, that."

"Tis th' strongest I could get in Thurwick," Sean said. "It'll have tae do."

"I guess you only live once."

Holding the hook, Tom grabbed a steak.

"Make sure ye get those hooks in there." Sean demonstrated with his own hook and bait.

Tom worked the hooks into the steak. He was surprised how easily the points sliced through the flesh. If something big got this thing lodged in its mouth, it would develop a major bad attitude.

He studied the bowline know around his waist. *I'd be better hope Sean was crazy. No monsters, no getting wet.* He shook his head.

This whole thing is nuts, he thought. Then, he lifted the steak over the rail and dropped it over the side. It plopped into the water, and he watched and listened as the line unwound into the depths below.

"Woa!" Sean said.

"What!" Tom jumped. Had the monster had surfaced?

"I lost hold o' my hook on this line and it swung near ye. Sorry abou' tha'."

Tom tensed. Flying hooks versus going overboard. What am I doing?

Sean worked the hook into the steak.

Tom was claustrophobic. The boat was very small, and the fishing gear made it smaller. If something large came up from underneath, they could capsize.

Sean said, "Ye seem jumpy. Ye think we'll find him t'night?"

Tom felt surprised by the question. "Do you?"

"Oh, I hope so," Sean said. "Bu' remember thirty years passed between sightings. Scientifically, th' odds are against us."

After all the lines had been baited, Tom decided now would be the perfect time to talk. "Mr. Paterson," Tom said. "If you expect to find the creature once every thirty years, don't you wonder if you're missing out on more important things?"

"Did my daughter tell ye tae ask me tha'?"

Tom was taken aback. "Well, I…"

"Wait," Sean interrupted. "Do ye hear tha'?"

Tom stopped. Though they were faint, he heard the sound of voices coming from Saint Michael's Church. It sounded like singing.

"Tis th' priests again," Sean said. "They do this on occasion."

"Will they ruin our chances?"

"Don' know. But tha' does give me an idea." Sean grabbed the fishing net behind him."

Tom laughed. "Your net's too small."

"Aye," Sean said. "But, lest weekend this was wha' I used tae make noise. I heard fishermen say tha' sometimes bangin' on th' bottom o' th' boat will attract fish. I was doing tha' with th' handle o' this net lest time when they came. I wonder if tha' had somethin' tae do wi' it."

Tom shook his head. "We need to talk about…"

"Shhhh," Sean said, raising a finger to his lips. "Now, we need tae stay quiet. Na talkin'. Let's let th' bait and th' tappin' do th' work fur us."

The rope was still tied around Tom's waist. The poles swayed with their baits in the water. The sky darkened, and the stars flickered behind the overhanging clouds. At least there was no rain.

Just stay dry and get back to the car.

Sean tapped the net's handle on the floor of the boat, making a thumping sound. Sean's rhythm naturally went with the rhythm of the chanting priests. Often, when Tom worked out in a gym, he had exercised at the rhythm of the music in the room, and he thought it interesting how people will sometimes move with the music without thinking about it.

So he sat quietly, uncomfortable in the dark surroundings. The lights from Thurwick reflected off the clouds above, and the windows were lit from the small rooms in the rectory next to Saint Michael's. Beyond, the dark shapes of the Highland hills descended into the black waters of the Loch.

The chanting ceased for a moment, though Sean continued to tap. Then the priests changed to a new song. Would Sean change his tapping to the new rhythm?

He did.

MATT KUNZ

Tom mentally prepared himself in the event he'd have to stay quiet a long time. Sean was determined. Tom imagined Sean was also experienced in patience. If the man had to wait thirty years to recapture his experience, then Sean Paterson was a model in perseverance.

Tom decided he'd have to learn the same. It was his idea to pretend to help Sean, all the while trying to convince Sean that his priorities were wrong. Tom knew they wouldn't find anything. There was no monster. After another failed attempt, Tom knew he could convince Sean to better spend his days…

A thump hit the boat. The boat rocked in the water. Tom caught his breath. He felt his adrenaline rush through his body. The hairs on the back of his neck stiffened. Sean, who a second ago had appeared calm, had dropped the net and grabbed the sides of the boat. His eyes were wide.

"What was…what was *that*?" Tom said.

Sean said nothing. He examined the ripples in the water. None of the poles indicated anything had taken the bait. As the boat rocked silently in the water, Tom heard the chanting from the priests.

"Maybe we just hit a log," Tom said.

Suddenly, a reel from the pole next to Tom spun. It whirred loudly, its line running up the pole and down into the water. The sight of it made Tom's hairs stand on end. He rose from his seat, and his eyes widened.

Sean said, "Grab it, lock it in, and jerk th' line."

Tom grabbed the pole and said, "What do you mean, lock it in?"

Then another pole's reel spun beside Sean. The loud whirring from the reels confused Tom. "Jesus!" He grabbed the pole, and hit the lock.

In a flash the pole jerked out of his hand and flung into the shadows.

The flying pole splashed in the darkness. The splashing sound was overcome by the sound of the spinning reel next to Sean.

Sean grabbed near the handle of the pole with the spinning wheel, keeping it in its socket. The whirring of the line running mesmerized Tom.

Sean tensed. "Hang on!" He locked the reel.

The pole bent hard and the boat tipped. Water poured into the rowboat over the side. Sean screamed and fell into the water. Tom felt a tug on his waist as the rope tightened. The water was cold as it soaked through his shoes and socks. Then, Tom lost his balance as he was yanked out of the boat and into the water.

His entire body went below the surface.

"My God!" he screamed, but water entered his mouth. His thoughts ran wild.

Prehistoric monsters! No lifejacket! Where's Sean! They're going to eat me!

He kicked and swam to the surface. When his head exited the water, he gasped for air. All round him, all was chaos. The boat was sinking. Sean was yelling and splashing toward the boat, his life jacket keeping him afloat.

"Dammit. Come here and help me!" Sean said.

Tom swam to the boat. He had an image from the movie, Jaws. He pictured rows of razor sharp teeth rushing at his legs. He imagined his legs being cut from his hips, his lifeless upper torso bobbing at the surface. He felt his breathing go out of control. Despite his anxiety, he grabbed the edge of the boat. Much of it was below the water. The coolers floated in the waves next to him.

One of the fishing rods remained in its boat socket.

The rest were gone.

Then he felt something hit his leg thigh. It was hard, and solid. It felt like a hammer, and he knew it would bruise. He felt water currents swirl around him. Something swam past him.

Tom yelled, like a construction worker who had just been in an accident.

"There's something in the water with us!"

"I know. I know!"

"Get in the damned boat!"

"Tis already capsized!"

Tom pulled himself up over the edge of the boat. "Get in!"

They heard a monstrous sound. It came from the waters below them. It was a sound Tom had never heard before. It sounded ancient. Tom felt his air leave his lungs as he gasped in fright.

Sean screamed.

"Help me in!"

Tom grabbed Sean's hand and pulled. Sean slid over the edge, his legs kicking the air. The rowboat was capsized, its rails centimeters above the surface. Both oars were still on the boat, so Tom grasped the handles and rowed towards the shoreline.

Another roar came from the water below. Then a smell of rotting fish hit his nostrils.

"Good God. What is that smell!"

"Hurry!" Sean said. "Ge' us out o' here!" Sean cupped water and flung it over the rails. It did little good.

Tom felt his shoulders ache as he rowed with everything he had. The water resisted with every stroke.

Suddenly, the final pole's reel whirred. The sound and the speed of the reel's spinning shocked them both. Sean didn't waste time. He picked up the rod and threw it into the water. "He can have it!"

Tom continued to row, his adrenaline pumping, his muscles aching.

This boat is sinking!

"We're goin' tae have tae swim," Sean said.

Tom panicked. "We can't make it!"

Then the boat dipped.

Tom stood, but the boat disappeared below his feet into the depths. His shoulders sank below the surface.

"We're done!"

"Just swim!"

Tom kicked and swam, splashing with everything he had.

Sean said, "We're close tae th' shore. Come on!" His floating life jacket keeping him afloat, Sean swam towards land.

Tom felt the tug from the rope around his waist. The shore was twenty yards away. He kicked and writhed and paddled to get out of the water. His lungs were about to explode. He swallowed, and he coughed to keep the Loch out of his lungs.

"Get me out of this water!"

Tom kicked. His hand touched something.

A rock!

He clambered. The shoreline was under his feet. He stood to run, but fell down. The rope connecting him to Sean tugged and knocked him off balance. He got up again, splashing his feet. Then he found solid ground, and he fell.

He felt grass and mud.

Next to him, Sean lied on the grass, his chest heaving with each breath. Tom worried Sean might have a heart attack. Heck, he worried that *he* might have a heart attack. Then Sean sat up, and laughed.

Tom said, "You're out of your mind."

"Am I?" Sean said.

Sean wasn't crazy. He, in fact, had been right all along. Everyone else had been wrong.

"So, wha' do ye think o' th' Loch Ness monster now?" Sean asked.

Tom rolled on the grass and put his hands on his head. He tried to catch his breath. His leg was sore from whatever hit him on his thigh.

"What's Marella going to say?"

"She won' believe us."

"This changes everything."

"Wha' did I tell ye, laddie?"

Tom sat up. "We need to get your boat back." He rubbed his bruised leg.

Sean stood, untying the rope around his waist. Water poured from his wet clothes onto the ground as he threw the rope into the mud. "Aye. In th' mornin'."

"After that, I have no idea what we do next."

"It'll come tae us." Sean said. "Come on. Let's go get th' car."

Tom also stood. He noticed his legs felt weak. He reached out to Sean to steady himself, but Sean had already moved up the hill. Tom put his hands on his knees.

As Sean walked away, he said, "I knew I liked ye." Then Sean appeared giddy as he disappeared behind the trees and into the shadows.

Tom took one step to follow him before he bent over and heaved.

CHAPTER 16

Tom's body shook. After having escaped the Loch, they had walked to the car. Tom had lost a shoe, and he'd have to hop along the rocks and the cobblestone streets. It was a mile away, but the clouds overhead had opened up, and rain had fallen upon them. The wet clothes caused him to experience the first hints of hypothermia. Once they arrived at the car, Sean had climbed under the driver side door and pulled out a small box.

"Spare key," he said.

"Did we lose the other one?" Tom asked.

"Na. Tis still in my pocket. But tis wet, and I wanted tae make sure we had an extra just in case."

Sean had sat in the car and turned on the engine. "I'll start the heater. Get inside."

Sean shook. The cold weather had affected them both. Sean went to the back seat and found the towels. "Here. Co'er yerself. Get warm."

Tom had done as he was told, shivering all the way to Sean's cottage.

When they arrived, Sean opened the door to his cottage and went inside. Tom followed. Marella had been asleep on the couch. When she opened her eyes, she frowned. "Wha' in th' world happened tae th' two o' ye?"

Sean and Tom didn't answer. They rushed past the den into the back rooms. Sean said, "Ye can change in Marella's room. I'll grab some warm clothes fur ye."

Tom's immediate thought was to get warm. The shaking persisted. Sean tossed him some clothes, and he shut Marella's door. He undressed, dried off, and put Sean's clothes on. He still felt chilled, but his body noticed an instant improvement.

Tom went to the den. Though he shook he felt some warmth return to his body.

Marella said, "Ye look like ye drowned."

"We did."

Tom found a blanket and sat on the couch. He noticed his teeth chattered.

"Do you have anything warm to drink?"

"I'll make some coffee."

Sean walked into the den. He didn't appear cold. Was he handling the hypothermia better, or was he just good at faking it?

"Alright. Foremost thing we need tae do is retrieve th' boat and whate'er we can find that's left o' th' coolers and th' rods."

"Do you think we'll be able to get it?" Tom asked.

"Wait," Marella interrupted. "Wha' happened tae th' boat?"

Sean said, "Aye. Tis still there. Likely just under th' surface o' th' water near where we left it."

"Will the rest of the gear wash up on shore?"

"It should. Let's just hope th' currents wash it all up on our side o' th' Loch."

Marella raised her voice. "Will someone please tell me wha' happened?"

Neither Tom nor Sean said anything for a moment. Sean gestured to Tom. "Why don' ye tell her?"

Tom paused.

"Tell me wha'?" Marella said.

I can't believe what I'm about to say.

"We found the Loch Ness monster," Tom said.

"Ye're lying."

"It's true. It capsized our boat."

"Oh, really?" Marella said. "Look a' me and tell me ye saw it wi' yer own eyes."

Tom shrugged his shoulders. "Okay," he said. He recounted the events: the spinning reels, the thump below the boat, the rushing water.

"Wha' did it look like?"

"Well, actually, I didn't see it."

"Terrific."

"We're serious."

"Am I a fool or somethin'? A couple o' hours on a boat and now ye two are in collusion together."

"Wait," Tom said. "When we were in the water, he hit me in the leg. Hard in the thigh." He reached down and unbuckled his belt.

"Don' take yer pants off in front o' me," Marella said. "Just because ye followed me halfway across th' world doesn' give ye that right!"

Tom stopped removing his pants.

Sean walked up to Marella. "My dear, we heard it. We smelled it."

Tom said, "That's right. I was in the water when I heard that sound. And that smell. I've never smelled anything like it. I tell you I was never so scared in my whole life!"

"Ye're both insane," Marella said. "I should leave both o' ye here tae fend fur yerselves while I go back tae America."

Tom said, "Marella, I don't know that I can explain everything that happened to us tonight, but I believe your father was right all along."

Marella's eyes fell to the floor as she shook her head.

"Marella," Sean said. "Look in Tom's eyes and tell me he didn' see something that he can' explain."

"So what o' it?" she said. "Wha' are ye two goin' tae do now? Catch it and brin' it home as a pet?"

Tom said, "Your father has found a way to bring this thing to him. He's done it twice now, and I can at least confirm one of those times. If he can do it a third time, maybe I can get a device that will allow us to catch it on camera."

"Like wha'?" Sean said.

"Maybe there's a place around here where I can pick up a Go-Pro. Something light I could wear on my head but is also water proof."

"Great idea. I think I saw one at th' store when I picked up th' extra poles this mornin'."

"Perfect. Let's run and pick it up first thing tomorrow."

"Sounds like a plan." Sean heard the coffee finish brewing, and he went to the kitchen to get a cup.

Marella frowned. "Wha' happened tae helpin' him with his priorities?"

"I was trying to...."

"Bu' ye promised."

"Things happened…"

"Men!"

Tom held his breath. He didn't have an answer. He had hoped tonight he would be her hero.

But he had new information. He did not expect Sean Paterson to be right. All that had changed. Tom could not deny his own experience, and he worried whether or not what happened would hurt his chance with Marella.

"Marella. I…I don't know what to say."

Sean brought them two cups of coffee, and he handed one to Tom.

"We'd better do all we can tae go out again t'morrow night," Sean said. "We don' know if it migrates, but we do know it's in th' area. If we hurry, maybe we'll have th' same luck so long as we don' wait."

"Ye call wha' happened tae ye t'night 'luck'?" Marella sat on the couch. "I'm surprised ye both didn' drown." She buried her head in her hands. "I'm surrounded by idiots."

Sean sat on the couch next to Marella. "My daughter," he said. "Let's look at this a differen' way. If we go out there and find this creature, and if we can get proof tha' it exists, everythin' will change. I'll na longer be disrespected by th' scientific community. I'll be able tae sell my inventions again. Tha' would help my business, and I could always use a good hand or two tae help." He nodded at Tom. "And, who knows? Maybe th' town of Thurwick will thrive from this discovery. They may even name th' museum or th' library after us."

"But, Da'. Look at ye. Ye almost drowned t'night. Wha' if ye come back t'morrow night with a chunk of flesh taken out o' yer backside?"

Sean patted her on the leg. "Well, my dear, ye always said I needed tae lose a few pounds. Tha' would sure do th' trick, wouldn' it?"

"Na' funny."

He hugged Marella with one arm.

She resisted at first, but then acquiesced. "Okay, then. Ye two are goin' tae go out t'morrow tae capture proof o' Nessie. I don' believe either o' ye, but I want ye both back alive. Wha' can I do tae help?"

Sean pulled out a piece of paper and a pen. As he made plans and put them into checklists of the items to do before going out the next evening, Tom appreciated Marella all the more. She had once had faith in her father, but she had lost it somewhere along the way. In these last few moments, her eyes flashed a new hope, a hope of her having a family.

And Tom wondered if he wasn't falling in love.

CHAPTER 17

Tom climbed out of his bed at Annabel's Bed and Breakfast. He hadn't slept. The adrenaline from the past few hours never subsided, and he had tossed and turned, trying to wrap the experience together in his mind. When he arrived at Sean's cottage he discovered that Sean hadn't slept either. He had been too excited. Only Marella slept that evening. She was ready to go. Sean, on the other hand, was gulping caffeinated coffee.

Sean had set down his coffee cup and said, "Alright then. Are ye two ready tae get goin'?" Tom nodded, and the three of them climbed in the car and drove to the Thurwick shoreline, recovering the gear that had washed up. They also drove to an outdoor store and purchased new fishing rods and coolers. Later, they went to a butcher's shop and bought several large flanks of steak.

When they finished their shopping checklist, they drove back to the cottage. When they arrived, Tom had forgotten the Go Pro.

"How could we forget that?" Tom said.

"Ye're rushing. People make mistakes when they rush," said Marella.

Sean climbed out of the car, and leaned back in before shutting the door. "Why don' ye two take my car? I've got things tae do here before t'night."

Tom said to Marella, "You okay with spending some time with me?"

"Don' get yer hopes up. Ye're both insane."

"Is that a yes?"

She sighed. "Aye. That's a yes."

Sean shut the door and Tom turned the car around. He tried to be extra careful, not wanting to damage or scratch Sean's car. As they drove into Thurwick, Tom tried to keep the car at the exact speed limit.

"I'll bet this wasn' wha' ye expected," Marella said.

"What do you mean?"

"This."

"Riding in a car with you?"

"Aye. And nearly drownin' across th' ocean from yer home."

"I will concede they left the whole Loch Ness drowning experience out of the brochure."

"So why are ye here?"

"I took a chance," Tom said.

"Do ye always take chances?" Marella said.

"Only if it's worth it."

Marella blushed enough for Tom to notice the dimples in her cheeks.

"The Go Pro's in there," Tom said, nodding to the small outdoor store where they had picked up the fishing rods earlier. He parked the car, climbed out and hurried to open Marella's door, but she didn't wait. She climbed out, shut the door, and walked to the store.

Marella said, "Go get what ye need. I found somethin' I need tae take a look at." She left him between some cloth racks.

"Okay." Tom shrugged. He walked through some aisles, when he came upon a life jacket. "Thank God," he said. He tried one on, and it fit.

As he was about to remove the jacket, Marella appeared before him, holding a bag. She grinned. "I bought a surprise fur us."

"What did you get?" Tom said, sensing her playfulness.

Marella pulled the item out of the bag. It was a hat, and on the front was a silhouette of a plesiosaur, the Loch Ness monster.

"I love it!" Tom put it on his head. "This is perfect!"

* * *

By early afternoon, their checklist complete, Tom and Marella returned to the cottage. Sean was on his cell phone, pacing around the den and the kitchen. "Look, I was th' one who had th' accident," he said. "Ye don' have tae rub it in!"

Marella frowned.

"Go ahead then. Send me th' invoice!" Sean hung up his cell phone. "Can ye believe it? We almos' drowned out there, and they want tae charge me a fine fur reckless conduct." Sean fumed a few more seconds, and then he said, "I like th' hat."

"Thanks," Tom said, "Did you tell them what happened?"

"Na. I told them I took ye fishing tae show ye around th' Loch. Na' sure they believed me, though. I suppose a reputation sticks with ye fur a while."

"How's the boat?"

"Oh, it's alright. Another fisherman spotted th' last remainin' fishing rod stickin' out o' th' water. He said he almost flipped when he saw it bobbin' up and down in th' middle o' th' Loch. When he went tae investigate, that's when he found th' boat floatin' just under th' surface."

"Were there any marks on the boat? Anything unusual?"

"Didn' see any," Sean said. "I went tae th' dock as th' fisherman was hauling in th' boat. That's where th' authorities decided tae fine me fur reckless conduct."

Tom chuckled. "I guess searching for the Loch Ness monster is rather reckless."

"Did ye two get everythin'?"

"Aye," Marella said. "And I got ye this." She handed Sean his hat.

"Oh, ye got me one!" he said. He slipped it on. "We all look official now. Someone needs tae come up wi' a team name."

Tom said, "Are we ready for tonight?"

"Aye," Sean said.

"Are ye certain?" Marella said. "Lest night was quite an ordeal fur th' two o' ye. Why na' give it a day and rest?"

Tom hesitated a moment. Marella had a point. It was true he hadn't slept in a while. The adrenaline from the night before had kept him restless.

"Na, we canno' wait," Sean said. "We don' know if these animals migrate or na'. We know they are in that area. If we wait, we might miss our chance."

"I agree," Tom said. "It's now or never."

Marella said nothing.

"Alright then," Sean said. "Let's get goin'."

Tom readied the Go Pro, and then they packed the car, stuffing every square inch with supplies while leaving room for the three of them to fit in the seats.

Once everything was loaded, Tom sat in the back seat, waiting. He was anxious now that his mission had changed. He watched Marella. She appeared hopeful, but he knew she did not comprehend what he and Sean had experienced. Tom closed his eyes for a second to take it all in when he heard Sean start the engine. Then he sat silently as they drove to the dock.

When they arrived, Sean said, "Marella, ye sure ye wan' tae do this? It could be a long night."

"Someone has tae keep an eye on ye," she said. "I'll watch from th' shore in case ye need rescuin' again."

Sean nodded, and then he exited the car and went to unpack the supplies. "Here we go," Tom said. He put his hand on the door handle, but he stopped when Marella spoke.

"Tom," she said.

He paused. It was the first time he had heard her say his name.

"Ye promise me ye'll be careful t'night and keep him out o' trouble. He's all I have."

Tom put his hand on her shoulder and squeezed. Then he let go, hoping a gentle touch would be reassuring.

Marella blushed.

Tom winked, and then he exited the car and helped unpack the supplies.

He carried the coolers and the fishing rods across the wooden dock. The fisherman who found the rowboat had brought them to the same spot where they shipped off the day before. It was tied to the dock between the speed boat and the pontoon. The last time he was in this boat it had sunk below the surface. After what had been a sunny but cold and windy day, the boat had dried. It was as though nothing had happened the night before, which was too bad. It would have been nice to have had a mark or a dent or something on it to showcase the drama which had unfolded the evening prior.

"Don' forget this." Marella handed Tom his life jacket. He put it on. "Ye two had better get goin'. Sun's about tae set, and ye wan' tae catch them before they migrate."

"You're going to drive to the church and watch us from the shore?"

Marella held up a pair of binoculars. "They're na' much, but I should at least be able tae tell if ye're in some kind o' trouble."

Marella's hair shimmered from the sun's light, and Tom felt an urge to lean in and give her a kiss.

"Ye about ready?" Sean stood a foot from Marella. "Nice life preserver." Sean grabbed the rope and tossed it at Tom. "Doesn' mean ye get away from tyin' another bowline knot, though."

Tom smirked and helped load the boat. Marella said goodbye and walked away to the car. Tom took a second to watch her go.

"Don' screw it up, laddie." Sean grabbed a cooler and set it in the boat. "I think she likes ye."

"What do you mean?" Tom said.

"Ye know."

Tom shook his head. Then he helped set up the boat for another round.

The preparations went more quickly this time. However, Tom felt his energy waning. The excitement from the night before propelled both of them throughout the day, but there were dark circles under Sean's eyes behind his glasses, and he figured he had some under his own eyes as well.

Sean untied the boat and rowed away from the dock. Tom put his hands on the seat underneath him. He didn't say anything, and neither did Sean. The sounds they heard were the creaks of the oars moving in their sockets, and the sounds of some gulls near the Loch's shoreline as they floated overhead in the breeze. The air felt chilly. It was still spring. The smell of mist and muck filled the air. Tom decided that staying dry, even if they didn't find the monster again, would make it a good night. Perhaps Marella was right. Perhaps they should have waited…

Sean said, "Ye're na' goin' tae give up on me t'night, are ye?"

Tom was taken aback. "Don't plan to. Why do you ask?"

"Ye just don' look like yer mind's wi' ye, that's all. If we have a surprise, I canno' be responsible fur someone who might lose his wits about him."

Tom took a breath. His trip had been a whirlwind ever since he got off the bus, culminating with a prehistoric monster that whacked him in the leg under the cold waters of Loch Ness.

Maybe it was better to admit he was losing energy.

Maybe it would be better to consider a rest.

Then he thought better of it. "No. You don't have to worry about me. I'm all in."

"Glad tae hear it."

Sean strained as he rowed. Neither spoke until they reached the spot in front of Saint Michael's twenty-five minutes later.

The sun had set, and the sky turned a deep purple. Sean said, "Okay. Let's hook up th' bait." He reached into a cooler and pulled out a steak.

Waves splashed upon the moonlit shore. A pair of vehicle headlights moved behind some small trees to the left of the church. *Must be Marella.* There were no windows lit at the rectory this night. All of them were dark.

"Are ye goin' tae help or are ye goin' tae just sit there," Sean said.

Tom opened the cooler behind him. Three steaks rested on the ice. He reached down to pick one up and held it in his left hand. Then he grabbed the fishing rod, and removed it from its socket. The rod swung forward, and he couldn't find the hook in the dark. He raised the pole.

Sean let out a yell. Tom's hairs on his neck stood up, and he felt his last remaining rush of adrenaline pump through his body.

The monster!

Tom jerked the rod back.

Sean stood up screaming, fell backwards, and landed in the water.

The rod bent downwards.

Tom didn't know what was going on. He jerked the rod back up, perplexed.

Sean screamed.

Tom said, "Where's the monster? Sean, are you alright?"

"Drop th' pole! Drop th' damn pole!"

Tom reacted, and dropped the pole. It clanked on the edge of the boat before it splashed into the water.

Sean, appearing angry, clambered back on into the boat.

Tom offered to help, but Sean slapped him away with an angry arm.

"What happened?" Tom said. Something clung to Sean's face. "What's that?"

His heart sank.

"Oh, no." Tom had caught his hook at the base of Sean's jaw. "Can I help you get that out?" Tom said.

"Don' ye come near my face."

"What are we going to do?"

Sean paused. He grabbed a pair of clippers from his pocket, and he cut the string attached to the rod. He grabbed the rod out of the water, placed it in the boat. Then he waved at Marella, motioning to head back to the dock.

Tom said, "Are we going back?"

"I don' have a mirror tae get this thing out o' my chin, and ye're na' goin' near me. We'll have tae try again another night." He grabbed the oars, steered the bow eastward, and rowed back towards the dock.

The trip back was quiet. Neither said anything. Tom sat, guilty. Earlier in the day, he felt heroic, having helped Marella's father. Now, he felt a hole in his gut. He could do nothing but apologize and hope for another chance.

When they docked the rowboat, Marella was waiting for them. She sat upon the wood dock as it lifted and lowered with the waves, her bare feet hanging above the cold water.

"Back so soon?"

Sean stood up out of the boat and onto the dock. Marella laughed when she understood what clung to Sean's face.

"What's so funny?" Sean said.

"Looks like somebody finally hooked a monster," she said.

Sean glared at Tom. "Take me somewhere where I can get this thing properly removed."

Marella said, "Ye both are walking disasters. Ye should've waited another night before going out." She giggled as she helped unload the boat. "Th' day's goin' tae come one day when ye're goin' tae listen tae me. One of us has tae be th' voice of reason."

Tom hung his head. *This project was too much*, he thought. They only had the three of them.

They were going to need help.

Tomorrow, he intended to find it.

CHAPTER 18

Tom awoke and stepped through Annabel's front doors. The day was cold. Tom smelled the ozone in the air from the threat of rain. He once again borrowed Annabel's umbrella. He wanted to see Marella, but after he had implanted the hook into Sean's face, and after they had sat in the waiting room, and after he had watched the night-shift doctor remove the hook, and after Sean hinted he was displeased, Tom decided he needed to act alone.

Tom admired St. Michael's across the street. The more he was around the church, the more he appreciated it. He imagined its stones had been placed upon each other ages ago, and even though it wasn't always occupied, there was something about it that drew him to explore the inside.

But not today.

Today, Tom decided he needed to get help, and he felt the person he should ask was Chairman Gordon Briggs.

Briggs was a man of power, and he had been kind enough to offer assistance several nights ago after the special called meeting outside of Dorlan Hall when Sean's tires had been slashed. Even though he had voted to deny Sean's request, he had said he was rooting for Sean. Whatever that meant, Tom decided he would find out.

He walked into the central part of Thurwick. A few people walked past. Whereas before when he first got off the bus and no one had paid him any mind, this time Tom noticed the eyes of the pedestrians. They were watching him. Did they know he was associated with Sean? Probably.

He imagined word travels quickly in small towns like this, especially after he and Sean had had their spill and needed their boat retrieved. Neither he nor Sean had publicly declared they were hunting for the Loch Ness monster on that particular night, but he gathered they had rightly guessed at what they were doing.

A man walked past him. "Excuse me, sir," Tom said. The man pretended he wasn't being called and kept walking. Tom decided to press the man. "Sir, I could use some help."

The man stopped. "Ye were talkin' tae me?"

"Yes." No one else was within earshot. "Where can I find Chairman Briggs?"

"Briggs?" The man pointed across the street. "His insurance office is o'er there. That's where he is when he's na' campaignin' fur Highland Unitary Council."

Tom hesitated. "What's that?"

"Tis th' next higher level o' government. Wha' we have here is th' Thurwick Community Trust. They ge' together and vote, bu' all they vote tae do is make recommendations tae th' Highland Unitary Council. Thurwick's council doesn' have any real power. Bu' Highland, that's where one becomes important."

"So he's trying to advance his position?" Tom said.

"Aye."

Tom thanked the man and headed across the street. In a corner of an old collection of buildings, a rugged green sign with "Briggs Insurance", displayed in white lettering, swung from two small chains. The sign had been weathered, which was why it was not visible from across the street. How much time was Briggs spending on insurance versus politics? If the sign gave any indication, it wasn't business.

Tom opened the door. A small bell rang above him, indicating his presence. He heard the voice of a woman sitting behind a cubicle. She sounded as though she was on the phone. He gathered she was alone.

After a moment, the woman appeared from behind the cubicle. She looked Tom up and down. Then she asked if she could help him.

He said needed to find Chairman Briggs for a local matter. The woman frowned and pointed him back across the way towards Dorlan Hall. She gave the impression that was where he spent most of his time, confirming his suspicion.

Tom left, and the doorbell rang a second time as he passed through. Cars drove past him on the street. Dorlan Hall was across the square. It stood historic amongst the other parts of Thurwick. Tom believed it had been built before the discovery of more recent construction techniques. He liked the ambiance of the old stones, though. Had the builders who built Dorlan Hall also witnessed the Loch Ness monster? The legend must have begun sometime, from someone, even if it originated many centuries before.

He walked to Dorlan Hall. The door was made of old wood. It was solid, and Tom guessed it was oak. He opened it, and he was surprised at how heavy it was. There were paintings and the statues in the breezeway. A door blocked his way on the other end. To the right were more heavy doors and he remembered they led into the chamber where the council had voted the other night.

The door in the breezeway opened. Chairman Gordon Briggs and Alex Vaas strode into the room. They were conversing with each other. When they noticed Tom, they both paused. Briggs approached Tom and offered his hand.

"Well, hello my American friend." Briggs flashed a toothy grin as he stuck out his hand.

Tom said a hearty hello as he shook Brigg's hand.

Vaas appeared somewhat nervous, but Briggs's charming personality more than made up for it.

"I heard ye survived a boatin' accident," Briggs said.

"That's right. Mr. Paterson took me fishing, you know, to try to acclimate me to the natural surroundings."

Vaas rubbed his red beard. "Did ye catch anything *unusual*?"

"Well," Tom said. He hesitated. "Actually, yes. Mr. Paterson was right all along."

Briggs and Vaas glanced at each other before Briggs grinned and put his hand on Tom's shoulder. "Is it out there?"

"The Loch Ness monster?" Tom said.

"That'd be th' one," Briggs said.

"I can't tell you I saw it with my own eyes, but when our boat tipped and we fell in the water, something large and powerful hit me in my leg, bruising my thigh. Would you like to see the bruise?"

Briggs put his hand to his side and chuckled. "We won' need tae. We were just talkin', and we had an idea."

"What's that?" Tom asked.

"Th' problem with Mr. Paterson's request was that he asked fur funding. Here at th' local council, we don' have any control o'er funding."

"I see."

"However, that doesn' mean we're castrated."

Briggs walked over to the wall.

"Do ye see these portraits up here? Each o' these people was a chairperson before me. Most o' them moved on up tae th' Highland Unitary Council, and a few even wound up in Parliament. They didn' let somethin' like a bank account stop them from makin' great accomplishments."

The portraits were all done in oil. They represented stoic dignitaries, all of whom rose to political heights higher than a local councilperson.

"So, what are you proposing?" Tom said.

"I'm announcin' a contest, fur one day only."

"A contest?"

"Aye. Tomorrow is Saturday. Tis fitting we invite th' people o' Thurwick tae get on their boats, and hunt fur th' Loch Ness monster."

"I'm not so sure that'll work," Tom said.

"Sure it will."

Briggs walked past the portraits and stopped next to a bronze one-foot-tall statue of a Scottish warrior. It stood on a tall skinny stand, which held several books. Was the statue a representation of William Wallace?

"Oh, I canno' guarantee it will lead tae Nessie's capture. But I do believe it will bring some attention tae our town, along wi' some tourist revenue during a period when things are slow."

Tom frowned. "Should we give the people any instructions? I mean, the types of steaks and hooks we've been using…"

"Oh, they'll be alright. Most o' them have gone fishin' before." Briggs laughed and ribbed Vaas with a playful punch. "And, I'll bet none o' them capsized their boat in th' middle o' th' night."

Tom didn't like where this was going. A contest would bring attention to Thurwick, and bring some seriousness to the possibility of the Loch Ness monster. On the other hand, it could make a mockery out of his and Sean's experience.

"Maybe ye can make an annual holiday out o' it?" Vaas said. "Call it 'Nessie Day'."

Tom said, "Chairman Briggs. There's something in that water. I'm being serious."

"Oh, I'm serious, tae," Briggs said. "If there's somethin' in th' Loch, th' town o' Thurwick is goin' tae benefit. When we find it, we'll all benefit."

Briggs and Vaas walked past Tom. Briggs opened the heavy oak doors, letting the sunlight in from the outside. "See ye t'morrow."

Tom watched them leave, and then he went to admire the portraits. He studied the eyes of the prior leaders. Were they trying to tell him something?

One thing was for sure. If someone found evidence of the Loch Ness monster, Chairman Briggs would find a way to get the credit.

CHAPTER 19

Tom hurried in the rain to Annabel's, and then onto Sean's cottage. As his feet splashed in the puddles between the cobblestones, he felt nervous about running into Sean again. He had been doing so well, making an impression on Marella's father. More importantly, Marella appeared to be warming up to Tom.

But the hook in Sean's face didn't help.

Heck, it could be worse, he thought. *I could have taken the man's eye out.*

When he reached the cottage, he hesitated before knocking on the door. To his surprise, the door swung open. Marella, standing in the doorway, appeared as beautiful as ever. Tom relaxed when she did not appear angry. "Come in. Hurry," she said. There's been some sort o' announcement!"

Tom walked in and stood in the den. He heard Sean in the back hallway. Sean walked into the den holding a printed piece of paper. On his face was a white bandage where they removed the hook.

"Says here they are goin' tae have a 'Nessie Day'. Who th' hell's idea was tha'?"

Tom raised his hand, but Sean continued. "Don' they realize bringin' all those people here is likely tae scare it away?"

Tom said, "I know where it came from."

"Oh, come tae poke holes in my face again?"

Marella said, "Dad, don't be too hard on him."

"Well I was doin' fine until he showed up."

"Until he showed up ye also had no other witnesses. So, if ye want him tae testify on yer behalf, ye'd better apologize tae him," Marella said.

Sean took a step back.

"Ye want *me* tae apologize? He's th' one who threw th' damned hook in my jaw."

Tom said, "Mr. Paterson, I'm terribly sorry for that. I had no idea it flew at you the way it did."

"Daughter, ye can do better than this one."

Marella rolled her eyes.

Tom said, "Maybe I can explain. I just came from talking with Chairman Briggs at Dorlan Hall."

Sean said, "Oh. I bet ye're goin' tae say this whole idea was yers."

"No, I swear. I wanted to ask him if he'd offer help, and he told me he had already planned on doing a contest to find the monster. In fact, Alex Vaas was with him. He is the one who called it a 'Nessie Day'. Did they announce what time tomorrow?"

"Tomorrow?" Sean said. He held the paper to Tom, stiff armed. "Th' announcement said th' contest runs fur twenty-four hours, wi' th' winner declared t'morrow evening. It started five minutes ago."

"What?" Tom said. He took the paper.

It read...

Attention!

Chairman Briggs hereby declares noon of the second Friday of March to be the annual "Nessie Day" contest. We invite all interested parties to come and hunt for the Loch Ness monster in the township of Thurwick, Highlands in Scotland. A $1,000 prize and naming rights to the monster will be granted for anyone who catches the creature and presents it by noon the following day. The capture must happen within that twenty-four hour period. If no monster is presented, the town will spend the following twenty-four hours celebrating the legend of the Loch Ness monster.

Good luck and happy hunting!

The clock read five after noon. "You're right. It's already started."

"That's wha' I said." Sean could not hide his agitation. "We need tae pack up and get tae th' dock right away."

Tom said, "Will people will look for it?"

Marella shrugged. "Yer guess is as good as mine."

Sean said, "We need tae load up th' coolers and th' fishing rods right away, and get tae th' Church..."

"Woa. I'm not so sure we'll want to do that," Tom said. "If we do that, we'll be playing their game."

"Wha' are ye sayin'?" Marella said.

"Everybody knows we had our boating accident two nights ago. Some may know it happened by the Church, but not everybody. If we don't go, it's possible those who do know will go to the Church to look for the monster. We don't want them to do that, right?" Tom said.

"Go on," Sean said.

"Here's what I say we do. People will be watching us, not anybody else. After all, we're the ones everyone is talking about, right? If Sean and I get on the boat, act like we're hunting for the monster, but instead we go somewhere other than Saint Michael's, we'll lure everyone away from the Church. Then, we can keep our hunting spot a secret."

Marella said, "So, ye two get on th' water, but ye only act like ye're huntin' fur Nessie?"

Sean said, "I don' wan' tae lose another night findin' tha' creature, but we canno' do anything if there's a bunch o' people out on th' water. Tha' could scare it away fur good." Sean frowned, and then said, "I hate tae say it, but th' lad's got a point."

Tom said, "And the good news is we don't even have to bait any hooks."

"Thank God," Marella said.

"Okay, then," Sean said. "I'll grab a few fishin' rods and a couple o' empty coolers. Ye put on yer life jacket." Sean went down the hall. "Whate'er happens, this whole thing has become one giant mess!"

* * *

"Unbelievable," Sean said as they arrived at the dock. Cars were everywhere. The place was buzzing with activity. Would-be monster hunters wore their fishing gear, baseball or fishing hats, and everything in between. They carried fishing rods and heavy coolers onto several of the boats tied to the dock. The announcement had been sudden, so everybody took off from work and rushed to their boats at the chance to catch the Loch Ness monster and win the prize.

Tom said, "Remember the plan. We lure them away from the church. If anybody asks why our boat capsized, blame it on me, the American, being clumsy. I'd bet they'd accept that, but they'd still follow us."

Sean agreed.

Marella said she'd drive the car away, just in case somebody tried to press her for information. "I may just do some shopping in Foyers fur several hours," she said. "Tha' means, though, that I won't be able to rescue ye if ye two happen tae have another disaster."

"We'll be fine," Sean said.

Sean and Tom exited the car and unloaded the equipment. Marella drove between walking pedestrians carrying their fishing poles and coolers.

As Tom surveyed the scene, he felt penetrating eyes. Someone was watching him. But who? Men and women loaded their equipment, but paid him no mind. Boats bobbed up and down on the dock. One man swore at another when two boats bumped into each other.

And then Tom spotted the albino. The same man from Dorlan Hall. He stood still, holding his large "Keep Nessie Free" sign in front of him. The albino didn't speak, didn't move, and didn't give any indication of emotion other than displeasure coming from his piercing eyes.

A chill ran through Tom.

"Who is that guy," Tom asked.

"Who?"

"That guy over there, holding the sign."

"Him? I think his name's Martin. He's English."

"Is he someone we should worry about?"

"Na. Been in and out o' trouble. I heard he's heavy intae drugs."

Tom watched. The albino's lips moved. Standing fifty yards away from him, Tom couldn't make out what he was saying. The albino lifted his right arm and pointed at Tom. He shouted some impassioned words that caused the nearby fishermen to stop what they were doing. Then the albino ceased pointing at Tom and walked away.

The fishermen were puzzled. They watched the albino leave. One of them scratched his head, as though he was unsure what to make of the scene. Others laughed, and went back to their gear.

"What was that all about?" Tom said.

"I told ye. He's on drugs," Sean said.

"He gives me the creeps."

"He's a strange one. Don' let him get tae ye, though. He's got his own problems."

"Then why is he following us?"

Sean shrugged. "Is he?"

Tom watched as a few of the fishermen returned to their activity. Others noticed Sean and pointed. Some of them gossiped.

Others laughed. Tom was uncomfortable being the center of attention.

"You ever get tired of people staring at you?"

"Are they?" Sean said. "I hadn' noticed." He lifted the empty cooler on one end. "Grab th' other end and act like 'tis heavy. If they're watching, we might as well give them a show."

They walked with the cooler and rods over the dock. As they approached the rowboat, a man on the speedboat waved at them. The man shouted, "Hey Paterson. McGregor and I found yer monster."

McGregor appeared on the pontoon boat. "Aye, he's a good one, tae." He pointed at Sean's rowboat.

In the middle of the boat sat a green four foot long inflatable toy plesiosaur.

"Aye, I see ye found it," Sean said. "Then there's no need tae go out hunting fur another one, is there?"

Sean stepped into the rowboat and grabbed the toy. He tossed it onto the speed boat. "Hey, Thomson. I found a girlfriend fur ye."

Thomson stepped across his speedboat and kicked the toy into the water. It floated upside down behind the rowboat. "Don' let it capsize yer boat," he said.

"Hey Paterson," McGregor said. "Where'd ye say this thing was anyway?"

Sean said, "If ye leave th' dock and head northeast about a mile, ye'll find an old building on th' other side o' th' Loch. It used tae be a church. It was in front o' there."

Thomson said, "I had heard ye saw it in front o' St. Michaels?"

"Ye must've misheard, then," Sean lied. I was referring to the old church."

"Th' one on th' Watson property?" McGregor said.

"That's th' one."

Tomson said, "When was tha' e'er a church? Since I've been here tis always been an old barn."

Sean said, "Trust me, I've done my research. They wanted ye tae just think it was an old barn, but in reality people gathered there hundreds o' years ago and worshipped."

McGregor said, "Tha' building's supposed tae be cursed, isn't it?"

"Aye," Sean said. "It wasn' a Christian church."

McGregor and Thomson appeared puzzled. *Were they having second thoughts?*

Thomson said, "Tha' whole story is phony. I don' believe a word o' it."

"Suit yerself," Sean said. "But if ye're goin' tae look fur a monster, spending time near a cursed building might be a good place tae start. Tha's where we're goin'. Ye can do as ye please."

Sean stepped into the boat, and Tom followed. They sat down and Sean rowed the oars. "See ye both on th' other side," he shouted. Then he nodded at Tom, and grinned.

CHAPTER 20

"Tell me about this building," Tom said. "You were just kidding when you said it was cursed, weren't you?"

Sean didn't answer.

Tom shifted on his seat. The conversation at the dock left him more uneasy than he anticipated.

Sean rowed moving the boat in the opposite direction, away from Saint Michael's Church. After several minutes, he said, "Legends say tha' some in th' past practiced witchcraft in there. Tis been abandoned fur years. E'ery now and again, though, someone reports strange sights in and around tha' building."

"Do you believe it?" Tom said.

Sean rowed several more strokes before he said, "E'ery mystery can be explained wi' some sort of scientific explanation." Sean rowed a few more times, then he said, "But na' e'ery man thinks like me. Give them a little mystery, and they become curious. If they're cowards, they won' bother tae search. If they're fools, we can lead them tae where they won' do any damage."

Several motorized boats had entered the water. Tom heard their engines running. More than twenty large boats set off at the same time. Another thirty large boat owners made their last preparations before untying from the dock and joining the hunt.

Other smaller non-motorized boats had left the dock, too. Some had sails, and others were rowboats. They all headed southeast towards Saint Michaels. One speed boat passed them. The driver appeared puzzled at Sean rowing in the opposite direction.

The speed boat passed, and then slowed down. The driver picked up a radio, all the while studying the direction of Sean's rowboat. Was he asking other boaters where to go?

The speed boat veered left, and headed northeast away from Saint Michael's.

Tom said, "It's working. It appears the word's out that we're going somewhere other than Saint Michael's." The other boats slowed and reversed course, heading northeast. Those leaving the docks didn't bother going southwest. Word had gotten out, and those captains steered the ships starboard and headed in the direction of the cursed building.

The rowboat splashed in the water. Water surges caused by the other boats made the small rowboat bounce upon the waves, and Tom felt seasick for the first time. "Geez, this is crazy!" he said.

Sean continued to row, but his efforts became more burdened by the rolling waves. "This Loch has a depth o' two hundred twenty-seven meters in some places," he said. "And if I were Nessie, I'd be at a depth o' two hundred and twenty right now."

A large wave crashed into the side of the boat. The water splashed over the side and fell upon the two of them, soaking their clothes. The cold water shocked Tom. The boat shifted to the starboard side. Tom's torso tilted, and he grasped the port rail to keep from falling into the Loch. His heart pounded.

"Hang on!" Sean yelled.

The boats crowded the waters around them. The width of the Loch where they were was a mile wide, but the boats circled around Sean's small rowboat. The other boat's captains watched them, anticipating Sean's next move. Tom noticed a shadow block out the sun. To his right, a large white hull passed them just feet from their oars, its shadows blocking out the sun. The rowboat swayed to the port side from the large boat's wake. Party music echoed from the deck above. Several pretty women were waving to them and laughing. Though the weather was cool, most of them donned bikinis.

Sean let go of an oar and shook his fist at the boat. "Damned Ewan Coffee," Sean said.

"You know him?"

"Aye. Fur tae long." Disgust was on Sean's face.

"He came awfully close to us," Tom said.

"Twas no accident. He knew wha' he was doin'," Sean said.

As the boat passed and moved on ahead, Tom got a better understanding at how large the boat was. It was a large white yacht.

Obscenely large, Tom thought.

When the aft of the yacht had passed, he noticed something on the back right corner. It stood on a stand on the deck, but it had a white barrel that appeared as though it swiveled. *Was it a large gun?* At the end of the barrel, the sun reflected light off a piece of metal with what was a large point and hook. "What's that?" Tom said.

Tom pointed at the object.

"Sheesh. Th' man's gone mad. Tha's a harpoon gun. Used fur whales. He must think he's goin' tae kill it."

While many of the other boats had fishing contraptions bought and paid for by experienced fishermen, none of them compared to the size and the technology of Ewan Coffee's yacht. As the bikini clad women danced to music on the deck, Tom said, "Are you sure he's not just trying to show off?"

"Na," Sean said. "Coffee is all about th' sport. He loves winning, but he's na' as good at business as he thinks he is. Canno' say fur sure, but tis been rumored he's been backing Chairman Briggs fur Highland Council. He's th' money in this area. Sometimes men like tha' are good tae help build a community. As fur Coffee, though, I can tell ye he's na' one o' those. I believe he's a dangerous man."

"Did something happen between you two?" Tom asked.

"Aye. He used tae be an investor in my business, though tha' was years ago. He came from a wealthy family. He tried tae make a name fur himself by investing in high risk ventures. At th' time, I was higher risk in tha' I wasn' established, and I had just had my first experience wi' th' monster. I think my celebrity attracted him tae me.

"Unfortunately, he was always more interested in th' money than th' science. He ne'er had an appreciation fur th' earth's mysteries. Tha' put us at odds. I always felt ye could do both, but he became tae impatient. We had been together fur several years, but one day he pulled his money, and tha' was tha'."

Tom said, "Looks like he's done pretty well for himself."

"Doesn' mean tis all legit," Sean said. "He's learned how tae buy favors. When he pulled his money from me, he also pulled it from many other businesses. Then he began tae hang around certain politicians. Th' good ones, th' honest ones, learned tae stay away from him. Others, though, proposed laws tha' benefited his family's estate. O'er time, he eliminated his competitors and became th' go-to guy fur many industries in this area."

"So he's learned to monopolize," Tom said.

"Aye," Sean said. "And I'm surprised he's out here t'day. Coffee doesn' like tae participate in public events. He likes tae think o' himself as a member o' th' elite class. But I'd bet it has tae do wi' Chairman Briggs. Gordon Briggs isn't high enough up th' food chain tae attract Coffee, but if Coffee thinks Briggs has a shot at winning a spot on th' Highland Council, there's a good chance he'd come out in public."

The yacht tore through the Loch as Tom and Sean bounced over the splashing waves. Other smaller boats made way for the yacht and followed it. Tom remembered Brigg's insurance company. "Is Briggs insuring that boat," Tom said.

"Aye."

Over Sean's shoulder, two men walk to the back right corner of the yacht. They examined the gun. A man dressed all in white, wearing a white cap, put his hand on the shiny harpoon, sliding it over the metal to feel its texture.

The other man, though, seemed familiar. The man in white had moved the harpoon gun, as if he was demonstrating to the other man how to use it. As the rowboat bobbed up and down, Tom had difficulty making out the second character. However, he continued to observe him: his height, his mannerisms, his clothing.

The red beard.

Tom knew who the man was.

He had to be Alex Vaas.

CHAPTER 21

Sean rowed through the choppy waves but they moved slowly. The motorized boats moved forward, and then waited, their captains growing impatient waiting on Sean's slow rowing. A few others in rowboats and kayaks congregated together and moved towards the destination Sean had intended. "Geez, there has to be over a hundred fishermen out here," Tom said.

Sean said, "Thank God they are all in th' wrong spot."

Tom admired the different types of water craft: pontoons, sailboats, speedboats, rowboats, kayaks, and the dominant yacht rising past them all in the center, owned and piloted by Ewan Coffee. They all settled around the opposite shore from Thurwick. There was a cluster of trees at the edge of the water. They stood alone in front of rolling green Scottish hills. Then, under the shadows of the trees, Tom made out what appeared to be a stone structure of some sort. It had ivy climbing up the outside walls, camouflaging its appearance in the shadows.

Tom nodded to Sean. "Is that the building you talked about?"

Sean said, "Aye," but Tom noticed that Sean didn't bother to look at it.

"What's in there?"

"Don' know," Sean said. "Hadn' been in there in ages."

"Should we go check it out?" Tom asked.

Sean stopped rowing. He appeared agitated, almost anxious, as though coming here was a bad idea. "It'd be best if we just drifted right where we are. If we act like we're looking fur Nessie where we sit, then we delay everyone else from findin' him."

The surrounding hunters were pretending to hunt, but in actuality they were listening to music and drinking beer. Others, however, were more serious. They acted methodical in their baits, dropping large steaks on deep sea lines. None of the hunters were banging on their boats.

"Hey Paterson. We in th' right spot?" said a nearby kayaker.

The man in a blue anglers kayak floated a few feet away. He appeared happy, if only to be out in the water on a Friday afternoon instead of working.

Sean said, "Ye'd better hope na'. It would sink yer toy boat before ye knew wha' hit ye."

The man said, "This whole thing's a show. Ye know that."

"Ye don' know a damn thing…"

"Wait," Tom interrupted. "What's that?" Something dark moved out of the corner of his eye. It moved by the old building under the trees. And then it was gone. He couldn't make out its size or shape. Still, something told him he needed to check it out.

"Sean, I saw something," Tom said.

Sean said, "Na, ye didn'."

The man in the kayak moved away, so Tom spoke up. "Yes. Yes, I did."

"And I'm sayin' ye didn'." Sean huffed, insinuating he didn't want to discuss it.

"How would you know? You're not even facing that way," Tom said. He was becoming agitated.

"We're na' goin' near tha' building," Sean said.

Tom chuckled. "I thought you didn't believe in curses."

Sean glared at Tom. "I don'. But I'm also na' foolish."

"What do you mean by that?"

"Tha' means tha' I at least know what I don' know, and there's somethin' about tha' building I don' know, and I don' want tae go near it."

The building stood amongst the ivy along the shore. Tom couldn't explain what he felt. Perhaps there was a calling, or a pull. Something was drawing him there. He told Sean, "Take me over there."

Sean said, "Leave it alone, lad."

"You don't have to come with me. You can take me over there and drop me off," Tom said.

"Is anybody else floatin' near tha' building?" Sean asked. Tom noticed a semi-circle of boats distancing themselves away from the building, none of them any closer than a hundred yards.

Tom insisted. "Well, take me to the edge far away and drop me off. I can walk the rest of the way along the shoreline. I want to go check out that building."

Sean said, "Somethin's grabbin' ye, lad. I need tae get ye away from here." Sean grabbed the oars to turn the boat around. "We're goin' back tae Thurwick."

Tom felt an urge. He wanted to go. He *had* to go.

Sean was turning the boat.

Tom examined his life jacket. They were away from the shoreline, but wearing a floatation device, he felt comfortable he could swim the distance. He stood up. The boat rocked.

Sean said, "Wha' are ye doin'?"

"Don't worry about me," Tom said.

Sean said, "Don' do it," but Tom jumped into the water. The cold water chilled him, but he kicked and swam. He forgot about Sean, and Marella, the monster, and the boaters. He thought he heard yelling, but he didn't care. He swam to the shoreline, his only mission to get to the building.

He maneuvered around the other boats, but soon swam past them, with nothing between him and the shoreline. He kicked until his hands felt mud. He climbed out of the water, and he felt his heavy clothes as the river drained from their material. He stepped and stumbled. Somehow, his shoes had stayed on. He moved through the grass. He heard more yelling, but he had to get to the building. Soon, he was under the shade of the trees. The outside was made of old stones, and they were covered with brown ivy, which he imagined would turn green once warmer weather arrived.

He went around the side, and found an open doorway facing away from the Loch. He went inside. The ground was stone and dirt. On the inside walls were several wooden rails, with hooks. Some of the hooks held old farm tools, such as rusted rakes and shovels.

The room was otherwise barren.

He stood in the middle, and a breeze entered the room. A chill came over him. Something felt strange. Was there something by the door? There was nothing there. Nor was the grass outside moving. He turned around again, but there was still nothing.

And yet Tom had this strange feeling.

He took a step backwards, and he fell on his rear. The room appeared to spin. The chill felt worse. He crawled out of the building. He thought he heard laughter. Once he exited the doorway, the chill subsided. Behind him, there was only the empty room, but everything appeared dark. Outside, the Scottish hills brightened, having been uncovered from under the shade of moving clouds.

He stood up, and decided to run, fast, and far. He sprinted south along the shoreline. Running along the water, he hoped he'd be spotted by someone in a nearby boat, someone to carry him back across to Thurwick.

But when he reached the water, he stopped at the shoreline. The Loch lay before him, a quiet body of water in front of the rolling hills to the southeast. But something was different.

Every single boat had disappeared.

CHAPTER 22

Tom walked southwest along the northern shore of the Loch. Most of the landscape was countryside. A couple of sheep bayed at him as he walked past. They chewed their grass, their eyes fixed on him. Tom imagined them asking why he was trespassing on their feeding grounds.

The sun still shone overhead. The buildings of Thurwick stood sturdy across the water on the other shore. Maybe he could find a boater near the dock. Perhaps he could wave someone down, someone who could pick him up and bring him back across.

As he walked, he spotted the dock, and a boat. He still wore his life jacket. He decided wearing it did him no good. He'd take it off, and wave it over his head until they saw him. He did so and the boat turned in his direction. When it neared the shore, the boater asked, "Are ye alright?"

"No," Tom said. "I need to get over to the other side."

When the boater heard him speak, the man was puzzled. "Ye sound like ye're an American."

"I am," Tom said.

"Are ye Tom Wayne?"

"I am."

The man paused. He said, "Tell ye wha' I'll do. I won' bring ye back myself, but I'll alert th' authorities. They'll pick ye up."

Tom thought that was strange. "Ok," he said. He shook his head and shrugged his shoulders. As the man in the boat picked up a radio, Tom said. "What is going on?"

"Someone's comin' right away." The man put down his radio. "I'm goin' tae head back across, but they'll be here in a few." The man in the boat then revved the engine, and the boat sped away across the Loch towards Thurwick.

In the distance, the small figures of several men ran out of a building on the opposite shore. They climbed aboard a boat. After several minutes, the boat left the dock, and turned towards him. Tom waited. Something was strange.

When they arrived, the men didn't appear friendly. They wore a similar uniform, one that had a strange shield emblem on its left chest area.

"Who are you guys?" Tom asked.

"Are ye Mr. Wayne?" said one of the men in the boat.

"Yes."

"Hang on."

They pulled the boat up and Tom jumped in the water to come aboard. They pulled him up, and wrapped him in a blanket as he sat on a seat on the deck. "We've been lookin' all over fur ye," the man said.

"Who are you guys? Are you with the police?"

The men didn't answer.

"I don't know what happened," Tom said. "This has been the craziest week."

"We'll ge' ye back across," one of the men said.

"Thanks. My plane leaves back to America this weekend. I'm glad I'll be able to see my friends one more time before I have to go."

The men paused. "Mr. Wayne, I'm na' sure wha' ye're sayin', but t'day's Sunday. Yer disappearance caused a stir. Ye've been missin' fur two days."

"Two days?" Tom said. "What are you talking about? It's Friday, Nessie Day. I left the hunt for about an hour, and I came back once I left that building."

The three men didn't say anything. One of the men had his hand on a belt holster.

"Who are you guys, anyway?" Tom said again.

"Don' worry, Mr. Wayne. We've been sent tae help."

"You with the police?"

"Ye needn' worry about us. We'll get ye across. We know Chairman Briggs will wan' tae see ye."

"Chairman Briggs has been looking for me?"

The men said nothing.

What did they mean that Briggs wanted to see him?

* * *

"Where th' hell have ye been?" Chairman Gordon Briggs sat across the table from Tom. His bald head reflected the lights above in one of the back rooms of Dorlan Hall. Next to him sat Alex Vaas. He scratched his red beard with his left finger, observing Tom and analyzing everything he said.

"I already told you. I was helping Sean Paterson during the Nessie hunt, and frankly, that was only a few hours ago," Tom said.

"Ye've been hidin' out fur two days, hopin' tae cause some sort o' international incident. Wha' did Paterson tell ye?"

"Nothing," Tom said. "We went out to hunt for Nessie on the day you said to hunt for him. That's the last I saw him."

Briggs sat back in his chair, perplexed.

Vaas said, "Where'd ye sleep last night?"

"In my room at Annabel's Bed and Breakfast, across from Saint Michael's Catholic Church." Tom was annoyed. "Check with her if you don't believe me." Vaas leaned over to Briggs, and the two of them whispered to each other. "Hey, am I on trial here or something? Are you two having me arrested?"

Briggs and Vaas separated. Briggs said, "Annabel called th' Highland police last night, claiming tha' ye skipped out on their services without signin' fur payment."

Tom said, "She said I was missing? That's ridiculous. I was there last night!"

"Look, lad. We don' wan' any trouble. Tis bad enough I've got a resident stirrin' up trouble wi' a mythical creature in th' waters off shore. Th' last thing I need is some American causin' an international incident in th' Highlands."

"So, am I under some sort of arrest, or not. Because, if I am, I'm calling the U.S. Embassy."

Briggs laughed, and then he sat back in his chair. "Mr. Wayne, ye don' understand. We're yer friends here in Thurwick. We're tryin' tae keep th' peace. If ye disappear, I'll have officials from th' European Union all th' way tae th' United Nations askin' wha' I did wi' th' American tourist from Atlanta. When I canno' find ye, wha' am I goin' tae tell them? Tha' ye were eaten by th' Loch Ness monster?" Briggs laughed again, and Vaas joined him.

Tom wasn't sure what to make of it, but he decided Briggs made some sense. Sitting in his shoes, Tom imagined how Briggs would be stressed if he was getting pressure from international governments.

Tom relaxed and to chuckled. He said, "I can see where you're coming from. I don't know what happened, but I'm on this side of the Loch, and I can tell you I don't want to go to that other side again."

Briggs said, "Tha's good." The balding man sat in his chair, thinking. His fingers rapped on the desk. "How long are ye stayin' in Thurwick?"

"I'm leaving tomorrow, Saturday," said Tom.

Briggs said, "Mr. Wayne, I hate tae tell ye this, but t'day is Sunday. Ye can go tae th' church at Saint Michael's, and I can promise ye'll they'll be happy tae take yer donation in th' collection dish at their Sunday Mass."

Tom shook his head. "Then I don't know how long I'm staying. I guess I'll need another ticket home."

Briggs said, "Tell ye wha'. If ye feel threatened at all, I wan' ye tae call Alex. He's one o' my helpers." Briggs rapped his fingers on the table. "Alex, give Mr. Wayne yer phone number." Vaas pulled out a card, and slid it across the table to Tom. "His phone number is on tha' card. I wan' ye tae call Alex if ye need any help."

Tom said to Vaas. "Do you work for the town?"

Briggs said, "He's just someone I trust, and I wan' tae make sure ye stay safe while ye visit Thurwick. But if ye can, get yer ticket home, and let us know when tha' is…" Briggs's eyes shifted over to Vaas, "…so, ugh, we can make sure yer stay is safe while ye're here."

Tom grabbed the card, and he put it in his wallet. "Okay. Thanks." He sat for a moment before he said, "So, can I leave now?"

Briggs stood up, smiling. His teeth shined like they had just been bleached. "Aye, o' course. We're glad tae have tourists visitin' Thurwick, especially from America. Just le' us know how we can help ye."

Tom thanked them both and shook their hands. He walked out of the back room, found himself inside the breezeway, and exited Dorlan Hall. As he exited, a woman passed him on the street. Tom said, "Ma'am. Sorry to bother you. Can you tell me what day it is?"

The woman, surprised by the question, stopped and said, "Aye. Tis Sunday."

What the hell?

"Thanks," Tom said.

He surveyed the area. Thurwick's square appeared the same, but so many things felt different. *It should be Friday,* he thought. *My plane leaves Inverness tomorrow.* But if everyone was right, he had missed his flight, and he wouldn't show up to work in Atlanta on Monday. That would mean he might be out of a job.

He decided he had to return to Annabel's Bed and Breakfast, settle payment so he would still have a room, and then he had to find Marella. As he took a step in that direction, he noticed some young men heading towards him. He paid them no attention, until one of them stood in front of him, blocking his path.

Tom tried to get by, but one of the men said, "Hey, ye go' any money?"

Tom said he was sorry, but he didn't and he had to get past.

That's when Tom felt one of them grab his shoulder. He heard another one of them say, "He wasn' askin'," and then he felt the first punch in the ribs.

CHAPTER 23

Tom had been in five fights over the course of his life. Most of the time, he avoided any physical attack with a clever verbal redirection, offering a way to avoid bodily harm while also letting his opponent know, if there would be a punch thrown, that he'd be ready to dish it out. However, sometimes verbal redirection did not work. In those instances, he'd find out if a man would move onto the next phase of force, or if he was all talk.

Tom was not all talk. As he examined his life, he should have been in well over five fights, more like thirty, considering all his conflicts. He didn't seek trouble. He just gave effort, and competitors either didn't want to work as hard, they didn't like losing, or both. When his opponent became angry, he'd stand firm, smile, and use his wit to avoid anything physical. He had a strategy, and he had over the years found he had many opportunities to practice it.

What bothered him when he was punched in the ribs was how fast it happened. This gang of thugs appeared out of nowhere. Their quick question gave him no time to realize a conflict was coming, and they attacked before he had any time to react. They came upon him too fast, too unexpectedly, and that threw him off.

The blows happened rapidly, first to the back, then to the shoulder, and then to the back of the leg. He fell to the ground, and one kicked him on his thigh, on the bruise he had from the lake, giving him a sharp pain that made him curl into a fetal position. He covered his head. They kept hitting. He felt a blow to the face. Then someone kicked him in the back. What had he done? Why the attack?

He stayed on the ground, absorbing the blows. He tried to make out their clothes, their faces. Everything was a blur, but he believed his attackers were part of a local gang, a group of young men who wore shabby clothing and were up to no good.

Then he thought he spotted the albino. He was standing under a tree in the distance, watching, enjoying the scene. Tom absorbed another blow to the gut, and he shut his eyes.

Then, all of a sudden the attackers fled. He heard a whistle, and shouting. His eyes stayed closed, his body aching. The sound of footsteps grew louder. "Are ye alright?" a man's voice said.

He opened his eyes. Two men and a woman bent over him. "We've go' tae get him tae th' medic," a man said.

The woman gasped. "Oh my. He's hurt bad!"

Tom opened one eye. "What happened? Who were those guys?"

The man asked if Tom could get up.

"Where's the albino?" Tom said.

"He's delirious," said a woman.

"Help me ge' him up," the man said.

The man grabbed Tom by his hand and arm and lifted him to his feet. Tom stumbled, his legs aching from all the kicks and bruises.

"Can ye walk?"

"Yeah, I think so." An aged uniformed policeman jogged around the corner.

One of the helpers said, "Did ye find them?"

The officer said, "Na. I rounded a corner, and they were gone." The officer took a few large breaths. He was out of shape. He said to Tom, "Lad, are ye able tae give me a description? How many were they? Wha' did they look like? How tall were they? Wha' were their ages? Things like tha'."

Tom said, "Five or six of them. Late teens, I think. Maybe early twenties. Dressed in brown or gray coats."

"Did ye ge' a look at any o' their faces?"

Tom thought, took a step, and stumbled. The man holding his arm helped him back up. Tom tried to picture the faces, but for some reason he had a hard time describing any of them.

"I remember the albino," Tom said.

"Did he hit ye, tae?" asked the officer.

"No," Tom said. "He watched. From over there." Tom nodded to the tree.

"The hospital is tha' way," said the man holding him up. "Can ye make it?"

Tom said, "Their faces. I can't remember them."

The officer said to the man holding Tom up, "Get this lad there fur treatment. I'll open his file and begin our investigation." The officer then said to Tom, "Ye get yerself bandaged up. I'll send Riley o'er yer way in half an hour tae finish th' report."

Tom nodded, and the helpers walked him across the street to the hospital.

* * *

The doctor examined Tom's face. "They go' ye good," he said. "Yer nose is bleedin', and ye're pretty bruised. But nothin' appears broken. Ye do have a good shiner, though. If ye walked into a pub, I don' think anybody'd want tae mess wi' ye. Heck, they may even buy ye a pint."

"Great," Tom said. He knew he should find the doctor's comments humorous, but he couldn't get himself to do so.

"How's yer head?"

"A little groggy," Tom said. "But not too bad."

The doctor rapped his pen on his clipboard. "I don' think ye sustained a concussion," the doctor said. "Ye're goin' tae be sore fur a while after all th' body blows. But I do believe ye'll be alright in a few days."

Tom didn't answer. He shut his eyes and took a deep breath. Who had attacked him? Why was he attacked? What did they want? They had asked for money, but they never took his wallet out of his pants pocket. The whole thing was like a ruse, with the sole purpose to cause physical harm. Did they want to scare him? Intimidate him? Or was it random, punks wanting to cause violence? He tried to picture the faces of his attackers, but they just couldn't come to him.

He pictured the albino, standing, staring, grinning. Tom felt a chill.

The doctor stood up and wrote notes on his clipboard. Tom lay on the table in his hospital garb. His clothes rested on the chair in the corner of the room. He felt aches all over. "Members o' th' local rugby team come here after e'ery match," the doctor said, "and ye don' look any worse than they do. Just go hang out wi' them, and ye'll fit right in."

Tom managed a slight chuckle. Then a nurse appeared in the doorway. "Doctor Ross. He has a visitor. Shall I let her in?"

The doctor said, "Ye alrigh' wi' tha'?"

Tom nodded, and the nurse left.

"I'm goin' tae leave ye wi' yer visitor," the doctor said. "Ye're free tae go, but ye need tae watch yerself. Learn tae get some eyes on th' back of yer head, will ye?" He rapped on his clipboard again, and then he left the room.

It had been about half an hour since the attack, and the investigator was due any moment. Tom tried to remember what had happened so he could tell Marella everything. She'd be there in a moment, and if he couldn't describe his attackers to her, the authorities would not be able to find them. He and his friends would still be in danger.

The albino hadn't attacked him, but Tom believed he was behind it.

Somehow.

It was just that he couldn't picture the faces of the others. He remembered the scene, the fists that punched him, and the boots that kicked him. He felt every blow. He had seen their eyes, but for some reason he couldn't bring himself to describe them, any of them.

It was as though they were all faceless. The more he tried to picture them, the more he felt a chill go through his body.

Then he noticed a movement by the door. A tear welled up. He took a deep breath, and his ribs pained as the air entered his lungs. He winced, but then he grinned showing all his teeth. "Am glad to see you."

Marella said, "And just where th' hell have ye been?"

CHAPTER 24

Tom propped himself up on his elbow. He felt so glad Marella came that he didn't pick up on her harsh tone. "I've had kind of a rough day," he said.

Marella walked in and shut the door hard. The sound of the door closing alarmed Tom. "Don' give me any Casanova bunk," she said. "I wan' tae know th' truth."

Tom said, "I'm not sure what happened. All I remember was crossing the Loch, and everyone told me that today's Sunday. Everyone's lost their mind."

Marella stood over Tom, and then she came and shoved him on his arm. "Ye're lyin', and I'm tired o' people na' bein' honest wi' me."

"Marella, it's been a crazy day."

"Ye'd better give me an answer where ye've been th' past two days, and if yer answer's na' satisfactory…"

"Look, as far as I know, it's still Friday. I swam away from your father around two this afternoon. Then I found my way back, and everyone's been acting weird. They are trying to trick me that it's Sunday."

"I'm tired o' yer games," Marella said.

Tom slid his feet off the side of the bed and sat up. He wore a soft hospital gown with small blue diamonds. Not what he wanted Marella to see him wearing, but what could he do?

"Please don't take this the wrong way, but I just got attacked by some Scottish thugs and I'm not all that great right now. I *wish* it were all just a game."

Marella paced, clenching her hands into fists. "My father became very scared when ye disappeared," she said. "In fact, he hadn' been tha' way since my mother left us."

Tom closed his eyes. He remembered the brief moment he had in the old barn, or church, or whatever it was. The thought bothered him. He wanted to try to forget it. "I bet I know why he was scared," he said. "In fact, I should go see him now."

"He doesn' wan' tae see ye."

"Is he mad I swam off without him?"

"He won' say. He just doesn' wan' tae see ye again."

"Why's that?"

Marella's face turned red. "Why are ye askin' me? Th' hell if I know wha' he wants. Or ye for tha' matter. I don' know what's goin' on wi' e'eryone around here. Here's th' deal, Tom. If ye don' tell me wha' is goin' on around here, I'm leavin'."

"Marella," Tom said, his voice elevating. "I came here to help."

"Na ye didn'. Ye were hopin' fur some cheap lay."

Tom blinked. "Wait, what? You think I was hoping for what?"

"Ye heard me."

"I don't care what you think." Tom put his hands behind head and interlocked his fingers, trying to figure out what he should say next. Then he dropped his hands to his side, exhausted. "Yes, I find you attractive, and yes, I want to get to know you more. But I just got pummeled by six people after spending a few days trying to help your father. I think you owe me an apology."

"Ye? An apology!"

"Yes."

Marella crossed her arms. "Alrigh'. I'll be honest. Th' lest time anybody disappeared fur two days withou' a word and came back was when tha' happened tae my father. Right after tha', my mother left."

Tom rested a second.

"If ye ask me," Marella said. "Ye both are cursed. This whole Loch Ness monster is a curse."

Tom chuckled. "Your father doesn't believe in curses, remember?"

"And wha' about ye? Do ye believe in curses?"

Tom frowned. "I'm not sure."

"Regardless, I'm leavin' tae go back tae America."

"You're what? You're leaving?"

"I bough' a plane ticket. It leaves next week."

"Well, what about your father?"

"Ye two should kiss and make up. At least then ye'll have each other. Whate'er happens, just leave me th' hell alone."

"Wait, Marella. I know it's been tough. But you're no quitter."

"I'm na' quittin'. I'm goin' back tae livin', and havin' a life withou' ye, my father, and this doolally town."

"You don't mean that."

"Goodbye, Tom." She opened the door and shut it behind her as hard as when she came in. Tom flinched. His mirror reflection on the wall vibrated and the jar of Q-Tips rattled.

Tom remained sitting on the bed. He put his head down into his hands and let out a moan. Everything ached. His bruises hurt, his head felt groggy, and now he felt like Marella's words punched him in the stomach. "How can a woman make a guy feel so bad," he said.

He shook his head. There's something real going on, but he couldn't understand it. Just a few hours ago he was in a rowboat with Sean. Now, it was Friday evening, but he was being told it was Sunday.

What's worse, he was beat to hell. Could he walk? He decided to stand. A sharp pain came from his ankle. He stumbled, but he put his hand on the bed and prevented himself from falling. "Ok. I can do this," he said.

He limped over to the mirror. His face reflected in the mirror, and he laughed. *I just received the raw end of a heavyweight boxing match.*

His clothes sat folded in a pile on a chair. "Just got to work it out." He moved his ankle. The soreness went high, but an acute pain struck him as he moved the joint. "Okay. That's going to take some time." He moved for the sake of moving until he managed to move through the pain. As he paced, he scratched his head.

What do I need to do next?

He had already missed his plane, according to everyone else. That is, unless everyone else was crazy.

Different options came to mind. Even if his plane did leave tomorrow, he would have to stay. Marella was under a lot of stress, and he believed she needed him now more than ever. And if what she said was true, that Sean didn't want to see him, he had to know something.

But what did he know? Did he have the same experience years ago? Is that why he tried to avoid that building?

He reached for his clothes. His body ached. But it wasn't enough to keep him still. He had an urge to search for the Loch Ness monster. It was more than an urge. It was almost like something inside him spoke to him that he needed to find it. He *had* to find it. Before, he wanted to find the monster to help Marella by helping her father. *It's different now,* he thought. *I need to find the monster because my life depends on it.*

"Sean would know this feeling," he said aloud. "This might be what he was experiencing." But Sean hadn't dealt with all that had happened to him very well over the years. There had to be someone who could give him some answers. Who attacked him? What was so strange about the old building? Who was the albino? Who else has seen the Loch Ness monster? Tom buckled his pants and left his hospital garb on the bed. He hesitated to leave the safety of the room. There was no telling if another gang of thugs had his number outside in the dark streets.

Should he wait? The investigator hadn't come as the officer had promised. He patted his back pockets, and felt his wallet. He had an idea. "That's right. We don't want an international incident, now, do we?"

He reached for his wallet. Vaas's card was in it. He found it, and pulled it out.

"Alex Vaas," Tom said. "It's time you told me who you are and what you know."

CHAPTER 25

Tom felt the pressure on his ankle as he stepped into Guthrie's Pub. It was the one place he figured would be open this late at night. Vaas had agreed to meet him there when Tom called him from the hospital. He didn't tell Vaas about his attack on the phone. He thought he'd let his swollen eye do the talking for him.

When he walked in, the musty odor of the pub opened his nostrils. Some of patrons flinched at the sight of his injuries. Tom paid no mind to their "Wha' happened tae ye?" expressions. He scanned the snugs, and found one with a lone man sitting in the far corner. He was drinking a beer. It was Vaas.

He walked past the bar. "Ye okay, lad?" asked the bartender.

Tom nodded, but stayed focused on Vaas. Tom's bad ankle made him limp, but he hid it well. He was right. The more he walked, the more he worked out the kinks. His ankle would be swollen in the morning. In fact, he knew he needed to ice it. He needed to ice his whole body.

Later. I've got business to attend to.

He walked up to Vaas, who did not acknowledge him. Tom sat down across the table, and that's when Vaas raised his eyebrows. "Jesus," he said.

Tom said, "Oh, this is nothing. You should have seen the other guy."

Vaas's eyebrows lowered. "Look, we told ye na' tae cause trouble."

"No. You told me you didn't want an international incident, whatever that meant. You said you'd protect me. Well, does my face look like you protected me?" Tom said.

Vaas leaned back, and then said to the bartender. "Alan, bring my friend an Old Mortality, and put it on my tab."

Tom appreciated the gesture, though he wasn't sure if it was genuine.

Vaas said, "We all need tae do better at doin' wha' we said we would do."

"I'll say." When the bartender brought the Old Mortality, Tom said, "Do you have any idea who would want to attack me?"

"I know o' a few gangs in th' area. Do ye think they knew ye were a tourist?" Vaas said.

"Maybe. I did ask to move past them when they approached me. My accent probably gave it away," Tom said.

"Did they take anything o' yers?" asked Vaas.

"No. They did ask for money, but they never took anything."

"Why do ye think they ran?"

Tom said, "Don't know. I didn't get the impression they were trying to rob me. It's like it was pure violence."

Vaas took a sip of his pint. His eyes made Tom insecure. Yet Briggs had told him Vaas would make him safe. "Who'd ye talk tae wi' th' police?"

"Tall guy. Older. Out of shape," Tom said. "Didn't get his name, though."

"Sounds like Anderson," Vaas said. "Did he take a report?"

"Not sure," Tom said. "He said he'd send an investigator to the hospital half an hour after the attack. No one showed up. So I called you."

Vaas said nothing.

"Do you know of an albino around town?" Tom said.

"Albino?"

"Yeah. He's about 5 feet 10. Skinny. White hair. Pale skin. Dark clothes. Long overcoat. He was at Dorlan Hall the night of the meeting holding a sign to keep Nessie free. I've seen him around a couple of times."

"Canno' say I remember him?" Vaas said.

"You can't miss him. He was at the docks before Nessie day, and he was there when I was attacked."

"Did he attack ye?"

Tom sipped his beer. "No. He stood under a tree, watching."

"Ye think he had somethin' tae do wi' yer attackers?"

"Yes."

"I'll be sure we find out who tha' is," Vaas said.

Tom said, "So what is your role in all this? What do you do?"

"I help Chairman Briggs."

Tom squinted. "With what, exactly."

"Whate'er he needs help wi'."

"So what's in it for you?" asked Tom.

"Wha' do ye mean?"

"I mean if Chairman Briggs asks me to leave so as to avoid an international incident, and he promises my protection before I go, but I don't get protection, what happens to the one who was supposed to do the protecting?" Tom said.

"Ye were supposed tae avoid trouble," Vaas said.

Tom laughed. "All I did was leave Dorlan Hall and walk back to Annabel's Bed and Breakfast. I didn't do anything to attract trouble. Trouble found me."

"So, wha' do ye want?" Vaas said.

"I want to make sure my friends and I are safe," Tom said.

"Until ye leave, right?" Vaas said.

Tom said, "No. While I'm here. I intend to stay to help my friends find the Loch Ness monster."

"Then I canno' promise yer protection."

"My black eye is proof of that," Tom said.

"Lad, ye'd be best tae give it up. If th' monster exists, ye should leave findin' it tae th' authorities," Vaas said.

"Why, so you and Briggs can get the credit?" Tom said.

Vaas glared. He put his hand on the table. His fingers tapped the table next to the glass. He sat waiting for what Vaas would say next. "Mr. Wayne, I can assure ye we don' want anything tae happen tae ye while ye're here. But if ye insist on engaging in reckless behavior, there's nothing we can do tae protect ye."

"Even if I'm just walking down the street?" Tom said.

Vaas said, "Have ye e'er thought tha' searching fur th' myth o' th' Loch might bring its own consequences?"

"What do you mean?"

"Wha' I mean is tha' certain endeavors heighten risk in and o' themselves. The Loch Ness monster is a myth, but th' myth o' th' monster does things tae people. It makes them act strangely, behave differently. When they believe it exists, they do strange things, and they don' know why." Vaas took a sip of his Guinness. "People forget th' law and order created by their government. Tis like their eyes get glazed o'er, and they lose themselves. Mr. Wayne, th' local authorities do a good job o' protectin' people from others. However, tis more difficult tae protect people from themselves."

Tom said, "So let me get this straight. You're saying it's my fault I got beat up because I had been looking for the Loch Ness monster. Is that what you're saying?"

"Ye elevated yer risk, Mr. Wayne. If ye intend tae keep tha' risk elevated, there's only so much we can do."

Tom considered Vaas's words. *He had a point*, he thought. For example, what on earth made him want to jump out of the rowboat to swim away from Sean this morning, or two days ago, whatever day it was? And what about Marella's frustration with her father after all these years? No wonder she was tired of the whole thing.

But something was different now.

Things had taken a darker turn, and his experience in the barn said something else was brewing. He thought back to the people on the Loch who were with him and Sean. He remembered how so many people were out there, with all the different kinds of boat. Then he remembered the yacht.

Tom said, "Ok. I hear you. But if what you're saying is true, then why did Briggs organize a day to hunt for the monster?"

"Call it an outlet," Vaas said. "And an economic ploy. Let me ask ye, why do ye think governments tax th' alcohol ye're drinking instead o' prohibiting it?"

"We tried that in the States," Tom said. "Didn't work very well."

"It ne'er works," Vaas said. "But by allowing it, people wind up helping th' economy. And th' myth is no different. E'erything must be done in moderation. We've made th' mistake o' na' acknowledging th' myth fur tae long. By having a day o' it, people will release their imagination fur one weekend, and then they can go back tae livin' their real lives." Then Vaas frowned and said, "Mr. Wayne, I'm afraid ye and Mr. Paterson are beyond th' point o' moderation. Ye've drunk o' this myth more than ye can handle."

Tom said, "I wasn't the only one out there. You were on that big yacht in the middle of all the other boats."

Vaas's eyes flashed, and he grinned. "It was th' best way tae make sure everyone stayed safe. On a boat tha' size, we'd be right in th' middle tae see e'erything. We'd know instantly if we needed tae call fur help."

"Did you see me swim to the shore?" Tom asked.

"Aye."

"Why didn't you radio for help?"

"Ye seemed tae know what ye were doin'," Vaas said.

Tom sat back. Vaas had an answer for everything.

"So you want me to tone it down," Tom said.

"Na. We wan' ye tae stop. I mean, look at ye. Ye're beat tae hell. Stay indoors until ye go home tae America. Leave th' monster tae th' authorities. We've been handlin' it fur centuries. We can handle it goin' forward."

Tom thought a moment. "You're not talking about handling the monster. You're talking about handling the people. The people of Thurwick."

"Aye."

"But the monster exists," Tom said.

Vaas chuckled, shook his head, and leaned back in his chair. He grabbed his beer with both hands. His shoulders slumped. He reached for his Old Mortality and finished it off. Wiping his mouth clean, he said, "Okay, then. Let's say I believe ye. Why don' ye tell me th' secret tae findin' th' Loch Ness monster?"

Tom felt himself get excited. Something about the monster consumed him, and he had to talk about it. "It's not the technology," he said. "Sean Paterson was right. It's the fishing technique that's been used over the centuries. That's what's been missing. We used large cuts of steak and pork. Then we found it in the spot by Saint Michael's Church. It was huge, and I'll never forget the sound it made, just before it hit me in the water."

Vaas didn't change his expression for a time. Then he laughed. "Lad, I hate tae tell ye this, but people have been fishin' in that Loch fur close tae five thousand years. They've used beef and pork as bait in those waters all tha' time. Ye mean tae tell me tha' somehow *yer* beef and pork is more appetizin' tae th' Loch Ness monster than all th' other fishermen who've come in th' centuries before ye? I'm sorry. Mr. Paterson's fishin' recipe isn't th' secret."

Tom sat back in his chair. He knew what he saw. He knew what he heard. And he knew what he felt. But there was more, now. He also knew that he had to spend his life, whatever it took, to prove the monster existed.

And he knew he needed help.

And he wouldn't get it from Alex Vaas.

Tom said, "You have a point. Maybe you're right. Maybe I do need to keep a low profile until I leave."

Vaas said, "Tha' would serve ye well."

Tom shook Vaas's hand, thanked him for the Old Mortality, and left the table. His body ached, and his eye remained swollen. He needed rest, but he also needed to think. He had no intention of laying low. Vaas made some good points, but Tom the creature was out there. He had to prove the monster for Marella, for Sean, and for himself.

As he left Guthrie's Pub, he scanned the street for people. The roads were empty, but Tom stayed cautious. He had to return to Annabel's Bed and Breakfast, get some sleep, and figure out what to do tomorrow.

Sean Paterson had trusted people in his search for close to thirty years, only to fail. Tom limped across the shadowed cobblestone streets of Thurwick. Should he find somebody else to trust?

Yes. But who?

CHAPTER 26

He woke up with a plan. Beat up and bruised, but with a plan. As he limped around his rented upstairs bedroom at Annabel's Bed and Breakfast, he remembered what Vaas had said the night before.

He had thought the government would be the way to go. After all, they had funds, and they had authority. However, they also had motivations, and if their motivations did not correspond with their desire for power, they would not direct the funds. Sean Paterson had believed the same thing. Being a part of the scientific community, and having been ostracized by Ewan Coffee's investment fund, Sean would seek assistance from government authorities. But it was to no avail. Sean was caught in a circular trap. First, he'd go to the scientific community for research ideas, and their connections with the government brought Tom to the powers that be. However, they would send him back to the scientific community. It was a never ending circle. Tom decided he would break it.

What Vaas indicated last night was the motivation for some governmental officials, at least the corrupt ones. It was money. More accurately, it was the desire to bring economic prosperity to the area.

And then take the credit.

Tom thought that, if he decided to run for office one day, he'd do it differently.

However, the economic prosperity thought tugged at him. Then, he had an idea. "Why hadn't I thought of that earlier," Tom said as he brushed his teeth. After all, that was the trick of "Nessie Day". People spending money on Nessie brought money to Thurwick, too. Then why do it for one day only? Why not make it continuous? If the local government wanted to play off the people's emotions, why not escalate those emotions?

Tom climbed out of bed. He needed to go to the business community. He had to get their buy-in. They would then put the pressure for additional funding on the politicians. It made sense. It should work. It had to work.

But which businesses? And who?

He knew nobody in the area. He sat down and took out a piece of scrap paper. With the hotel pen, he jotted down some ideas. The Chamber of Commerce. Tourist stores. What about any museums? Perhaps he contacted boaters or fishermen? He thought of finding Marella and Sean, but he remembered Marella's words last night in the doctor's room. They didn't want to see him again. If that was the way they wanted it, fine. Though her words hurt, he intended to keep trying.

Tom left the Annabel's. Saint Michael's Church loomed to his left as he walked towards Thurwick. Some people congregated in the church parking lot, dressed in black. He assumed it was for a funeral. He became solemn for a second, and then he moved along the cobblestone road to the center of town.

When he reached the square, he surveyed the scene. He had decided his first trip would be to the Chamber of Commerce. He stood outside a small shop. Above him, the wooden sign of a local barber swung in the breeze. He walked in and asked the men inside where he'd find the Chamber. Many grimaced when they noticed his injuries. Then one of them pointed past Dorlan Hall.

Tom's ankle continued to hurt, and he still limped. His eye's swelling had improved, though he had a good shiner around it. *People will stare*, he thought. *Just pay it no attention.*

Tom arrived at the building the men had indicated. Along the side was another wooden sign, this one vertical. It read, "Thurwick Chamber of Commerce" in white lettering amidst a green background. He stepped inside. The room was small. Two women sat in desks. There was a hallway behind them leading to other offices. The two women gasped at Tom. One of them opened her mouth and put her hand over it.

"Can we help ye," asked the other woman. Tom observed she didn't appear too eager to help.

"Yes," Tom said. "I had a business idea to help spur economic growth here in Thurwick. Who would I talk with about that?"

The woman asked, "Are ye a member o' th' Thurwick Chamber o' Commerce?"

Tom said, "No. I don't live here in Thurwick. You see, I'm from America…."

"Do ye have a business here in Thurwick?"

Tom said, "No. But I have friends who do."

"Really?" the woman said. "And who is tha'?"

"Sean Paterson. He's an inventor down on the other side of town."

"Is he a member o' th' Chamber?" she asked.

The other woman said, "Ahem," and motioned to her coworker to lean in closer. The women whispered to each other, nodding their heads.

You do realize I'm standing right here, right?

The women separated.

The woman on the left said, "I'm sorry, sir, bu' Sean Paterson is na longer a member o' this Chamber o' Commerce."

Tom played along. "He's not? Since when did that happen?"

"We're na' at liberty tae say th' details o' past members and their account status," she said. "Now, if ye have na further business here, we'll have tae ask ye tae leave."

Tom said, "Well, what if I wanted to open a business in Thurwick?"

"As a foreigner, do ye have all th' permitting documents?"

"Uh, which ones do you need to see?"

"All o' them," she said.

This isn't working, Tom thought.

"Can you tell me if you have any members who at all benefit from Loch Ness monster enthusiasm? That's where I have my ideas. If you can just send me there, that would be helpful."

"We have a museum ye can go tae. If ye'll walk out th' doors and turn left, go tha' way fifty meters, there will be th' sign fur it on yer left."

"Okay," Tom said. "I'll give that a try. Thanks." He left the door, disappointed in their reaction to his appearance. He had tried to dress well, and even though he limped, he thought he hid it well enough so that it wasn't noticeable.

It has to be my face.

He walked down the sidewalk towards the museum. There was a wooden brown "Museum" sign with black lettering. He walked inside.

As he entered, there was a large room, about the size of a small convention center. His eyes became dry, as often happened to him when he walked into a large open building. Before him were several exhibits, each cordoned off by red ropes held up by bronze stands. A red carpet circled the room between the exhibits, directing guests to the different themes.

He didn't want to take the tour, but a paying guest might get information. They might be friendlier than the chamber.

He went to the ticket counter and paid his fare. He asked the lady at the ticket counter if someone would be available if he had any questions. The woman's eyes stayed locked to her computer screen. Then she noticed Tom's black eye, and his bruised face, and she gasped.

"I didn't understand the local customs," he said pointing at his face, hoping she'd take his humor.

The woman didn't laugh. But she suggested that the museum manager would be in later, so Tom decided to walk along the carpet and read about the history.

As he entered the gates, he came to the first theme. To his right a display case held shiny armor from centuries past. He admired the polished metal. How would he fare if he had to wear equipment such as that in the heat of battle? If a joint moved wrong, he could be cut by his own equipment. Then he would suffer death by tetanus or gangrene. And that was if an opponent didn't hurl a blade through his skull.

What he also found interesting was the size of the equipment. People back then were just smaller than they were today. Tom wasn't a large man by any stretch of the imagination, but he still wouldn't have fit into the gear in the display if he had tried. *Maybe that's how legends were born,* he thought. People had to find ways to survive, and their stories created status, which created economic opportunities.

He turned the corner. Several black and white pictures hung on the walls. They were pictures of men in business suits as they stood together in ancient buildings. The large picture on the wall reminded him of his experience at Dorlan Hall last week, except the room was bigger and the people were more numerous. He guessed it would be a state legislature of some sort. He enjoyed reading the displays.

As he continued along, the displays held more and more information about the people of Scotland. Tom read information about authors, politicians, inventors, and actors. As he neared what appeared the end of the tour, he approached several pictures of Loch Ness.

And boats.

Lots and lots of boats.

Then, he noticed something different. He found strange black and white pictures of a creature coming up from the waters. He concentrated on the pictures, analyzing their texture. They were old pictures. The quality wasn't very good. *Too many strange shadows,* he thought. *Was that water, or sunlight?* He put his face close to the pictures on the wall. He searched for any evidence that would confirm what hit his leg.

He gave up and moved to his left.

"Woaaaaahhhhh!!!" Tom yelled. Teeth and a tongue and a snake-like head lunged at him just inches from his face. Startled, he fell backward into the brass stand holding the rope. He made a loud ruckus as he knocked over the brass and it clanged onto the tile floors. The noise echoed inside the museum. He knocked his head into the display behind him. Hanging in mid-air above him was a full-size replica of a plesiosaur. The museum staff had placed this replica in its location to scare museum patrons, and Tom figured the person who did this knew what he was doing.

"Can I help ye?" said a woman's voice.

A lady wearing a red business suit approached him. "Sorry," Tom said. "Your friend here scared me." he tried his best to maneuver the brass stand and dust himself off.

"He's been known tae do tha'," she said. "We have a video camera tha' catches people's reactions." She pointed at the ceiling to a small black box high in the corner. "Th' staff gets together and watches th' videos when things ge' slow. We can show ye yers as ye leave th' museum if ye'd like."

"Can't wait."

"Th' lady at th' ticket counter said ye migh' have some questions."

"Yes." He pointed at the creature hanging in the air above him. "How real is this?"

"Th' Loch Ness monster?" The lady was pensive. "I can tell ye those who believe in it, really belie'e it exists. Those who don',

don'. As fur me, it attracts visitors, and tha' helps pay my salary. So th' more he exists th' better it is fur me."

Tom laughed. "Well, I believe he does exist."

The woman held her breath. She smiled politely, but her lips pursed.

Tom said, "I want to get business owners to form a group that will prove he exists. Would you have any ideas?"

"Ye may wan' tae try th' Thurwick Local Council, or th' Chamber o' Commerce."

Tom dropped his shoulders. "Already been there." He pointed to his eye. "This is all I got."

"They didn' believe ye?"

Tom shook his head. He moved around the hanging plesiosaur. "Is this as large as they get?"

"Na. Their skeletons have been found all o'er th' world, ranging from one and a half tae fifteen meters. Th' one here is only abou' ten meters."

Tom thanked the woman, and said he wouldn't need further help. She walked away, leaving him alone with the plesiosaur.

The creature hung in the air, supported by several thin wires. He noticed the long neck, the open mouth, the four powerful fins, and the eyes. For a replica, its creators made it very lifelike. Was this what hit him that first night out in the water? Was this what rammed his thigh before he scrambled to get back into the boat? What was it that made them come to Sean's boat in the first place?

There was so much to take in. He reconsidered his plan. His economic pursuit wasn't panning out.

Sean admired the model of the plesiosaur hanging above him, and he scratched his head.

The government was against him. A gang of thugs were after him. Some strange albino guy showed up in places to haunt him. Marella and Sean abandoned him.

He had to figure out what he'd do next.

A new tactic was needed.

But what?

CHAPTER 27

Tom walked out of the museum. The day was cloudy. Storms threatened Thurwick again, but as the falling rain cast shadows off in the distance, he decided he'd take his chances.

He would walk outside.

And think.

It hadn't always been that way. When Tom was a child, living with his family in Arizona, the outdoors was a place of adventure. He'd run off and play with his friends in the woods, searching for one thrill after another. It wasn't until his father got a job in the city that the woods became the place to think. He would try to get away from the pavement and lights of the city streets just to hear his own thoughts. His trip to Scotland, so far, had been like his childhood. One challenge came after the next. However, with his pursuit of Marella, and now the mystery of the Loch Ness, and whatever mystery was in that building across the water, he realized he never took time to just be outdoors and think.

Tom knew he was a longshot to win Marella's affections. No doubt about it, though, she had his. He had wanted to just show up, get to know her, and maybe be a shoulder for her to cry on if she was having troubles with her family. He had no idea he'd be in the middle of where he was.

Tom walked to the boat dock. As the boats swayed in the choppy waves, he admired them for their craftsmanship. People had been using boats for economic development and prosperity since man first found bodies of water. Though the styles of boats had changed, they remained the same as those built during earlier centuries. The waters hadn't changed, nor the weather.

And neither had the Loch Ness monster changed. Tom hadn't given much thought to a prehistoric creature surviving a calamitous event that wiped out the dinosaurs sixty-five million years ago. The museum information said that plesiosaurs lived from two hundred million years ago until the asteroid hit the earth. Wouldn't it be possible for some remnants of plesiosaur to survive?

Something had hit him in his leg the other night. It was the fin, or so he thought. He had heard the roar. He had smelled it when it surfaced. Heck, he had the bruise to prove it.

It had to be the Loch Ness monster.

It *had* to be.

Then again, everybody says I'd been missing for two days. Maybe I am losing it.

He thought of his roommate, Bob, back in Atlanta. He hadn't given any indication that Tom had abnormal behavior prior to his leaving for Scotland. In fact, it had been Bob that gave Tom the idea.

Or had it? He couldn't remember all the events that had happened. Was he imagining things? Was his passion for Marella causing him to lose his mind?

Was he even able to think?

He left the dock walked along the Loch Ness shoreline towards Annabel's. A fish jumped above the surface of the water and made a splash upon reentry, causing ripples to expand along the surface. A cold wind hit Tom in the face. Tom thought the water was beautiful. He admired the Scottish hills. The small town of Thurwick made him think. Had things not been so unusual, this would be a nice place to raise a family. If things did work with Marella, would he consider moving to Scotland?

"I'm probably out of a job," he said aloud. "What would I have to lose?"

Sean may not like it if he stayed, though. He wasn't sure of Sean.

Yes, Tom had launched a deep sea hook into Sean's face. Not many fathers would overlook an offence like that.

Tom suspected Sean would behave like most fathers would toward a daughter, even if he happened to have a peculiar obsession for the Loch Ness monster.

It was an obsession he now shared with Tom.

Ever since the barn experience across the Loch, something had happened to Tom. He felt it. Something in his gut demanded he find the monster, to search for it, to capture it.

He couldn't explain why.

For some reason, it became the only thing that mattered. His thoughts led him to the monster. His daily activities were a means to finding the creature. His rest was to restore energy to learn more about it. The monster was consuming him. He knew it was happening, and it scared him.

A shadow bobbed in the water. Tom thought it was Nessie, and he jumped. He got on all fours, ready for a large serpentine head to reach out of the water.

It was just a stick.

Tom stood tall again, his arms by his side. He felt like a fool. *How long will this go on?*

He walked along the Loch when he heard a voice nearby. "So are ye tired yet o' lookin' in all th' wrong places?"

Tom flinched at the sound of the voice, but he had heard that voice somewhere before. On a hillside behind a tree, he spotted a bench. An unassuming patient man wearing a brown leather coat and a fedora sat on it. Tom recognized him immediately.

It was Caleb.

"Where have you been?" Tom said. "First, you come out of nowhere at the city meeting to tell us all sorts of conspiracies, and then you disappear? I could have used more information about this time last week."

"Ye weren' ready fur it," Caleb said.

Tom threw his hands into the air. "I don't have time for these games. I need to know what's going on, and you may be my last hope."

"I'm na' yer lest hope," Caleb said.

"Great," Tom said. "So are we going to play twenty questions until I figure out what I'm supposed to do next?"

Caleb remained sitting. He picked up a pebble and threw it into the Loch. It splashed in the water, rippling the waves.

Tom grew impatient. "This whole town is crazy. No one tells me what he thinks, except Sean, and he's the one claiming he's found the Loch Ness monster. Yet he makes more sense than anybody."

Caleb said, "Maybe yer answers are in other places."

"Answers?" Tom said. "I don't even know what questions to ask!"

Caleb watched the waves.

"Okay. I'll ask a question." Tom scratched his head. "Do you have any idea what's with that barn across the river?"

"I do," Caleb said. "It may be cursed. We wondered wha' would happen tae ye, if it would be th' same thing as happene' tae Sean Paterson thirty years ago. When ye disappeared, we had our answer."

Tom crossed his arms. "A curse? You've got to be kidding me. Are you sure I wasn't just breathing fumes from a pot house or something?"

"Aye. Pretty sure."

"I'm not going to believe that."

"Suit yerself."

"What do you know about the albino?"

"Th' albino? He's around. Strange one, he is."

"So you know him?"

"Aye. He shows up from time tae time."

"Are you sure we're talking about the same guy?"

Caleb raised a flat hand to the height of the albino. "About this lanky? White locks? Pale face? Wears rags?"

"Yeah. That's him."

"He calls himself th' White Warlock."

"The what?"

"Th' White Warlock. Strange, I know. He meddles in divination."

"What's that?"

"Witchcraft."

"Okay. So why does he watch me?"

"Ye're a threat."

"Threat to what?"

"Revealing th' secret tae th' creature."

"He wants to keep it hidden?"

"He thinks tis his."

"Unbelievable." Tom laughed. "Did he have anything to do with this?" said Tom, pointing to his face.

"More than likely," Caleb said. "But he's probably a tool fur th' curse."

"So, let me get this straight. I'm cursed?"

"Aye. And Paterson."

"How's that?" Tom said.

"Tis na' a curse tha' marks ye fur death, but tis one tha' serves a purpose. Tis a cruel curse, really. We call it an 'obsession curse'."

"What do you mean?" Tom asked.

Caleb reached down and picked up some grass near his feet. He tossed the grass blades, and the small breeze landed them to the left of the bench. "Are ye familiar wi' Cassandra, from th' Iliad?"

"No. Never heard of her."

"Cassandra was a princess who was gifted wi' prophecy. She was always right, except she was cursed because na one woul' believe her. Durin' th' Trojan War, she'd have visions o' her loved ones dyin'. Tae protect them she'd tell them wha' would happen. Instead, wi' her information, her loved ones woul' do th' opposite, and find themselves dying exactly as Cassandra had prophesied. Her ability tae predict th' future also became her curse."

"So, how does this relate to me?" Tom said.

"Well, wha' do ye think?" Caleb said. "Ye've go' an obsession fur a monster ye ne'er cared abou' until lest week, and now ye're facin' all sorts o' calamities and social stigma. By th' way, where *are* Sean and Marella? Don' they wan' tae be wi' ye anymore?"

"Marella told me that she and Sean don't want to see me again."

"And yet ye keep lookin' fur th' monster. Why?"

Tom shuddered at the words as they came out of his mouth. "I *have* to," he said.

As soon as the words left him, he knew he had changed. Tom noticed a chill run through his body.

Fear.

He didn't understand any of this. The waves of the Loch leapt upon the shore. The clouds overhead grew darker. Shadows covered the landscape with the oncoming storm. A most cold wind blew from the west. Tom put his hands in his coat pockets.

Caleb sat on the bench, waiting for Tom's next move. Could Tom trust Caleb?

Why all this information? Why now? Why me, here across the ocean.

How'd I get in all this mess?

Tom said, "I don't want to be this way, Caleb. I know I've changed. What can I do?"

Caleb said, "Ye have th' free will tae choose where tae look. All I can tell ye is ye haven' searched e'erywhere. Unless ye open yer heart, ye will be cursed like Sean Paterson fur th' rest o' yer life." he stood up. "That's all I can tell ye. I just hope yer heart is open enough tae find th' answer." Then he stepped up the hill and walked away from Tom.

"Wait. What do you mean by that?"

Caleb didn't respond. He marched around a corner, and disappeared from Tom's view.

Tom picked up a rock and threw it hard into the water. It splashed into the water. He decided to catch up with Caleb. He sprinted up the hill. When he reached the crest, he scanned right and left, but Caleb was gone.

"Is my heart open enough to find it?" Tom said aloud. "Just what the hell did he mean by that?"

CHAPTER 28

Tom went back down the hill to the bench and sat and watched the waves as they crested on the Loch. His mind raced in many different directions. He thought of Marella, and Sean, and Briggs, and Vaas. He tried to picture the Loch Ness monster. He tried not to picture the barn, or the albino. So much had happened, and he felt himself losing control.

He found himself in a foreign country, with no family, and no friends. His hope was waning.

He remembered a similar time from his past. He was a young boy, who had decided he would run away from home. His parents had just moved to the city, and their schedules had changed. He was seven, and upset he had to spend so much time on his own. So, one day, he just packed up a peanut butter and jelly sandwich, wrapped it with tin foil, and put it in a brown paper bag. Knowing he'd soon be thirsty, he also grabbed a can of Sprite from the refrigerator. He put them in the bag, and he walked out the door.

He had no idea where he'd go. He decided to go back into the woods, since the city was the cause of all his troubles. He found a patch of trees, and walked through them. In half an hour, he knew he had made progress, but then he was disappointed when he heard the sound of motors echoing on what was a busy nearby highway. A few more steps later, he was out of the cover of the trees, and facing the back of a large building. There was a dumpster nearby. It was covered with cardboard boxes. The air smelled putrid. He examined the building. At first he thought it was a warehouse, but later he imagined it was the back of a grocery store.

There was movement by the dumpster. A man wearing ragged clothes was bent over the side of the dumpster. His head was focused on the trash inside, and he picked at the garbage with his hands, examining an item, and if he found it unsatisfactory, threw it over his shoulder. When he found something he liked, he put it to his mouth and ate it.

Tom's stomach heaved as the man ate from the garbage. His noise caught the attention of the man. The man walked briskly, but stumbling, towards him. Tom backed away.

"Hey," the man said. "Can you get me some liquor?"

Tom's eyes widened.

Liquor? What's that?

Tom's innocent mind had no knowledge of alcohol. He ran. He heard the man call out to him again and then swear at him as Tom ran over the pavement along the back of the building and around the corner.

When he rounded the corner, he was at a busy intersection. He had found the highway. Cars sped past. Drivers did not notice at him. He knew they would run over him if he found himself in their way.

He went to the corner at the crosswalk. He stood alone, holding his paper bag, waiting for the crosswalk light to turn green. After several long seconds, it did. Large semi-trucks stopped at the light. The trucks' hoods towered over him. Tom felt the heat coming through their metal grills as he walked past them. He stood on his tiptoes to see the drivers, but he was too small see above the edge of the hoods.

Maybe hitchhike, he thought. Then the crossing light flashed, and he decided he didn't have time. *Best get to the other side.* He ran, clutching his paper bag.

When he crossed the other side, he gathered himself. *Where should I go?* Should he go left, or right, or straight into the woods ahead? That's when he noticed a stray dog at the edge of the woods, its nose to the ground. It wasn't a small dog. Its shoulders went to Tom's waist. Tom had an idea. He and the dog could be friends, and take on this world together. He decided to pull out his sandwich. He tore off a portion of it and, holding it between his fingers, walked to the dog.

"Here, boy. I've got something for you."

The dog picked its head up, its body flexing, but its ears raised out of curiosity. Tom moved closer. Then the hairs on the back of the dog's neck rose, and the dog flashed white teeth. Its eyes showed aggression as it growled. Tom stepped backward, and fell down. The dog moved closer. Its teeth grew larger. Sharper.

Tom found a stick next to him and he picked it up. He scrambled to his feet, and held the stick in his hand.

The dog did not advance.

Tom decided to walk away to his left along the road, keeping his front to the dog in case it decided to charge. He heard the cars continue to drive past on the busy highway.

Then Tom ran. He was terrified the dog would give chase. Some signs were up ahead. *Get to them, then figure out what to do.* His heart pounded. His breath was fast. He came to another intersection, this one a minor road off the main highway. On the other side was a McDonald's. Cars were in the parking lot. The dog was not following him. Tom stopped.

He decided not to go inside. A minor road went up a hill and around the bend. He decided to follow it. A car drove past him. The people inside gave the expression one does when they notice something unusual, but they don't want to do anything about it.

Tom kept his eyes straight ahead, pretending he wasn't lost or that he didn't need any help. He noticed the car slowed down. Tom didn't want their help, so he ran the other direction. He rounded the bend.

A parking lot was on his left. It was a fancy building, different than the grocery store strip malls. Its structure had elegance to it, and it felt safe. The building's ambiance welcomed him to go inside. He came to the doors. They were large. He imagined they'd be locked, but when he pulled on the door, he was surprised that it opened.

He went inside. There were some stands with pamphlets in a room. Through the open doors was an auditorium. He walked through the door, and at the other end of the auditorium there was a large table on a raised platform. Behind the table, hanging on the wall, was a statue of a man who had died. His arms were stretched outward.

"Hello, young man." It was a deep voice. Tom turned around. A large man wearing a black outfit stood next to him. His hair was gray, and his face was round. He had a big smile. It was the gentle face that kept Tom from running. "Are ye here tae have a picnic?" The man pointed at Tom's paper bag.

"No," Tom said.

"Well, I was abou' tae have a picnic," the man said. "Ye're welcome tae join me if ye'd like."

Tom scrunched his paper bag. He was alone. He had no friends. The world was dangerous. He didn't want to admit it, but he had made a mistake. The man introduced him as Father Kenny. He was the pastor at the church. He spoke in an unusual accent. It had been the first time Tom had heard an Irish accent. Father Kenny was kind to listen to Tom. The man didn't talk about the church, or anything. He simply asked where Tom's parents were and if they knew he was gone. Tom to sniffled, and then he cried. The priest told a receptionist in the main lobby to find his parents. They spent some time together outside the building, sitting at a table in a small garden off to the side.

Soon, Tom's mother drove up. Her face was worried. She had been crying, too. He felt mad at first, and then sad for what he had done. But when she ran up to hug him, he knew he was safe. He was embarrassed. She had put him in the car. He never even had time to thank Father Kenny for listening. But he was happy he had.

And that's when Tom realized what Caleb meant. As he sat upon the bench, the sunlight reflecting off the ripples of the Loch's surface, he knew his heart hadn't been open. Yet the clue had been there all along.

Tom stood up. There were no people around, but was he being watched? He was alone by the Loch. At least he thought he was. He did not want to risk being followed. He didn't want to expose those who might have the answers.

He would first go and find Marella. Whether or not she and Sean would listen to him would be up to them. He considered them his friends, and though they were frustrated, he hadn't given up on them. He had to tell them about the barn, and the albino known as the White Warlock.

And then he had to tell them where he would go next.

CHAPTER 29

Tom hurried back to the cottage. Above him, the rain clouds shifted, and he heard nearby thunder. His ankle continued to hurt as he took his steps, and he felt it swelling inside his shoe. When he arrived at Sean's cottage, a slight drizzle landed on his face. Drips of rain trickled down his forehead. The windmills spun in the breeze, signaling an oncoming storm.

He knocked on the door. His heart felt sadness, worried that Marella would reject him forever.

I still have to try.

The door opened, and Marella said, "Go away." She moved to shut the door.

"Wait," Tom said. "I know you're tired of all this. But I think I know what's been going on."

"Aye? And who made ye God? Why don' ye just leave?"

Tom noticed how, even in her disappointment, Marella still had a fire in her green eyes that made her radiant. "Marella, believe me when I say this that I want to help you. You're in pain.

You've had it so long. You may not notice anything else. Maybe that's why I'm here. Maybe I'm here to bring you relief."

Marella said, "Na one tells th' truth. Na' my father. Na' ye. Na' anybody. I'm tired o' bein' lied tae, and it's time I just left all o' ye alone." Marella opened the door wider, not to let Tom in. Suit cases rested on the sofa. "Ye see these? I'm leaving fur Inverness t'morrow. I'm already packed. I'll stay there wi' a friend until my plane leaves." She shrugged. "I'm sorry, Tom. I just don' believe anybody anymore, and I need a fresh start."

"What about your father?" Tom said.

"He's na' well. He hasn' come out o' his room since ye disappeared. I don' know what's come o'er him, and I don' have wha' it takes tae take care o' him anymore. I canno' help someone who doesn' wan' tae help himself. When I leave, I'm goin' tae call th' local authorities, tell them what's happene' tae him, and le' them figure it out," Marella said.

"Can I see him?" Tom asked.

"T'would be best if ye just left," Marella said. "Just forge' this whole thing, and get on wi' yer life."

"Marella, look," Tom said. "I woke up this morning, and I had a plan. Granted, it didn't work. I tried getting help from the Chamber of Commerce, and the Thurwick Museum, but neither had the answers."

Marella rolled her eyes.

"Just stay with me a moment. When those didn't work, I went for a long walk along the Loch." Tom paused a moment. The air was cold, and a fog had covered the countryside. "I admit something has changed in me. I have felt different since everyone says I disappeared. Quite frankly, I'm a little nervous. I don't know what happened. I just know something inside me is different. I don't know what it is, but I've got to find out."

Marella frowned.

Tom wasn't getting through to her.

"Regardless, I ran into Caleb. You remember him? The one we met after the meeting in Dorlan Hall? He just showed up. And he told me what could be happening."

Marella sighed and shook her head. "Just le' it go."

"Marella, I believe your father and I have both been cursed."

Marella laughed. "I've said tha' all along. Now I must be goin'…" She pulled the door to shut it, but Tom held up his hand to keep the door from closing. Marella said, "If you don' let me shut this door, I will call th' police."

"Both of them?"

"Don' tempt me."

"I'm not so sure the police run this town."

"That's why tis na' safe here."

Tom removed his hand from the door. "Please hear me out this once, and I'll be gone forever."

Marella didn't answer.

"It's just hard for me to put all this into words." Tom said. Marella's green eyes flashed with anger. He knew his next few words to her could very well be his last. "I believe I know where to find the answers to this whole thing."

Marella said, "I'm glad ye do. Send a postcard tae me in American when ye find them."

"Wait, Marella. Please, come with me. It would be good if you came."

"I'm na' goin' anywhere wi' ye. As I said, my bus leaves t'morrow. I'm spending wha' time I have left here wi' my father, and then I'm leaving this God forsaken place."

"So I've got one day. That may work."

"Just leave."

"Please give me just one day, and I may have a solution to all your problems."

Marella frowned. "I've been dealin' wi' this obsession all my life," she said. "I'm done wi' it. Ye do wha' ye must. Bu' I'm finished. Now, if ye'll excuse me…"

Marella pulled the door, and this time it shut with a loud bang. The door closed inches from Tom's face. Then he heard the door lock.

Tom said, "I'm not giving up."

She said through the door, "Good luck tae ye."

Tom leaned his head against the door for a few moments. The rain drizzled, and strands of his hair fell down over his forehead. Water ran over his black eye. Another rumble of thunder echoed between the hills surrounding Loch Ness.

In the distance, the skyline displayed the tops of the tallest buildings in Thurwick. While many of them were ordinary, one stood out above the rest. That one just happened to be his next destination. It had been there all along, but he hadn't been open to walking through its doors.

Tom took a deep breath. The building's peak elevated a simple cross below the storm clouds. Then, as the pain of his ankle increased, he walked in the direction of Saint Michael's Catholic Church.

CHAPTER 30

Tom reached the front of the church. Large stone walls loomed before him, rising to a point on its face which held the cross that stood high in the sky. It was visible from Sean Paterson's cottage, and just about everywhere else in Thurwick. Though the rain had let up some, a new wind picked up that was fiercer than before. Dark clouds congregated above Annabel's. They extended east over the town of Thurwick.

As the wind blew, he stood outside. He shrugged to keep the moist air and the cold wind from hitting his neck and chin. The heavy doors were made of heavy wood. He reached for a door handle, and pulled.

The door was slow to open, but as he pulled the handle, he felt a rush of musty air. The outside pressure was dropping, and so he went inside just as the sound of hard rain crashed to the ground. He pulled the door shut behind him. The sound of its closing echoed in the chamber. He was in a small entryway. Beyond the entryway, several wooden pews aligned facing a front altar. Just like his childhood memory of the day he ran away, a crucifix hung on the wall behind the large altar.

He stepped forward. No one was in the church with him. He moved forward between the pews. Several statues stood on opposite walls. Overhead, colorful windows, darkened by the storm outside, shone what little light came through. Shadows danced inside the church, energized by a few well-placed candles which lit the front. He walked toward the candles. As he neared the front, he admired the crucified Christ hanging on the wall. Tom flinched at a clap of thunder which came from the storm outside, its power echoing between the church's stone walls.

Something moved to his left. He heard the sound of footsteps, and he peered into a side room, trying to make out the shapes in the shadows. A man wearing a brown robe with ropes tied around his waist stepped towards him. He was a man in his early sixties. The man didn't say anything. He put his finger to his mouth, instructing Tom to stay quiet. He then moved his fingers, and motioned for Tom to follow.

The man led Tom through a door and into a lit hallway. The stone around the walls reminded Tom how old this place must have been, but they did have some more modern electrical components.

At least they upgraded in the last half-century.

He followed the man, who opened the door to a side room. "Come inside," the man said. Tom walked in, and the man shut the door behind him.

Tom was in an office. A desk with some chairs sat inside what was a small room, with a single window facing the Loch Ness outside. Large drops of rain hit the window, making the view of the loch blurry. Flashes of lightning erupted outside, lighting the room within.

The man in the robe sat down behind his desk. A large bookshelf filled with books covered the wall behind his chair.

"Please. Sit," the man said.

Tom obliged, admiring the old world globe on the edge of the desk.

Tom said, "So, who are you?"

The man said, "I'm Father Ross Gibson. I'm th' pastor here at Saint Michael's Church."

"Well, I'm Tom Wayne. Maybe you can tell me why I'm here."

Father Gibson nodded. "We know well who ye are. In fact, it took ye long enough tae come tae us."

"If you wanted me, why didn't you come and get me?"

Father Gibson paused. He reached for a small refrigerator near the door. "Could I get ye somethin' tae drink? Water? Maybe a glass o' wine?"

"No thanks." Tom shook his head. "I'm good."

Father Gibson pulled out a small glass and a bottle of cabernet. He poured himself the wine, and set it next to the globe that adorned the edge of his desk.

"Suit yerself, lad. Le' me know if ye change yer mind." He reached for the glass and took a sip, and then he set the glass back on the desk next to the globe.

There were a few moments of silence. Tom heard the sound of ticking, made by a small desk clock which sat on the bookshelf behind Father Gibson.

"Ye know, Mr. Wayne, we've been here fur centuries. Ye've been in Thurwick now fur o'er a week. In fact, ye sleep across th' street at Annabel's Bed and Breakfast. How come ye ne'er came through these doors until now?"

Tom said, "So, you've been watching me? Why? What's with all the secrets?"

"Well, we coul' have been more direct and dragged ye in here, bu' then ye wouldn' have believed us."

"What are you talking about?" Tom said. He sat back in his chair. "Believed what?"

"All sorts o' things."

"Such as?"

"Mr. Wayne. Tis our job and duty tae help people have meanin' in their lives. We study and explore th' mystery o' God and all his Creation, and how tha' affects our eternity."

"Great. You're going to give me a lecture."

"If ye wan'."

"I don't."

"Okay then. Wha' do ye wan'?"

"I want to know what's going on around here."

"In Thurwick?"

"Yeah."

"Very well. Where shoul' I start?"

"How about the Loch Ness monster. What do you know about him?"

Father Gibson nodded, and then he took another sip of wine. "We think God wants th' Loch Ness monster tae be discovered by man."

Tom chuckled. "Now this is getting weird."

"I'm only answerin' yer question, Mr. Wayne."

"Okay. I'll humor you. God wants the Loch Ness monster to be discovered. Why is that?"

"Canno' say."

"Well, that doesn't help"

"Mr. Wayne, we don' know why. We just believe He does."

"Okay, that's a start, I suppose. But if God wants him discovered, tell me how you know the monster exists."

"We know how tae call him tae us."

Tom nearly fell out of his chair. "You've got to be kidding me. You know how to call him? To you? Really? I'm sorry, but I don't believe that."

Father Gibson shrugged his shoulders. He took his finger and spun the globe on the desk. "Th' world is a big place, wi' many secrets. If *ye* have a complete understanding o' th' creation o' th' world, maybe ye can be th' one tae enlighten us?"

A few seconds passed. Tom said, "He came to us as we were fishing. We had steaks in the water. I can't tell you all the fishing tricks Sean Paterson used, but he had used the same tricks the week before, and whatever he did attracted the monster to our boat."

"Steaks? So th' secret tae lurin' th' Loch Ness monster, in yer opinion, is steaks." The priest chuckled. "So, tell me. Did ye use filet? Ribeye? New York Strip?" He laughed again, took a sip of wine from his glass, and put it down. He smiled, shaking his head. "Don' ge' me wrong, lad. I enjoy a wee good sirloin myself. But do ye really think th' answer tae a centuries old myth is steaks?"

Tom didn't respond.

Father Gibson said, "Ye're forgettin' a few details."

"How would you know if I'm forgetting details?" Tom asked.

"Because I could see it all through tha' window."

Tom tried to remember. It was a crazy night. Many details ran through his mind since their boat was capsized. Had he forgotten some of them?

Tom said, "Okay. I remember some lights shone through the windows that night."

"And wha' else?"

Tom tried to think.

Father Gibson rapped his fingers on the desk, waiting for Tom to speak.

Then Tom remembered.

"The music! We heard singing. In fact, we were tapping the bottom of the boat to the music. Some fishermen will bang on their boats to attract fish."

"Aye," Father Gibson said. "Tha' is correct."

"That was you singing, right?"

"Aye, it was all o' us here in th' rectory. Do ye remember wha' we were singin'?"

"No. There were several songs. In fact, I remember Sean banging to the rhythm of your music, and it changed with each song. It's funny how someone's beat will change with the song."

Father Gibson nodded. He took another sip of wine, set it on the table next to the globe, but remained silent.

"So, is that the secret? To bang on the boat with steaks in the water while you sing in the rectory?" Tom said.

Father Gibson chuckled. "Oh, th' steaks had nothin' tae do wi' it," he said. "Neither did yer bangin' on th' boat, except fur maybe a little. Wha' we've found is there is one hymn which, when we sing it, will attract th' Loch Ness monster e'ery time."

Tom chuckled, unable to believe him.

"Le' me play something fur ye." Father Gibson spun his chair around. Tom noticed a small CD player on the book shelf behind him. Father Gibson turned the CD player on, and he hit a few buttons. Tom heard music. It was the sound of several male singers singing a tune in a foreign language. "Do ye know wha' this is?" Father Gibson said.

Tom shook his head.

"This is a Gregorian chant. This particular one is called 'Veni, Veni, Emmanuel'. We sing it a lot durin' Advent, which happens in th' weeks leading up tae Christmas. Maybe ye'll remember it?"

Tom hadn't been to church in years. He felt uncomfortable admitting it. He just shook his head, hoping the priest would continue.

Father Gibson said, "Well, fur whate'er reason, we sang this song durin' Lent a long time ago. Lent is the Church's season leading up tae Easter, which happens in th' spring."

"I know when Easter is," Tom said.

"Okay. Just checkin'. Well, thirty years ago, th' priests here practiced tha' song. That's when th' Loch Ness monster appeared out o' th' water. And that's when Sean Paterson saw it."

"You're kidding."

"'Tis also th' song we sang when ye and Sean found it o'er a week ago, and when Sean Paterson had his encounter wi' it th' weekend before tha'."

"You mean to tell me that the Loch Ness monster comes to the surface when you sing that song?"

"Aye. It has happened e'ery time."

"Every time?"

"Aye. E'ery time." He took another sip of wine, and the glass clinked as he set it back on the desk.

"No offense, Father, but that makes no sense at all. Why would a prehistoric monster come from the depths of the Loch just because you're singing a song?"

"I know. I admit it doesn' make sense. We wondered that as well. Maybe there's something in th' rhythm o' th' music tha' mimics it's mating call. Or perhaps 'tis a distress call. There's na tellin'. All we know is when somethin' happens regularly enough, ye begin tae accept it as fact."

The priest sat back in his chair as the rain streaked against the window. "We canno' always comprehend God's mysteries, bu' he does delight when we discover them."

"How do I know you're not lying to me?"

"Na offense, lad, but wha' else do ye have? Ye've been beaten up badly. Th' local authorities aren' helping ye. Na one outside these walls believes ye. It doesn' appear ye have any other choice but tae hear me."

Tom paused. The priest made some sense, at least by helping to move his thought pattern to a new possibility. But he still felt unsure. "Tell me what you know about curses."

"Och aye. Ye wan' tae know abou' th' barn and th' White Warlock."

"You know about him?" Tom said.

"Aye, we know abou' him."

"Am I cursed?" Tom shifted in his chair. He wasn't sure he wanted to know.

"Th' Catholic Church acknowledges th' existence o' curses. That's why we have prayers tae help remove them. If ye'd like, I'd be glad tae pray wi' ye."

"Thanks, Father, but I'm just not ready for anything like that."

"Very well," said Father Gibson. "Th' Faith is ready fur ye, when ye're ready tae choose th' Faith. God ne'er interferes wi' yer free will."

"If you don't mind, I'd better get going."

"Ye're free tae leave." Father Gibson lifted himself from his chair and extended his hand. "Just remember, ye're also free tae come back any time."

Tom shook hands, thanked the priest, and walked out the door. He followed the hall to the main church. As he walked past the pews, he stopped and examined the crucifix. It hung upon the wall behind the altar in triumphant sacrifice.

Did God really exist?

At that moment, the sound of church bells rung in the air. The timing startled him. Tom shook his head.

Sean Paterson. I need to find him.

He walked out the church doors into the rain.

CHAPTER 31

As the rain fell, Tom hurried through the mud. He felt his damp feet inside his shoes as his socks soaked up the water with each step. Regardless, he had to get back to the cottage. He had to tell Sean what Father Gibson had told him. Would it work? He had to try one more time. He had to…

It was the obsession again. Tom felt it in his gut. He couldn't control his desire. He had to get out on the Loch again, just one more time to prove the existence of the monster.

It consumed him.

He knew he would get on a boat that night. He would borrow Sean's rowboat and go alone if he had to.

But he didn't want to go alone. He wanted to get Sean Paterson on the water with him.

He turned the corner and went to the cottage. He ran to the door, ignoring the pain in his ankle. He knocked on the door. Then he waited.

No one came to the door.

He knocked again. "Marella, if you're in there. I need to talk with Sean. It's important."

The door stayed closed.

Tom backed up. The windows were dark. He decided to run around the side and peek inside them. As he ran around, he noticed the rear window blinds were closed. Tom went to the window he believed was Sean's, and he banged on it. "Mr. Paterson. It's Sean. I know what happened to you. I know about the barn. More importantly, I think I have a way to prove the existence of the Loch Ness monster!"

There was no answer. If Sean was in the room, and he was cursed with an obsession, then any chance to prove the monster existed would draw him out.

Several moments passed, and then the blinds opened. Sean's face appeared through the blinds as he opened them with two fingers. Tom said, "I need to talk with you." He pointed around the front of the house.

Sean made a motion to meet him around front. Tom nodded, and took a step to his left just before a fist hit him in the face.

He felt pain in his eye as he fell backwards. It was the same eye where the shiner was. The pain was sharp. His rear splashed in a puddle when he hit the ground. He felt vibrations in his back, and he winced when his muscles spasmed, flashing some pain up his spine.

He recovered quickly, though. Sitting in the mud, he put a hand on his eye. Marella stood above him, displaying her fists. "Well, that's a nice warm welcome," he said.

"I told ye tae stay away," she said.

"I did, and then I came back."

"Well now I'm tellin' ye…"

Sean Paterson ran around the corner. His clothes and his hair were disheveled, as though he hadn't taken a shower in several days. "Wha' do ye mean ye know th' answer?"

Marella said to Sean. "This is ridiculous!" She took several steps away from Sean and Tom. She stiffened her body and clenched her fists.

Tom rubbed his face. The pain in his eye lingered, but he was grateful that Sean had appeared around the corner.

Yes, he was still obsessed. Tom's trick to get Sean's attention worked. Now, would Sean believe him?

"There are others," Tom said.

"Wha'?" Sean said.

"Several who say they have spotted the monster. Not just last week, but thirty years ago when you first saw it."

"Who? Why didn' they speak up about it then?"

"The priests," Tom said. "The priests at Saint Michael's know about the Loch Ness monster. They claim they saw it thirty years ago, and they saw it last week, both times."

"Th' priests?" Sean said. "Bu' they have their own superstitions. Why would they care anything abou' th' Loch Ness monster?"

Tom picked himself up off the ground. His jeans were covered with mud and dark blue patches where they were soaked by rain water. "I just met with Father Gibson, the pastor at the church. I have to tell you, he didn't seem superstitious to me. In fact, he says they called him."

"*Called* him?" Sean asked.

"That's what he told me."

Sean checked on Marella's reaction. She had her hands on her hips.

Sean said, "How'd he do it?"

"He said there's a song they know. When they sing it, the monster surfaces."

Sean laughed. "A song? Really? Ye don' believe that, do ye?"

Tom brushed off some of the mud from his pants. "Mr. Paterson, I have to tell you I don't know what to believe anymore. Since I've been here I've had my leg bruised by an underwater monster. I've been beaten up. I've been laughed at by locals. I've been threatened by authorities. And I've had the you-know-what kicked out of me." He turned to Marella. "Not to mention I was just punched in the face?"

Marella said, "Don' ye drag me intae this." She huffed and stomped in the mud, marching away from them. "I'm going inside and waitin' in my room until t'morrow. Don' bother comin' tae my door. Good luck tae both o' ye!"

She swung her fist and hit the outside wall before she rounded the corner. Tom shuddered. Over the roof, they heard the front door slam. He shuddered again.

So much for feeling guilty.

He wanted to call her to stay, but he knew she was in no frame of mind to listen.

Tom said, "Mr. Paterson, I know about the barn."

Sean blinked. "Wha' do ye mean?"

"You know."

"We don' need tae talk abou' it."

"Mr. Paterson, I know you were in there before. Marella told me you once disappeared for two days, and when you returned you didn't even know you were gone."

Sean's shoulders dropped, and he leaned against the house. "I'll ne'er get it o' my mind. Tha' moment changed e'erything. Before I went inside, I was havin' all sorts o' success as a scientist." Sean cleared his throat.

"What do you mean?"

"I was makin' money. Th' monster was just a fun hobby. My family was doin' well. Bu' when I went into tha' barn, e'erything changed. Twas like I was *driven* tae find th' monster. It had taken on a whole new meaning, a priority above e'erything else." Sean paused. Then he stared out into the countryside. His eyes glazed over.

Tom stood quietly, believing it would be best for Sean to gather his thoughts.

Sean continued, "Ye know, e'er since then, bad things happened tae me. Things I wouldn' want fur anybody. Foremost, my wife left me and Marella. She disappeared. It devastated me, and I know it devastated Marella."

Sean wiped a small tear from his eye. His lips quivered some, but soon he gathered himself and continued.

"Bu' then other things happened. There was Coffee. He left, and things dried up. But tha' wasn' it. I was ridiculed by th' community. Twas like an economic wall appeared, and 'twas just enough tae keep me hopeful, but ne'er enough tae get me by. No matter how I budgeted, my money came up short."

Sean took in a deep breath as if he was finally letting out thirty years of stress.

"And, despite all this, I felt th' only way tae solve th' problem woul' be if I could find th' Loch Ness monster. I don' know why. My reason says tis foolish. But somethin' happened after my time in th' barn tha' threw reason out th' window."

"Mr. Paterson. Do you believe in curses?"

"Na. I believe e'erything can be explained. Don' fault me fur tha'. After all, I am a scientist." Sean rested against the wall. What was it like for Sean to admit something he'd concealed for thirty years?

Sean said, "Howe'er, tha' doesn' mean tha' e'erything has been explained. We just haven' found all the answers yet."

"Mr. Paterson, the same thing has been happening to me."

"Wha' are ye sayin'?"

"The Loch Ness monster. It's an obsession. I feel it in my gut, and I don't know why. Nor do I want to feel it. Yet, ever since I left you in the boat I've had obstacle after obstacle. Like you, everybody has been telling me I've disappeared for two days. Heck, I don't even know what day it is right now. But I'm the same way. I feel I have to find the answer to this creature or else my whole life will be one big disaster." Tom was glad to share his thoughts with Sean.

Sean nodded. "So, wha' do we do?"

"Father Gibson said he'd pray for us."

"That's nice."

"He says he knows prayers that will help lift the curse."

"I'm na' sure I wan' tae do tha'."

"Me neither. But the other idea I have is to find a copy of that song. Then, let's hope it works."

"Alright," Sean said. "Let's get ye dry, and I'll take ye where we can search fur tha' song."

Tom rubbed his face where he still felt soreness. "When do you want to get back out on the water?"

"Why, t'night, o' course. After all, we've go' a curse tae conquer!"

CHAPTER 32

S ean Paterson's blue car pulled outside of the white building. It was a newer building, not one that had any of the ancient features like some of the other centuries old buildings in Thurwick. There was sliding glass door out front, and several rows of shelves through the glass.

"This is th' drug store," Sean said. "If we have any chance tae find tha' CD, tis here."

"Do they have a good selection?" Tom said.

"Tis na' a popular genre. If they have any church music at all, we'll know soon enough if tha' song is here."

Tom nodded. "I'll scan the CDs. Why don't you ask the clerk if they can do a search for the song? It's 'Veni, Veni, Emmanuel'."

"Ye got it."

They exited the vehicle and hurried toward the door. Just as they were about to enter, a young man stepped through the door carrying a white plastic bag. Tom bumped into him. A brief moment passed when Tom thought he recognized him, but he hurried inside to find the CD. Sean was right behind him.

Tom scanned the rows of shelves, and found an aisle with several CDs. The categories were pop, rock, country, and gospel. There was no Gregorian chant.

"I'm not sure they have it," Tom said, flipping through the CDs.

"Let me ask th' clerk," Sean said.

From the front, Tom heard Sean discuss their search with the clerk. "Gregorian chant?" the clerk said. "I don' have a way tae find it in my system, but th' guy who just walked out th' door bought a CD wi' Latin songs. I remember because after I scanned th' barcode th' name popped up, and I though' it was unu…"

Sean didn't wait. "Tom. Th' guy tha' just left!" He pointed out the door.

That's who the young man was. It was one of the faceless characters who attacked him out in the street!

He hurried to the front. His ankle felt stiff from the swelling, but he did his best to ignore the pain. He ran through the doors, and Sean exited right behind him.

Tom scanned right and left.

"There!"

He caught the character walking around a corner. Tom ran. His ankle seared, but he pushed through.

As he neared the corner, he slowed. He expected he might be jumped again, so he stopped and put his back to the wall. He motioned to Sean, who caught up with him. Tom heard Sean as he tried to catch his breath.

Tom motioned for Sean to keep quiet. "That's one of the ones who attacked me," he whispered as he pointed to his eye.

"I thought Marella gave ye tha'."

Tom peered around the corner. There was another road, and trees. There were cobblestones and old buildings. Some cars drove past. But the man with the CD had disappeared.

"Damn. He's gone."

Sean moved around Tom. "Where is he?"

"Strange," Tom said. "Too many people know how to disappear around here."

"He couldn' have gone far," Sean said. "Maybe he jumped in one o' those buildings."

Tom said, "Are you certain he was human?"

Sean didn't answer.

"I have another idea," Tom said.

"What's tha'?"

"How good's your singing voice?" Tom asked.

"Depends on how many pints I've had."

"I'll keep that in mind," Tom said.

They returned to Sean's car. Just as they neared the vehicle, Tom heard a voice. Two uniformed men hurried towards them. The uniforms had the strange shield emblem on the left chest pocket, the same as were on the men on the boat.

"Who *are* these guys," Tom said.

Sean shrugged. As the men approached, that's when Tom noticed the non-uniformed man behind them. It was Alex Vaas.

He did not appear happy.

CHAPTER 33

"Is there a problem?" Sean said.

The men did not answer. One of the uniformed men held a baton in his hand. The other was large enough and muscular enough that he didn't need one. They spread their distance between them, and Vaas appeared in the middle. Who was working for whom?

"I thought I told ye tae lay low until ye disappeared," Vaas said. "Ye should be on a plane o'er th' Atlantic by now. Yet ye're still in Thurwick?"

"No offense, but what have I done? I wasn't ready to leave just yet," Tom said.

"If ye thought I wasn' serious before, ye need tae understand this time I am. If I catch ye out in Thurwick again, we'll have ye arrested," Vaas said.

Sean said, "Wait a minute. This young man is a guest o' mine. He's done nothin' wrong. Why are ye threatenin' him?"

"Ye'd better watch who yer guests are, Mr. Paterson, else we'll arrest ye as well fur harborin' a fugitive," Vaas said.

"Harboring a fugitive?" Tom said. His voice elevated. "What the hell are you talking about? You're not even the police."

Neither Vaas nor the uniformed men spoke.

"I've met the chief here. I'm going to pay him a visit." Tom made a move to get in the car.

Vaas grinned. "Laddie, ye might wan' tae think again abou' who runs this town."

Tom stopped, his hand on the door handle.

The larger uniformed man spoke. "Wha' do ye wan' us tae do, Mr. Vaas?"

Vaas stood silently, then nodded like he knew he had the upper hand. "Nothin' now. They get my point." He pointed at Tom. "If this one doesn' stay out o' th' public realm, though, ye two are free tae take care o' him."

"And what do you mean by that?" Tom said. "I thought you didn't want to create an international incident?" Tom grinned. "Besides, Thurwick is beginning to grow on me. Maybe I'll decide to live here. What are you going to do then?"

"We don' accept foreigners who have a record fur battery," Vaas said.

"Battery?" Sean said.

Tom frowned. Sean appeared puzzled. Tom turned to Vaas. "So you've been doing some homework on me. Well, you didn't work hard enough. I served that time."

Vaas said, "We're watchin' ye. If ye do one thing we don' like, ye'll find yerself at th' mercy o' th' court."

"You mean Chairman Briggs," Tom said.

Vaas frowned. The two police officers appeared worried. "Come on," Vaas said. The three of them backed away, and they left and walked towards Dorlan Hall.

"I'm beginning to not trust that guy," Tom said.

Sean appeared worried.

"We need to get ready for tonight," Tom said. "I have one more idea."

Sean said nothing. He opened the car door, and climbed inside.

CHAPTER 34

"I'll be right back," Tom said. Sean had turned on the engine. He motioned that he'd stay where he was and wait for Tom to return. Tom went back into the drug store and went to the sales clerk.

"Back again?" the clerk said.

Tom waived and went to the refrigerator. He found the alcoholic beverages. He grabbed two six-packs of Guinness, and he went to the clerk.

"Did ye get yer CD?" the clerk asked.

"No," Tom said. He motioned to the two packs before him. "Going to drink our sorrows away, I guess."

The clerk chuckled. Tom thanked him, and stepped outside. To his surprise, Sean was standing outside the car. A white van with a TV station design on its side was parked nearby. A reporter held a microphone to Sean's face, and a cameraman pointed his camera at Sean.

"Sean Paterson, please tell us wha' ye saw," the reporter said.

"Well, I was on th' Loch around two in th' morning, when I felt…"

"Wait a minute," Tom said. He walked to the reporter. "Can you give us a moment?" The cameraman pointed the camera at Tom, and then at his two packs of Guinness. The reporter nodded and stepped back. Everything would be captured on video.

Tom motioned for Sean to step out of earshot, but Sean didn't move. Tom shrugged. "Are you sure you want to do this?"

"Aye," Sean said. "Quite sure."

"But what about the public? You don't want to bring more bad publicity on yourself. I know what we believe is true, but those people? They'll never believe it," Tom said.

"Lad, I've been in this fight now fur thirty years," Sean said. "I know wha' this search has done tae me, and tae my family. I know I've been laughed at, and I know it's hurt my business. Heck, I'm barely livin' now. Bu' I know what's true. If a man fails tae defend th' truth, how can tha' man look himself in th' mirror?"

"But you can't control these people. No telling what they'll say about you."

"Doesn' matter." Sean paused, taking a deep breath like a man who knew what he had to do. "Lad, ye're still young. There are many things ye'll experience. Bu' when ye get tae be my age, ye'll come tae find tha' in th' end all a man has is his character."

"Okay," Tom said. He stepped back and watched as Sean told the reporter and the cameraman that he was ready.

The reporter was a young man. He gave the impression that stories were few so they were going with anything interesting to put on the evening news. "Mr. Paterson, tell us wha' happened tae ye lest week."

Sean said, "My cohort and I went out and we had an experience tha' was hard tae explain," he said. "We believe our boat was rocked by a creature below th' surface. We heard a roar, we smelled somethin' strange, and a fin splashed."

"A fin?"

"Aye."

"Wha' did it look like?"

"Like a large fin."

"Was it Nessie?"

"Whate'er 'twas, it capsized our boat, and we both wound up in th' water. In fact, my friend," and Sean pointed at Tom, "said he felt somethin' large hit him in th' thigh. It left a bruise."

The cameraman pointed at Tom. He felt embarrassed, and he remembered his shiner.

I have a face for radio right now.

The reporter and the cameraman came up to Tom. "Did th' Loch Ness monster really hit ye?" the reporter said.

"Yes. It did."

"Did it do tha' tae yer face?"

"No. Sheesh," Tom said.

"Wha' happened tae yer face?" the reporter asked.

"Someone else did that."

"Na' th' monster?"

"No. The monster got me in the leg."

"Wha' happened?"

Tom cleared his throat. He sought approval from Sean, who nodded to the reporter, insisting he answer the question. "I was in the water. I saw and heard something strange and powerful. But it was dark. All we knew was we were not alone. And, yes, something hit me in the leg."

"Ye're wearin' jeans, now," said the reporter. "Can we record an image o' th' bruise?"

"It's pretty high up," Tom said. "I'm not sure it would be appropriate for your viewing audience." The reporter frowned. The cameraman peered out from behind the camera to get instruction from the reporter. Tom unbuckled his belt. "But, if you insist—"

"Oh, na, na, na," said the reporter. "That'll be alrigh'."

Tom stopped what he was doing. Sean managed a mischievous smile.

"No really. I don't mind."

"That's alright. We have yer face. That'll be enough."

"Great." Tom shook his head.

The reporter said, "Mr. Paterson, do ye believe th' Loch Ness monster exists?"

"I'm a scientist, foremost," Sean said. "I believe th' world consists o' many wonders, all o' which have an explanation. Tis our job, our privilege, tae explore them and discover their explanations. I believe I've spotted a creature in th' Loch on several occasions. I believe tha' creature has an explanation. I just haven' discovered exactly what tha' explanation is. Perhaps my methods have been incorrect. Perhaps I need tae explore other avenues. But I know wha' I saw. I can promise th' people o' Thurwick tha' I will na' stop until I find an explanation tae wha' is in those waters. I owe tha' tae my city o' Thurwick, and I would hope my fellow residents would appreciate tha' effort."

"And what would ye say tae all those people who say ye're a quack?" the reporter said.

"How does any man leave a legacy withou' challengin' th' status quo?" Sean said.

The reporter motioned for the cameraman to stop filming. "Tha' was great, Mr. Paterson. Can ye and yer friend stand o'er here while we finish filmin'?"

"If ye don' mind, we must get goin'," Sean said. The reporter and the cameraman thanked Sean and Tom. Then they moved to the side of the van to plan how they would finish their report.

"Not bad," Tom said. "I'm inspired."

"Ye'd better be," Sean said. "Because if somethin' happens tae me, this mission we're on becomes yers alone."

Tom did not respond. Sean's comment struck him for some reason. What would happen to him if Sean could not physically continue with the search? Would Tom wind up like Sean, frustrated and impoverished for the next thirty years?

What about Marella? Surely, she would leave across the Atlantic and he'd never find her again. Tom felt he and Marella were bound by a destiny they did not choose. It was a destiny that lasted so long as her father obsessed over the monster. If Tom could find the monster, somehow break the curse, and free her father then he could also free Marella of her worry, a worry she'd felt for years. He, too, could be free of this new obsession that occupied his thoughts. Maybe, then, they'll both be free to explore a normal relationship, one in which they could get to know each other, without any of the outside forces causing friction between them.

"Do you have internet connection and a printer at home," Tom said.

"Aye. They're basic, but they work," Sean said.

"They'll have to do," Tom said. "We need to print off some copies of that song. Then, I suggest we don't wait any longer. We need to get on your boat and call for Nessie."

"Ye mean sing? Ye're na' goin' tae want tae hear me sing," Sean said.

"Why do you think I picked up the Guinness?" Tom said.

Then they climbed into the car and drove out of the square.

CHAPTER 35

"Tha' was awful," Sean said. The piece of paper in his hands displayed the words of "Veni, Veni, Emmanuel".

"We're not performing for an audience," Tom said. "We need to try this one more time."

Tom also held his sheets in his hand. He and Sean sat in Sean's car in the dock parking lot. They had driven to the cottage to look up the words to the song, printed off four copies, two extra in case something happened, and went to find Marella.

Marella had refused to open the door to her room, so Sean and Tom had left together for the dock. When they had arrived, Tom had insisted they practice a few times at the behest of Sean.

"This whole thin' is in Latin," Sean said. "I know some Latin, bu' I just feel foolish. How do we know this is e'en goin' tae work?"

"We don't. The priests said they didn't know the reason either. Father Gibson said the thing they did know was every time they sang the song, the monster surfaced."

"That's just absurd."

"That was all they said."

"Tha' makes no scientific sense," Sean said. "I may na' have made a lot o' money wi' my pursuits, but I know th' scientific process. I have tae tell ye, singin' on a rowboat won' do anythin' bu' embarrass me further in my profession. I'm just glad we'll be out in th' middle o' th' Loch so tha' nobody will be able tae hear us."

"I thought you told the reporter that you were open to exploring other avenues."

"I am. I just don' believe in magic. How does a song brin' a monster tae th' surface? This goes against e'erything I believe as a scientist."

"Maybe you're thinking about it wrong. Don't think of it as magic. Maybe there's something in the rhythm of the sound waves that echo through the water. Maybe that rhythm is similar to their calling mechanisms, and that song just happens to have the right rhythm."

Tom, too, didn't want to appear foolish. The last time he sang was in his car back in America when the windows were rolled up and no one heard him. However, after all that had happened to him the past several days he didn't care anymore. His black eye, his walking with a limp, the accusatory glances from locals, the punch in the face from the girl he was attracted to, his hooking Sean in the face.

I've already lost my pride. What else do I have to lose?

"We should go for it, and sing loudly," Tom said.

"Maybe ye're right. Heck, after thirty years, I should have found th' answer by now. Maybe tis worth a try," Sean said.

"Come on. The Guinness is in the trunk." Tom exited the car while Sean popped the trunk. Tom grabbed the Guinness and the life jackets.

The hairs on the back of his neck stiffened. Someone, or something, was watching them.

Sean came around to the trunk. Tom stopped what he was doing and turned around. He scanned the area. Several cars sat in the parking lot. A few cars drove around the roads, and the trees swayed in the breeze. But that was all. He could not justify his suspicion.

"Ye alrigh'?" Sean said.

"No. I feel something," Tom said.

Sean lifted his head and scanned the area. "I don' see anythin'. Ye sure tis na' just yer imagination?"

"I don't know. After all we've been through, I'm learning to trust my gut. Do me a favor. Take the Guinness and the life jackets to the boat. Let me sit here a moment. I just want to make sure we're not being followed."

"Okay," Sean said. He grabbed the Guinness. "I'll be back fur th' jackets." Sean left him alone by the car and walked to the dock.

Tom continued to watch the scene from the car. Nothing rational appeared that would be threatening, but the feeling persisted. There was nothing unusual about the distant buildings. Maybe there was someone in the windows watching them, but he was hiding behind the dark windows. He scanned the hills in the distance, but they showed nothing unusual.

Not that there couldn't be someone observing him with a set of binoculars. But if they were, they were well hidden.

He peered around the cars and the trees.

Nothing.

Or was there?

Did he spot movement behind one of the cars? *Was that a brown jacket?* Then more movement by another red car caught his attention, only it was thirty yards from the first.

What was that?

Paranoia entered his subconscious. Fear gripped him. There was an urge to run.

But he decided to stand firm. He had to face his attackers. He positioned himself to fight. He decided if any one of them appeared, he'd rush them. If they beat him again, he wouldn't go down without taking one of them with him.

But they did not appear. The fear grew stronger as he fought the urge to run.

"See anybody yet?"

Tom jumped.

It was Sean. He had come back and was reaching for the life jackets.

Tom exhaled. "I thought I did, but can't confirm it."

"Well, th' sun's about tae set. We don' want tae be in the parking lot anyway."

Tom still felt his neck hairs. Something was out there. Suspicion overcame him.

Sean said, "Come on. I've got a surprise waitin' fur ye down by th' dock."

"What's that?"

"We're goin' tae have access tae a bigger boat."

What did that mean? As they moved along the dock, Tom's suspicion grew. Were his attackers trying to push them to the dock? Was it a trap?

As they neared the rowboat, someone stood up in the pontoon boat next to Sean's rowboat. It was McGregor. Sean waved to McGregor, who jumped off the pontoon boat and onto the dock.

"She's all ready fur ye," McGregor said.

"Are ye sure we can use it?" Sean asked.

"It'll be a better ride. Ye'll get tae yer destination quicker. And, I've go' a sonar ye can use. Tha' way, if anythin' shows up ye can see it comin'."

Sean became excited to use the boat. Tom scratched his head. Why was McGregor so willing to help them?

"You know the last time we ran into the Loch Ness monster our boat capsized," Tom said.

"Maybe that's why ye need a larger boat," McGregor said.

"Do you believe it exists?"

"Don' care if it does or doesn'," McGregor said. "Bu' if it does, it would make a fine story tha' 'twas found on my boat."

"Would ye want tae join us?" Sean said.

"Na' t'day. I've been workin' on th' boat all day, and th' wife's expecting me home fur company. Bu' she's all yers. Take her out and good luck tae ye both." McGregor shook their hands, and walked along the dock away from them.

"Maybe 'tis just wha' we needed," Sean said.

The pontoon boat was tied to the dock. It was so much larger than the small rowboat floating next to it. He observed the two boats as they rocked in the waves. Sean and Tom had been successful at finding the monster in the rowboat. Should they stick with what already worked?

But the rowboat was so small compared to McGregor's pontoon boat. Maybe it was worth a try to use the larger boat, at least for safety reasons and the use of McGregor's fishing sonar. If it didn't work, they could always use Sean's rowboat another night.

The sun set in the west. Sore from his injuries, Tom was anxious to get back on the water. The lure to search for the Loch Ness monster beckoned. He wanted to get on the water right away. "Okay," he said. "Let's load up and get moving."

Sean nodded. They brought the packs of Guinness, the song sheets, and the life jackets on board. Tom thought it weird that this time they did not have to bring fishing poles and heavy coolers filled with packed meat.

Tom buckled his jacket. Sean did the same. Sean sat in the captain's chair, and started the engine. Tom untied the ropes from the dock. As Tom sat down, Sean said, "Should we say a prayer before we go?"

Tom didn't give an answer.

CHAPTER 36

The motor was too loud as Sean drove McGregor's pontoon boat. The sun had just set behind the horizon. They passed some fishermen heading the other way, going back to the dock after a day's fishing. The sky was clear, and the first stars in the sky glimmered above. He remembered as a child how he'd wish upon the first star that twinkled above him before night set in.

Maybe they'd have luck tonight.

He went to the cooler and picked up two bottles of Guinness. He tapped Sean on the shoulder, and offered him one. Sean put his hand up, implying that he'd pass on it for now. As they neared the area of the Loch outside Saint Michael's Church, Sean stalled the motor. The boat drifted. The sound of crickets echoed near the shoreline.

"It was nice of your friend to loan us his boat," Tom said.

Sean nodded, but he didn't answer. He appeared focused on the mission.

"We should have brought our fishing poles and steaks anyway, just in case," Tom said.

"I thought about tha', tae." Sean got up from his chair, and walked around all the edges of the boat. Was he gauging the perimeter, getting a feel for the layout in case the monster did come?

Sean returned to his seat. Tom offered him his bottle.

Sean said, "Before I take anythin', I need tae ask ye a question."

"Okay," Tom said. "Fire away."

"What did Alex Vaas mean when he said ye were arrested fur battery?"

Tom shifted in his chair.

"Mr. Paterson," Tom said. "That happened a long time ago. It's not something I'm proud of, but I'm also not going to shy away from it, either."

"If ye plan tae date my daughter one day, I insist I'm goin' tae have tae know. We're in this together now, but when it's o'er, I'll still be her father, and she'll still be my daughter. I'll have na problem sending ye away if I think she'll be in any danger."

Tom nodded. "I can appreciate that." He hesitated.

Sean waited.

Tom said, "I was just out of college, and some friends of mine and I went out for the night to have a good time. We didn't have much in the way of money. Most of us had just gotten our jobs, and after a few weeks we had this idea to go out on the town. You know, blow whatever money we had saved up until that point, but have an adventure to tell.

"While we were out, we ran into some girls, and one of my friends asked them to tag along. They did. Personally, I thought they were a little drunk, but they came with us as we went from bar to bar. Well, we went into one bar that was packed. A little too crowded, if you asked me. I wanted to leave, but my friends and the girls were inside, so I thought I'd stick around. I wasn't drinking much, actually. I did have one beer up to that point, but some of my friends were overdoing it. If you ask me, they had had too much.

"Then, one of my friends was pushed. A group of guys were in this bar with us. They had too much to drink. They seemed pretty well off. Some of them were wearing nice watches, could have been Rolexes. I didn't have anything against them. I just knew one of them pushed my friend.

"But then, the one that pushed my friend grabbed one of the girls in a way that, and you can relate to this as a father, you wouldn't approve. She was mad, but he continued to put his hands all over her. No one else would do anything. Some of his friends were laughing. I don't know what happened, but something came over me. I walked between them and pushed him away from her. She fell down. He started to swing, and before I knew what happened, I slugged him right under the jaw. He never saw it coming, and he went down hard. I knocked him unconscious.

"What I found out later was that the guy's family was in with some pretty powerful attorneys. They filed a police report, had me arrested, and tried. The girl I helped was too drunk to remember anything, but every one of his friends showed up to testify that he never swung at me. Instead, they all said I hit him, that I was the aggressor. It was their word against mine, and I lost the case.

Tom took a swig of his Guinness.

"I spent some months in jail. I had to do two hundred hours of community service. I lost my job. And it took me the past few years to rebuild my reputation. Mr. Paterson, I had been in five fights in my whole life before I came to Scotland. Most of them were hardly anything. Mostly, I talk my way out of it. But if a fight is coming, I intend to back up my words with action. The guy deserved it. Looking back, I didn't know enough to do anything other than what I did. I'm a lot wiser now. I've learned to use my words rather than my fists to stop trouble. But I still don't let people get away with being jerks, and I'm ready to back it up if I need to."

Sean nodded. "Le' me have my bottle."

Tom nervously reached for the Guinness and handed it to Sean.

Sean opened his bottle and raised it up over his head. "Tae th' good guys," Sean said.

"To the good guys," Tom said, relieved. He raised his bottle in the air, then brought it to his mouth and took a swig. "Now I have a question for you."

"What's tha'?"

"What did you mean when you mentioned you might not finish this mission?"

"Well, wha' do ye think I meant?"

"Sounds like a premonition."

"Na' quite," Sean said. "Wha' we're undergoing has a lot o' risk. Th' risk keeps getting' bigger th' more we pursue. There's a possibility tha' risk can get th' better o' us. If it does get tae me, I wan' tae make sure Marella is goin' tae be okay."

"I can promise you, Mr. Paterson, if anything happens to you, I'll make sure she's taken care of."

"Alright. Bu' on one condition."

"What's that?"

"Ye need tae stop callin' me 'Mr. Paterson',"

"No offense, Mr. Paterson, but your daughter's a lady. She may have a mean right hook, but she's still a lady, and a lady's father should be called by his last name."

"Let me put it this way. When this is o'er, and ye want tae court my daughter, I won' let ye unless ye call me 'Sean'."

Tom smiled and raised his bottle. "To friendship."

"Aye, tae friendship," Sean said. "I'll drink tae tha'." They both enjoyed the Guinness from their bottles.

"Okay. One more question for you," Tom said.

Sean took another swig from his bottle. He wiped his mouth. "Alright. Shoot."

"How's God involved in all of this?"

Sean paused. "Don' know. I've ne'er been against God. I just wonder how He's relevant."

"When I spoke with Father Gibson at Saint Michael's, he said something that keeps sticking in my mind. He said they believe that God wants the Loch Ness monster to be discovered."

Sean laughed. "If tha' were so, lad, then why didn' he let *me discover* him thirty years ago?" Sean lifted his bottle and finished his Guinness. "He sure as hell could have saved me a lot o' time, trouble, and heartache o'er th' years."

"Well, what about faith? Maybe this whole thing is a test of faith?"

"Maybe 'tis. But who's th' judge o' faith?"

"What do you mean?"

"Faith can mean a lot o' things. Fur example, I may have faith th' sun will come up t'morrow. I canno' see it comin' up o'er

234

th' horizon right now, but since it's happened every day I've been alive I can have faith tha' it will come up t'morrow." Sean took another swig from his bottle. "Bu' that's all scientific. It can be explained by rational forces which exist in th' universe."

Tom thought a moment. "I understand we should have faith in reason. Maybe we need to also have faith in things which science can't explain?"

"That's preposterous. Maybe we should have faith in th' Irish leprechauns, or th' tooth fairy, or Santa Clause."

"Or the Loch Ness monster?"

Sean paused. He remained silent for several uncomfortable moments.

Tom heard the sound of the boat as it rocked in the water. "Where's the rope to tie us together."

"There isn't one," Sean said. "We'll have tae do withou'. Hopefully th' boat's big enough we won' need one."

Tom scanned the shoreline. The lights to the rectory of Saint Michael's Church were dark. The sun had set, and the Church's silhouette stood tall in front of the soft glow of the Thurwick city lights.

Would the priests come out and sing? Their lights were off. He and Sean were on their own tonight.

"Sean," Tom said.

"Aye?"

"I want you to know, no matter what happens, that I'm going to finish this mission. If we're cursed, I'm going to find a way to break it. I'm not going to give up until Marella, you, and I are all free. I promise you that."

"That's good tae know," Sean said. "Now give me another Guinness."

CHAPTER 37

Tom and Sean sat on the pontoon boat. The night darkened, and a full moon rose over the eastern horizon. The light from the moon reflected the rippling water of the Loch towards the town of Thurwick.

Somewhere under the moon, on the opposite shore, stood the barn where Tom had disappeared. He tried not to think about it. In fact, the only real time he avoided thinking about it was when he thought about the monster.

An hour had passed since they reached the spot outside the church. Sean and Tom shared more stories, and unusual experiences. But they were not singing. Tom said, "Why are we hesitating?"

"Wha' do ye mean?" Sean said.

"I mean, it's been an hour. We could have brought the monster up by now."

Sean kept quiet.

"Are you afraid it'll work? I mean, what if we start singing and it actually surfaces?" Tom said.

"Maybe that's part o' it," Sean said. "If we discover we have th' secret, that's an awesome responsibility tae have."

The moonlight danced upon the surface. "You're right. We have to be careful that no one else knows but us. We also have to be careful about the priests. They took a gamble sharing their suspicion with us. If we hint that they know, too, that could be bad for them," Tom said.

"'Twould especially be bad fur th' monster."

Tom knew what Sean was saying. If word did get out, then someone would abuse the music and lure the monster to the surface in order to kill it. Not everyone would, but someone would. No telling when it would happen, but it would. Letting the secret out would become the monster's death sentence.

"We have to make a pact. No one can know the song. If it works, we tell nobody," Tom said.

"I have a better idea," Sean said. "We tell them th' wrong song."

"What do you have in mind?"

"We sing another Latin religious song while we're out here. Tha' way, if anybody catches on, we send them on a wild goose chase. They'll ne'er know. More importantly, if we're successful and someone asks us wha' happened, we tell them th' other song we sang. If we're e'er held tae a lie detector test, we tell them what we were singing, and no one will believe us. If by chance they do believe us, it'll ne'er work."

"Okay. But I don't know any other religious Latin songs. Do you?"

"Maybe it doesn' have tae be Latin. Maybe we can try another Christmas song and go wi' that. Marella always liked

'Hark the Herald Angels Sing'. Let's try tha' one foremost. It'll be a warmup."

"I don't know the words."

"Well, just hum it then!"

Sean stood up.

He cleared his throat, and stuck out his chest.

Tom imagined him pretending to be an opera singer. Then Sean bellowed the words to "Hark the Herald Angels Sing" so it was heard in Thurwick.

Tom put his head in his hands.

He did not feel like singing.

Sean motioned for Tom to stand up. Tom sat, refusing to get up and join him. Sean then sang, "If ye want tae court my daughter, ye'll get up and sing a-long."

Tom got the hint and stood. He tried to sing, but only mustered "fa-la-la, fa-la-Ta-da!"

They continued singing together, loud and uncoordinated, until the song was complete. Then they sat down.

Tom said, "Thank God it's dark and no one in Thurwick can hear us."

Sean said, "Oh, get o'er it, lad. Ye did great. Now we're goin' tae try th' real thing."

"Did great? I didn't even know the words."

"Does Nessie care abou' yer English? Ye Americans have funny accents, anyway." He stepped towards Tom. "Hand me those verses, and I'll show ye how a real Scotsman sings!"

"You know the priests are probably watching us from the rectory, laughing their asses off," Tom said.

Sean lit a small flashlight. He studied the verses. "Are ye ready?"

"No, but let's do it."

Sean stood, and cleared his throat again. Tom decided the two cases of Guinness had done the trick. Then Sean sang the notes to "Veni, Veni, Emmanuel". He sung them slow, and deep, as he imagined an amateur choir singer would during a Christmas Eve service.

Tom joined in.

He had thought he'd be ready, as he practiced in the car. But this time it was Sean who was eager to sing. Maybe it was thirty years of pent up energy coming out. Maybe the arts were a way of self-expression, and Sean's singing was his chance to express that he would persevere to the end to find his treasure.

Maybe it was just the Guinness?

Tom sang the words. He remembered the banging of the net on the base of the rowboat. Since they left the net behind, he bent down and banged his fist on the side of McGregor's pontoon boat. They kept the rhythm, and when the song was over, they sang it again.

The boat shifted. Its normal rocking in the water had been disturbed.

Sean and Tom stopped singing.

Tom felt a rush of adrenaline through his body.

Then there was a deep roar from below.

"Did you hear that?" Tom said.

"Aye," Sean whispered. "He's here!"

The two rushed to the side of the boat. The waves moved in odd patterns in the moonlight, as though something large underneath them was displacing the water.

Tom said, "I can't see him."

Questions ran through his mind. *How big was it? Where was its head? How fast did it travel? Was there only one?*

And then a wave of joy came over him. They had done it. Sean and Tom had discovered the secret, one which had been so hard to come by. Tom ran over to Sean. Sean was leaning over the edge of the pontoon boat, trying to watching for the monster to resurface. Tom put his hand on Sean's shoulder. Sean stood. Tom said, "We did it!"

"Aye, we did, lad. We did!" Sean said.

Tom reached out to fist bump Sean.

Suddenly, Tom sensed heat around his body. Fire obstructed his vision. Sean disappeared behind orange, white, and red flames. Immense pressure pressed his body as an explosion ripped through the boat. Tom yelled as he was thrown high and went end over end into the night air.

CHAPTER 38

Tom was stunned, unable to move as he spun head over heel. The sudden intense heat and the force of the blast had shocked all of his senses. He was paralyzed as he toppled end over end, flailing his arms and legs until he splashed into the water and sank below the surface.

He touched something solid, but it was gone before he knew what had happened.

Water filled his lungs.

His life jacket raised him to the surface. He coughed up water.

Flames jettisoned out of the hull of the pontoon boat.

He took his bearings.

He moved his legs and arms. That was good. The cool water shocked him back to the present.

What had happened? Where was he?

He remembered.

He was on that boat. He was with Sean.

Sean!

He scanned the area and he could not find Sean amidst the burning wreckage. He called for him.

Nothing.

He heard a loud ringing in his ears. He kicked and swam and searched.

Everything hurts!

He found debris floating a few yards from him. He smelled gasoline. He felt the heat from the flames as he moved through the debris.

As he neared, he found a body floating on the surface.

It was Sean!

Sean floated face down, his life jacket keeping his head near the surface. Tom pulled up Sean's face.

It was red.

Tom couldn't tell if he was dead.

He grabbed him by the jacket and swam towards the Church.

He heard a roar, but the ringing in his ears drowned out the sound.

There was that smell. He recognized the smell!

It was in the water with them!

Tom fought the urge to panic. He turned Sean onto his back, hoping the man was alive and able to breathe. Tom kicked at the water, pulling Sean with him. The heat from the flames burned Tom's skin. He worried about creature below the water.

He tugged and pulled as he swam. Sean coughed up water behind him. "Hang on," Tom said. "We're almost there."

Sean didn't answer.

The smell went away.

Tom gasped for air. He hurt all over. The glow of flashing emergency lights appeared over the ridge. They grew closer as they neared the shore.

Tom pulled and kicked. The weight of Sean was dragging him. His muscles burned. Pain struck him with each stroke.

Sean did not move. He floated lifeless behind Tom except for the recent coughing episode.

Tom reached the shallows. People rushed down the ridge from the glowing emergency lights. Tom yelled to them. He noticed he caught a man's attention, who signaled for the others. They ran to him.

Tom felt the mud under his feet. He pulled, working to get Sean to the surface. The emergency personnel surrounded Sean. They went to work on him, ripping off his life jacket and going through their emergency procedures.

Tom leaned back. He tried to stand, but felt himself becoming dizzy and falling. He couldn't hear what the men were saying. One of them came to him and asked a question. It sounded muffled. Tom nodded, and then he fell. The man caught him, and Tom found himself on his back.

The commotion around him bothered him. Sean was surrounded by several emergency personnel. Seven or more. They were working on him.

One was doing CPR, pounding on Sean's chest.

"Wait, what's wrong with him," Tom said, but he couldn't hear his own words. No one answered.

The night sky displayed thousands of stars overhead. A man's face leaned over Tom and shined a flashlight into his eyes. Tom noticed the man had a beard, and then the man's face was gone.

Then he saw the moon. Its light was so beautiful.
And then everything spun in circles, and the world went dark.

CHAPTER 39

Tom first heard the beeps. His eyes stayed shut, but the sound brought him back to consciousness. Then he remembered ringing. For some reason, the ringing wasn't as bad as it had been. He blinked several times before he opened his eyes.

There were bright lights overhead. It took a few seconds for his eyes to adjust. He was in a hospital bed. He turned his head. There were monitors and wires. An IV needle was strapped to his forearm. He was in a hospital gown. His feet protruded from under the white sheet, and he counted his toes.

Ten.

Good.

They were all there.

A nurse walked by with a clipboard. "Ah, Mr. Wayne. Ye're awake," she said. "How do ye feel?"

"Like someone tried to blow me out of the water."

"Well, ye're very lucky tae be here right now."

Tom didn't feel lucky.

"What time is it?" Tom said.

"A little after six in th' mornin'."

He closed his eyes. What had happened? He was in the boat. Then the water. Then the ground. Then....

"Where's Mr. Paterson?" Tom wasn't sure if he was ready for bad news.

The nurse frowned. "Th' doctor will be wi' ye in a moment," she said. Then she left.

Okay. Indirect answers are never good.

The ceiling above Tom was made of white panels. The beeping annoyed him as did the soft ringing in his ears.

I need to remember... he thought. They had sung, and brought the Loch Ness monster to the surface.

And then the explosion. Why then? Were they being watched? Were they being recorded? Was it just a faulty boat? McGregor's boat?

Tom ran through his thoughts.

Then he heard a familiar voice.

Marella!

Marella stepped into Tom's view. She had been crying. Before Tom said anything, Marella said, "Why do ye two have tae try tae be such heroes?"

"We've got to stop meeting like this," Tom said.

"Are ye okay?"

"Just another day in Scotland," Tom shifted. His body ached, but he worked to a sitting position with his back against the pillow and his legs out in front. "Where's your father?"

"They are operating on him right now. Th' news isn't good. They have tae remove his left shank."

"His leg?"

"Aye."

"Oh, no. Marella, I'm so sorry."

Marella wiped a tear from her face. She tried to manage a faint smile. "I'm hopin' this is it. Maybe this will convince him tae stop wit' his Loch Ness monster obsession."

Tom thought of the curse.

Marella wouldn't understand the pull both he and Sean had. He pursed his lips. Maybe she would be right, and the explosion would shock the curse out of Sean. But Tom knew the odds of that were slim. When he healed, Sean would get a prosthetic and be right back on the boat the next night.

"Wha' happened out there?" Marella said. "And why were ye on a different boat?"

"I'm still trying to figure that out," Tom said. "Has a guy named McGregor come to the hospital to check on us?"

"I don' know."

"It was his boat we were on. He offered it to us so we wouldn't have to go out in Sean's rowboat."

Marella sat down on the bed next to Tom. Her eyes were red from crying. He wanted to tell her something good. "But, Marella, before all that happened, it worked."

"Wha' do ye mean 'it worked'?"

"It worked. What the priest told me to do, it worked. We brought the Loch Ness monster to the surface."

"Now's na' th' time tae mess wi' me, Tom."

"I'm not. I'm telling you the truth. We saw it. We were about to celebrate, and that's when the explosion happened."

Marella paused. Her shoulders tensed.

Just then, a doctor walked over to them. Tom expected the same doctor who had treated him after his attack in the Thurwick square, but this one was younger. "Mr. Wayne," he said. "Ye're awake. How are ye feelin'?"

"I'd rather be out of here, if you want to know the truth."

"Ye're clear tae go. Ye had some shock from th' excitement, but other than some first degree burns, ye're okay tae leave. We can give ye some ointment fur those burns, and it would be a good idea tae find some ice. Ye're goin' tae need it."

Tom thanked the doctor. "I've been a walking medical case ever since I arrived in Thurwick."

Marella had stood up and leaned against the wall. She crossed her arms. "So, wha' do ye suppose we do, now?"

Tom moved his legs and sat on the edge of the bed. He rested his hands on the sheets. So many parts of him hurt. He ached every time he moved. But at least he *could* move.

As he gathered himself he said, "Don't know. My first thought is to make sure we're all going to be alright."

"How abou' we all pack up and move tae America?"

"Sounds good to me. Let's get a little place off the coast. Maybe we can bring your father's rowboat with us. Will they let us transport it on the plane?"

Marella managed a slight smile, which was a welcome sight amidst her tears.

Tom stood off the bed. He grunted when his feet hit the floor. His ankle still hurt. "I've got to get myself together. Truth is, I promised your father I'd finish this mission for us if anything happened to him." Tom scanned the room. "Where are my clothes?"

"Are ye insane? Someone just blew th' two o' ye out o' a boat, na' tae mention blew my father's shank off, and ye want tae keep goin'?"

"I don't have a choice." Tom winced in pain. "Ah, there they are." He found his clothes in a bag in the corner.

"Ye know ye canno' do it alone."

Tom grabbed the bag of clothes and hugged it to his chest. Then he grinned. How beautiful Marella was with her curly auburn hair and her green eyes. He wanted to free her of her struggles. "I know that, Marella. That's why I'm hoping you'll stick around to help me."

"I need tae stay in th' hospital fur now. My father needs me."

"True." He fitted his jeans on under his hospital garb. "I, on the other hand, need to get some reinforcements."

"Where are ye going?"

"Somewhere should have a long time ago." Tom limped past her and disappeared down the hallway.

CHAPTER 40

Tom hurried to Saint Michael's Church. His stiff feet loosened upon each step. The air was cool as the sun rose in the east behind the morning mist. He didn't know if the doors to the church would be open. If they were locked, he'd step into Annabel's Bed and Breakfast and wait, that was if they hadn't released his room. He had to admit he was a rather unstable guest. He could only imagine what Annabel must think of his coming and disappearing.

The stone walls of the church reflected the rays of the sun. He expected the doors to be closed, but when he pulled the handles, they opened. He walked in. There were some people sitting in the pews, scattered upon the wooden benches. He stood in the back, not sure what he should do. Then he heard a familiar voice.

"So ye've come tae join us fur Mass, have yr?" It was Father Gibson. "Oh, my. Yr look worse than when I saw ye lest time!" the priest said. He was dressed in his vestments. An altar boy was with him, carrying the crucifix.

"I need your help," Tom said.

"I'll bet ye do. We'll have plenty o' time after Mass, though," Father Gibson said.

"It's important," Tom said.

Father Gibson ignored Tom, sending his attention to the front of the church. He raised his hand high, and a speaker at the front of the church acknowledged the signal and issued commands. The people stood. Voices rang from inside the church. As the attendees sang, Father Gibson left Tom. He followed the altar server down the main aisle to the front of the church.

Tom stood, motionless. He felt uncomfortable. Should he sit and wait?

Do I have a choice?

He found a pew in the back and sat down.

As the Mass progressed, Tom picked up one of the books in the slot in front of him. He thumbed through the pages like a nervous child. There were songs and music notes, writings and instructions.

He closed the book and put it back. He decided he'd just observe. He didn't know the prayers, but as others stood, sat, and knelt, he did the same. While he wanted to appreciate the light as it penetrated through the stained glass windows, illuminating biblical scenes from centuries ago, he found his nerves getting the better of him. He was growing impatient. He needed to speak with the priest right away.

Should he interrupt the Mass?

He remained sitting. Had God Himself ordained Tom's attendance? Tom knew he needed all the help he could get.

As the words "patience" and "trust" kept coming to his mind, he decided he was being tested. He thought of Marella, and Sean, and his roommate Bob back home. He thought of his parents back in Arizona. Then he thought of all he had undertaken since he had arrived in Thurwick. "How the heck am I still alive?"

The Mass ended in about thirty minutes. The parishioners sang another hymn, and Tom watched as Father Gibson followed the crucifix carrying altar boy down the aisle to the back of the church. Tom hurried to the priest.

"Meet me in my office," Father Gibson told him.

Tom went back into the church and found the side door near the front, which led him through the hallway to the priest's office. Outside the door, he waited.

Another ten minutes had passed until Father Gibson appeared in the hallway. He wore his black clothes, his white collar protruding in a small square on the lower front of his neck. "Ye're up early this mornin', aren't ye?" Father Gibson said.

"It's been a rough night," Tom said as the priest opened the office door. They went inside, and the priest sat behind his desk. "Someone tried to blow us up."

"I know. We heard ye singin'," Father Gibson said. "We didn' want tae put on th' lights, just so ye'd stay in th' dark. We were all shocked when th' boat blew up."

"You saw that?" Tom said.

"Aye," Gibson said. "As soon as we heard th' explosion, we called fur emergency personnel. Quite frankly, I'm glad tae see ye alive. I wasn' sure ye two were goin' tae make it. How's Paterson?"

"He's losing his leg," Tom said.

Father Gibson's expression was blank for a few moments. Then he shook his head. "I'm sad tae hear it. Will he pull through?"

"His daughter's with him now. That's all I know."

The priest rapped his fingers on the desk. "So, were ye successful?"

"What do you mean?"

"Did he surface?"

Tom nodded. "Yes, he did. He did just before the boat blew up."

The priest leaned back in his chair. He folded his hands together. "So now ye know th' secret. That's a powerful thing tae know."

"I think so, too."

"Ye know, wi' tha' knowledge comes a lot o' responsibility. Will ye be able tae treat this secret wisely?"

"If someone doesn't kill me, first."

"Aye. That's somethin' tae consider."

"Father Gibson, I need to know what you know. I need to know who is trying to kill us," Tom said.

The priest twisted in his chair. Fog drifted past the window. "There are powerful forces at work here, many o' which we canno' comprehend."

Father Gibson stood up from his desk and walked to the window. Down below was the water where Tom had almost lost his life.

"Ye're caught between an eternal struggle. On th' one hand, there's th' wildness and th' mystery o' God. Tha', in and o' itself is a wonder tae behold. On th' other hand, there are those forces who oppose our Lord."

Father Gibson leaned his shoulder against the wall next to the window. The light from outside was gray as the mist covered the sunlight with shadows.

"Ye see, evil doesn't do th' opposite o' God. It mocks Him. It distorts Him. It doesn' shout th' opposite o' what th' Lord says. It takes wha' He says, and twists it in a way tha' sends mankind down a path o' destruction. I'm afraid ye've experienced na' only tha' eternal opposition, but also those who have fallen fur th' distortion and want tae capture th' mystery o' th' Loch fur their own selfish purposes."

Father Gibson returned to his chair. "It appears they have reached th' point where they are willing tae kill in order tae achieve their desires."

Tom closed his eyes. The vision of flames blowing up McGregor's boat replayed over and over in his mind. The priest was right.

"Father, what am I to do? I mean, I'm cursed. I'm hurting all over. I have an attraction for a woman who wants to leave the country and never see me again, and her father is losing a leg in surgery right now because we're supposed to find a mythical creature everyone says doesn't exist."

"And yet still ye persist," Father Gibson said.

"I don't think I have any other choice. I mean, I have this drive inside me that's unnatural. I have to find this creature or else my life depends on it. It always occupies my thoughts. If I'm not out there searching for it, I get nervous. Why is that?"

"Ye're experiencin' th' evil I just told ye about. Remember, evil mocks th' good. If God wants th' monster found, evil won' do th' opposite o' His plan. What it'll do is make God's initiative so important tha' it becomes an obsession in and o' itself, rather than a means tae bring one closer tae our Creator."

"I don't understand."

"Tha' means tis more important than God. Priorities are thrown out th' window. Tis a clever curse, really. It makes good ideas turn evil and destructive." The priest sat back and nodded. "We justify our actions because we think we're doin' good, when in reality we've fallen from righteousness."

Tom sat in his chair. What had the priest said? The priest's words were wise, but he still had trouble understanding everything. The one who shared his feelings was Sean, who was sedated in a Thurwick hospital operating room. Everyone else had an agenda separate from his.

"Father, am I all alone in this?"

"Our duty as priests is tae bring people tae th' glory o' God. Finding a creature, while exciting, isn't th' reason we took our vows. We are well aware o' wha' is goin' on in our communities, but our focus is on th' poor and th' hungry. Where appropriate, we try tae give guidance and direction," Father Gibson rubbed his hands together as he shifted in his chair. "All tha' being said, let me make a quick phone call."

Father Gibson picked up the phone on his desk and pressed some buttons. Then he held the receiver in his ear. "Aye… Aye… That's right… Aye… T'night..? Are ye sure..? Okay… Aye, I'll le' him know."

Father Gibson put the phone down. "Tha' was our man, Caleb. I believe ye've met him. He isn't a priest, but he serves th' Church as a layman. He's what ye would call one o' our soldiers. Most o' th' time he's just an informant. Howe'er, when he needs tae be, he's willin' tae get involved. He's been expectin' a request fur help from ye. He says tae meet him t'night at th' dock around sunset. Ye'll find him there."

"What does he intend to do?"

"Ye'll find Caleb is good at figurin' things out. Th' important thing is ye're na' alone. He understands wha' is happening, and he's reliable. Th' only thing we ask is tha' ye keep his identity a secret. Men like him don' come around often, and he's a great asset tae our cause in Thurwick."

"But Father, what am I to do? When I find the monster, what then?"

"When ye find what ye seek, lad, tae whom do ye give yer glory? One day ye'll have tae make a decision. Th' book o' Proverbs says 'he who wavers between two ways falls down in one o' them.' Tha' means tis best tae decide ahead o' time whose side ye're on."

Tom hesitated, but he found himself nodding anyway. He thanked Father Gibson and shook his hand.

As he walked down the hallway into the church, he tried to comprehend the meaning of his whole experience. He paused before he exited, taking one last look at the crucifix hanging behind the altar. It was an image of sacrifice and suffering. His eyes gazed upon it for several moments, and he found it difficult to turn away from it.

Then an idea came to him, one he should have thought of days ago. He left the church. As the sun shone through the mist, he knew he had to find Marella if he was going to have any chance at all.

CHAPTER 41

"I'll tell ye wha'. Na one can defeat a Gaelic knight. Na one!"
The voice came from down the hospital hallway. It sounded like Sean. Tom turned the corner. Sean was in a blue hospital garb sitting on the bed. One leg was covered with heavy white bandages to his knee, and the rest of the leg was gone. There was an empty space where Sean's leg should have extended.

Tom felt chills.

Marella stood next to the wall, dabbing the tears from her eyes. They were red from hours of crying.

Tom tried to say hello, but he could only muster a grimaced shake of his head.

"Well, they saved him, bu' he lost his leg," she said. "He woke up quickly, though. Now th' drugs are speakin'."

Sean turned to Tom. "Well, hello there my adventurin' companion. Are we off fur another excursion on th' Loch t'night?"

Tom struggled to speak. A part of him wanted to throw up. After a few moments of nausea, Tom asked Marella, "Does he know his leg is gone?"

"He hasn' mentioned it yet. He keeps talking abou' getting' back on th' Loch,"

Sean said, "That's right. Let's get back out on th' Loch t'night. They canno' keep us from our mission. We'll o'ertake them!"

"Sean, you're not going anywhere for a while," Tom said.

"Where did ye go?" Marella said.

"To find help. I think I found some."

"We know th' secret tae th' Loch Ness monster," Sean said. "We can call Nessie tae us!"

Tom shuddered. He told Sean to hush. He hoped no one would take him seriously since they had pumped him full of medicine.

Marella said, "Th' doctor said it will be a while before th' drugs wear off." She turned to Sean. "Da', ye'll need tae sit right where ye are fur a while."

Sean shook his head. "I've go' a mission tae accomplish!"

"Are you still leaving?" Tom said.

Marella didn't answer.

"She's na' goin' anywhere," Sean said. "My little girl is goin' on th' boat wi' me t'night. We're goin' tae find th' monster!"

Marella turned away, embarrassed, and put her hands to her face. She was crying again.

"He needs you right now," Tom said.

"This is tae much."

Tom didn't answer.

"I'm so afraid. I mean, what's goin' tae happen next?" Marella said.

"Don' be afraid," Sean said. "Ye're a mighty warrior, just like yer father. Remember? Wha' happened tae tha' little girl who used tae go out in th' woods and sword fight wi' me?"

Marella put her hands to her eyes as she held back tears.

"I can't imagine what you're feeling right now," Tom said. He watched as she released her emotions. "Maybe you should give it a few more days, just until he's set back home."

"My bus leaves in an hour," Marella said.

Sean said, "When we go out t'night, we'll call Nessie. Marella, how beautiful ye'll look when ye are riding on th' monster's back. Oh, wha' a sight that'll be!"

"Geez, Da'. Wha' did they give ye?"

"Marella, are you going to leave the country with your father in this condition?" Tom said.

Marella didn't respond.

"Aye, we're a family o' Gaelic knights. A Paterson ne'er retreats!" Sean said, waving his hand in the air as though he were carrying a sword.

Then his hand fell by his side and his eyes shut.

Within seconds his head leaned back against the pillow, his mouth wide open, and he snored like a locomotive.

Marella's eyes were swollen from exhaustion. "I'm tired o' runnin'. He may be doolally, bu' he didn' deserve this." Her face tensed, giving way to anger. "Do ye have *any* idea who was behind this?"

"I have a pretty good guess," Tom said. "But in order to confirm it, I'm going to need your help."

"Wha' were ye hopin' I would do?"

Tom scanned the room and peered out the door. "Not here. We need to go someplace where no one will be listening to us."

Marella said, "They aren' payin attention tae us."

"We can't take that chance. We need to go somewhere else."

"Where?"

"I have an idea," Tom said. He stood in the hallway and he waived for a nurse.

CHAPTER 42

"How long will he be asleep?" Marella asked. The doctor had come into the room. The doctor said it would be some time, but he could be off and on. "Will he be alrigh' if we leave and come back?" Marella said. She hesitated as she asked the question.

"We'll take good care o' him," the doctor said.

Tom took Marella down the hallway. They left the hospital and stood together under the open air. Cars and pedestrians moved around the square. He was suspicious that someone might be watching him, observing his moves.

He took Marella around a corner. A few yards later he found himself along the side entrance to the museum. "We're going in here," he said.

They walked inside and he paid both their fares. "Last time I was in here, it was pretty empty," he told her. They walked along the red carpet among the exhibits. "If we're talking, they might think we're discussing the artifacts or the pictures."

Marella nodded.

Tom noticed she did not resist.

They turned a corner and found an exhibit of the political history of Scotland. The large black and white pictures of legislatures at the UK parliament fit into Tom's plan. He stopped. "Okay. I'm going back out on the Loch tonight," Tom said.

"By yerself?" Marella said.

"Shhhh, not so loud."

"Are you doolally?" She pointed her finger at her head in the circular "crazy" motion.

"I want to find this creature. But if I'm being followed, maybe I can lure whoever or whatever it is that is trying to stop me. And I won't be alone."

"Ye don' expect me tae go wi' ye, do ye?"

"Of course not."

"Then who?"

"Do you remember Caleb from the local council meeting last week?"

"The guy wi' th' hat? Th' one tha' told us all those strange things?"

"Yes. Him. He's asked me to meet him at the dock tonight at sunset."

"So wha' do ye need from me?"

"I'm going to need you to find help for me at the US Embassy."

"Th' Embassy? Bu' they are hundreds o' miles from here," Marella said.

"It's the only chance we have. I need you to contact them," Tom said. "I don't care what you do. Tell them I'm American, and I'm being sought after and mistreated by local authorities. Tell them I've been beaten, threatened, and blown up since I've been in Scotland. Just get someone from America to Thurwick as quick as you can."

"This isn't a good idea," Marella said. "I mean, I still have tae take care o' my father. Ye've been injured also. Maybe we shouldn' separate. Maybe we should give it a few days before we do anythin'.""

"We don't have a few days. Whoever it was that blew up the boat knows we both made it. Sean's vulnerable in the hospital, but you and he are safer there than you would be at your cottage."

"But ye would be, tae, wouldn' ye?"

"I can't worry about being safe right now. Caleb says to meet him at the dock at sunset. I have to do it. He may know something that will help us."

"Tis just tae dangerous. Somethin' will happen tae ye."

"Whatever happens to me, the best thing for you and Sean is to get help from the US Embassy. Use my citizenship as leverage, whatever you have to do. My passport is at Annabel's Bed and Breakfast. Here's my key. Just get there when you can, and use whatever you have to get them to come to Thurwick."

Tom handed her his room key.

Marella nodded. "I'll do my best, but I don' know how quickly I can get them here."

"Just do what you can. I'm going to lay low and what I can find before Caleb and I go on the water tonight. I may try to pick up a few extra supplies. You won't see me until tomorrow. If you don't, promise me one thing,"

"What's tha'?"

"Send the US authorities to Father Gibson at Saint Michaels. If anybody will know what happened to me, he will. He knows a lot about what goes on around here."

"Okay," Marella said. "I'll go back tae th' hospital and make sure Da's alright. Then I'll do wha' I can tae get in contact wi' th' Embassy."

"We're going to solve this thing here and now. I promised I'd come to help you, and I intend to keep that promise."

"Then we'd best get tae work."

She followed the path back through the exhibits. Suddenly, the replica of the Loch Ness monster hung over her head. She gasped at the fake creature's teeth bearing down on her.

"Oh, don't worry about him," Tom said. "He and I go way back. He's the good guy in all of this." Tom took Marella by the hand. She held his and didn't let go and together they exited the museum.

They walked out into the sun. Mid-day storm clouds rumbled over the hills. Marella left him at the door and walked towards the hospital. Tom leaned against the wall as he watched her walk. He wanted to appear casual as he was observing the goings on in the Thurwick passageways. Was he being watched? He had no experience at spy games. He was too up-front. What you saw with Tom was what you got.

He felt awkward, though he tried to appear cool. As Marella left his sight, he decided to find a place to arm himself. That would come first, as there was no telling what awaited him at the dock.

CHAPTER 43

Tom surveyed the streets. He wanted a weapon. *A gun would be great to have right about now,* he thought, but there would be no way a government would allow a foreigner walking in off the street to purchase a gun. Nor could he get large knives. Maybe something smaller. He scanned the shops in his view, and he remembered the drug store. Maybe they had small knives. He'd try there first.

He moved along the cobblestone streets at a quick pace. He had become used to the aches of his body, and he found the more he moved, the less stiff he felt. A wind blew litter through the streets, a sign of another Scottish storm approaching. He found the drug store, and went inside.

In the front inside a glass case, he found them. Several brands of pocket knives were set in rows. Some were larger than others. Some had a single blade with a sheath. Others had fold-out mechanisms, including scissors, screwdrivers, and bottle openers. The single blades would be better for defense. The fold-out pocket knives could be useful in a pinch for several other reasons. He told the clerk he'd take one of each.

The clerk said, "Foremost, religious music. Next, Guinness. T'day, knives. Ye've kind o' done a one-eighty, haven' ye?"

"It's not easy being a renaissance man," Tom said. "Do you have a restroom in here?"

"Restroom? What's tha'?"

"You know. Where people can go to wash up?"

"Th' bog?"

"I suppose."

The clerk pointed to the back of the store. Tom paid for the knives, thanked the clerk, and walked to the rear of the store where he found the restroom. He walked in and examined his items. The single blade sheath had slits to slide his belt through. *Get it ready now,* he thought, *rather than go outside and hope for the best.*

He adjusted his belt and slid the sheath over it so that the knife would be on his left hip, then he buckled the belt again. He examined his bruises in the mirror. He was more protected than before, and he felt more confident. He opened the pocket knife and examined each of its tools individually, imagining scenarios which may come his way in which he'd use a particular tool to solve a problem.

He left the store. What should he do next? *Go to Guthrie's Pub and listen to some of the locals?* Maybe there he'd gather some information about of what was going on around Thurwick, alerting him to any potential dangers.

He also wanted to get back to his room at Annabel's. Annabel had to wonder why he disappeared some nights. But some of his things were still there, and he needed to make sure he still had his room.

He decided first his room.

Then, Guthrie's.

More people should be at the pub as the day grew later anyway. He headed across the square.

Then he heard them.

Footsteps.

Several of them coming from his right.

Five men wearing strange uniforms sprinted toward him. His instincts took over. He turned to his left and ran. His arches in his feet ached with each step. He planted his foot and cut ninety degrees into the street, dodging a red car that moved in his path. They were running after him. One of the uniformed men yelled and pointed, chasing him. Another was hit by an oncoming car, but the man rolled over the hood and landed on his feet before he continued to sprint.

"What do they want?" said Tom.

He turned to get away. An alley was on his left. He decided to take it. He found himself between two buildings, dodging a garbage bin. He ran around it, grabbing some of the garbage bags from the open cover and throwing them behind him. He had to delay them.

He turned right. Suddenly, two of men appeared in his left periphery. They had come around the building to try to intercept him.

He sprinted.

Up ahead, headlights sped toward him.

A car!

They had tried to cut him off. He turned right again into another alleyway. He found a door, and tried to open it.

Locked!

The pursuing men rounded the corner. "Halt!" one of them said. Tom ran. He felt himself breathing hard, but he was about to catch his second wind.

The alley ended. He turned left.

"What the hell!" he said.

Two SUVs had come and blocked his path, their passengers just getting out. One was about to fire a stun gun.

Tom heard a shot, and he ducked while he kept his legs churning.

Nothing happened.

The shooter missed!

He ran into the street. Cars had stopped everywhere, creating naturel blockades. The drivers became spectators, watching with awe all the commotion in the streets.

Twenty uniformed men cut between the cars and around the trees. Tom saw a gap between two cars.

He ran for the gap.

He heard shouting, and multiple screams. Pedestrians tried to get out of his way. A fat pedestrian tried to run at him and tackle him. Tom cut left just as the man dived and grabbed air. The fat man let out an "Ugh!" sound as his stomach landed on the turf, knocking the wind out of him.

A few more uniformed men appeared.

They're everywhere!

Tom discovered another alleyway. He churned his legs and sprinted to its opening. Just then, a man jumped in front of him.

It was Alex Vaas!

He had jumped in the alley escape route. Tom decided not to avoid him. Instead, he lowered his shoulder, prepared to ram his way through. "Let's show him how we do things in America!"

Then he heard a shot, and Tom hit the ground hard as an electric current zapped his senses. He felt his face scrape on pebbles. His body twitched. Men circled him. One grasped him and put cuffs on his hands behind him.

His pursuers surrounded him. The electric current churned his insides upside down. Several onlookers talked and pointed. Alex Vaas pushed aside a few of the men to stand in front of them. "Take him tae th' room."

The men nodded at Vaas, like they were taking orders. One of them mentioned he found Tom's sheathed knife. Another found his pocket knife. They told Tom he was in a lot of trouble. Then they picked him up by his coat and jeans and they threw him inside one of the SUVs.

Tom worked to speak, "What did I do?" but even he wasn't sure if he spoke or if he imagined it. He hurt everywhere, more so than before. He tried to catch his breath. The door slammed. Two muscular uniformed men climbed into the front seat, and the SUV pulled forward along one of the cobblestone streets.

The US Embassy. Please, Marella, get in contact with the US Embassy!

CHAPTER 44

The car stopped, and the uniformed men exited the vehicle. One opened the back seat door, and grabbed Tom by his collar. "Get out now!" the man said, pulling Tom out of the car and onto his feet.

Tom glared at the man, who yanked on his collar and threw Tom out of the vehicle.

"Inside!" the man said, pushing Tom through a door.

Tom stumbled, twisting his torso to keep his balance. His hands were still cuffed behind his back.

The building was old. It was an unmarked building, like a warehouse. They led Tom through some dark hallways towards a doorway.

Through the doorway was a dimly lit room.

"In ye go!" said one of the men. They shoved Tom into the room.

Inside the room there was a table and a man slumped on a chair. The man had bleached hair. His head was leaning on his shoulder atop a ragged coat. He faced away from Tom.

"Ye two have fun!"

His hands still behind his back, Tom stumbled toward the man in the chair. He heard the door shut behind him, echoing the slamming sound between the four walls.

The bleached haired man remained slumped in his chair.

He didn't move.

He didn't even flinch.

Tom turned around. "Who do you guys think you are? Let me out of here!"

He kicked the door.

The door was solid.

He stubbed his toe.

"Gawd dangit!" Tom said. Pain hit his toe and his aching ankle, and Tom sucked in air as he tried to manage it.

After a few moments, he recovered.

An old hanging light fell from the ceiling. The light it emitted was slight, not doing enough to brighten the room. Tom walked further into the room. The back of the man was between Tom and the door.

"Hey," Tom said. "What the hell is this place?"

The man was silent.

"How long have you been in here?"

No response.

Tom shuddered a moment, then he got a hold of his nerves. He stepped around the edge of the table. He kept his eyes on the bleach haired man.

The man remained still

When Tom reached the side of the table, he gasped.

It's the albino!

His head was leaning to one side, his mouth open. His eyelids were raised, and his eyes had glazed over. They stared ahead at the stone wall on the other side of the room, lifeless.

The albino had two dark blood stains that spread down from his chest. Two spots were dark red, and lighter reddish blood stained the ragged shirt and coat as it had run down into the albino's lap.

"Holy geez!" Tom stepped back. His instincts caused him to attempt to bring his hands in front of him, but his hands were still cuffed. He cut his wrists as he flinched. "Get me the hell out of here!"

His voice echoed between the walls. His heart thumped in his chest. His breathing grew heavier.

There's a dead guy in this dark room with me. Don't freaking panic!

Tom closed his eyes. He focused on his breathing. "Get a hold of yourself. Stay in control." He repeated the words for several moments until he regained control of his thoughts.

He opened his eyes.

There was the dead albino. And the blood. Shot twice in the chest.

Okay, don't look at him. See what else is in here.

There was the door. As he found out, it was solid. There were no other doors in the dimly lit room.

There was the window. It appeared unbreakable, and reflective. He could not see through it. Was someone was on the other side watching him?

What else?

Other than the window, there were no other cracks or vents. The air was stuffy without any ventilation. It was also cold.

Tom shouted at the window. "Did someone forget to turn on the heat?" He decided to stand in front of the window, his hands still behind his back. He thought he recognized shapes behind the window, but after a while decided it was hopeless. The shapes had to be either warped contours in the window or just his imagination.

"There has to be some sort of law against this," Tom yelled, directing it to anybody real or imaginary on the other side of the window. "So much for not causing an international incident. Boy, somebody screwed that one up!"

He examined the window for several minutes. He didn't want to appear weak, but the truth was his legs were tired, and, along with the pain in his ankle, his feet ached. His eye still hurt, and now he felt the scrapes on his cheek from where his face had skidded on the pebbles. He had to stay strong, but being locked up like he was, whether legal or not, they had the upper hand on him.

He decided to walk over to the table. An empty chair was pushed under the table opposite the albino. Using his legs, he kicked the chair away from the table and sat down. Then he shifted his weight with his legs and slid the chair back to the table.

Don't look at the dead guy. Just think.

He laid his head down and closed his eyes. His forehead rested on the flat surface. He banged it against the table several times.

Even then, the urge to find the Loch Ness monster welled up in his gut. "Not now," he said. "This has got to be like some sort of Chinese torture!"

He shifted, trying to pull his hands through the cuffs behind his back. Pain radiated from his wrists. He had pulled too hard, breaking his skin. He pulled harder, but they just wouldn't go through. He banged his head against the table again.

The albino stared at him with dead glossy eyes.

What the hell are they going to do to me? Think, dammit!

Vaas was behind this abduction. That had to mean Chairman Briggs was in on it. But wasn't there another authority?

The Highland Unitary Council?

He couldn't remember. What did they know? What was going on?

His mind grew foggy.

Were Marella and Sean in danger? Sean was vulnerable, having just had surgery to remove a leg. How were they holding up? Would Marella leave him to contact the US authorities in Scotland? Would his government even come to help?

He had no way of knowing.

The lamp above him lit the room with a dim light. The unbreakable window reflected the dim light, and the pale image of the dead albino. Was that a shadow through the window? He squinted. *Who the hell knows*, he thought. *Wouldn't matter anyway unless they opened the damned door.*

Think, Tom. Think!

He imagined someone coming through the door. Would one of those uniformed men come through the doorway and try to talk with him? What did they want? Would they try to intimidate him? Play good cop, bad cop? Would they threaten him?

Again, what were they after? Was it because he hadn't left? That had to be it. Vaas wanted to act like the tough guy. He wanted to force the US tourist out of the country as a favor to his Chairman buddy.

Or was it more? Did they want to capture him to get to Sean? Maybe Sean had more information on the Loch Ness monster, and kidnapping was their way to pry the information away from him.

Was that what happened to the albino? Did he have a secret? Did the albino not give up the secret? Or did he give it up, and they shot him anyway?

If they went after Sean, would he give up the secret if pressed?

Would I?

If the albino was anything, it would be an example of how they extracted information.

Like hell if they think they are going to do that to me!

Tom decided no matter what, he'd find a way to win. This was his mission. He wouldn't give up. He wouldn't let Marella down!

More time passed. He was thirsty.

Maybe they planned to keep him there. Just forget about him. Maybe someone would find his body twenty years from now, his bones on this chair with his hands cuffed behind his back and his forehead resting on the table. Across from him would be the albino's skeleton.

What would happen if, years from now, someone found them like that? The powers at be would never let that happen. They'd bury them both somewhere in the Highlands where they couldn't be found. Maybe put him in the Loch and feed him to the monster.

He'd never be heard from again.

Then, his anger gave way to sadness. What *if* he had never been heard from again? What about his chance with Marella? What about his life? He was only in his twenties. Did his life have any meaning? Was this going to be it?

"No," he said. "I'm going to finish this. I made a promise."

Tom raised himself up. He lifted his head. The ceiling above was old and stained.

"God, if you want the Loch Ness monster found, you're going to have to help me out of this." Then he shut his eyes, and he lowered his head so that his forehead rested on the table. He let out a small laugh. "I've never prayed before."

Time slipped away. Tom did not know how much, only that he knew it had to be hours.

Half a day, maybe?

He guessed it had to be late into the evening, possibly one or two in the morning. He had missed meeting Caleb at the dock. How long did Caleb wait for him. Did he call the authorities? Who would he call?

He had had nothing to drink. No food, no water. He felt hungry and tired and thirsty. Sleep sounded good, but he didn't trust whoever had locked him inside. He had to stay awake.

The albino creeped him out.

He had to think of Marella.

He had to...

The door opened. Tom raised his head, caught off guard. He had been asleep. His mouth was parched. His back ached, the way a crick would linger after having slept in a bad position all night. Two people walked in the shadows. He blinked, and he heard the door shut. As the people approached, Tom sat up straight.

He heard a voice. "Ye might wan' some o' this." A cup of water was placed in front of him. He tried to grab it with his hand, but he was reminded his hands were cuffed behind him.

His eyelids blinked in the light.

"You!" Tom said.

It was Chairman Gordon Briggs.

And next to him stood Alex Vaas.

CHAPTER 45

Vaas had carried a small chair through the door. He set the chair down next to the albino. Then, he shoved the dead man off the chair. The albino fell to the floor. His head hit the floor with a thump, and the body lied stiff and still.

Vaas grabbed the albino's chair and sat down.

Briggs sat on the other chair. The dim light that shone from the lamp above reflected off Briggs's balding head. He shook his condescending head. "Ye were supposed tae have left some time ago."

Tom didn't move from his chair. He knew he had to choose his words wisely. *Over thirty dangerous encounters, only five fights*, he thought. But this time, his hands were cuffed, and he had no idea of his whereabouts.

"Travel delays," Tom said.

"I don' know how ye treat authority in th' United States, but in this part o' th' world we have customs. Tis obvious ye haven' been paying attention tae them."

"Are they customs, or are they laws?" Tom said. "For some reason, I get the feeling the line between them is very blurred in Thurwick."

Vaas said, "Ye made a bad choice by na' goin' when we asked ye tae." He gave the air of confidence and control. "I warned ye a second time, but ye failed tae heed our direction."

Vaas was planning. He was on a mission, and he knew every tactic in the book. Should he play along, at least until he knew what their plan was?

Not yet, he thought. *First, spar with them and get them agitated. Find what buttons to push.*

"I'm sorry," Tom said, hinting sarcasm. "I didn't know Thurwick had a corrupt mafia running the local government."

Briggs and Vaas remained expressionless.

Unbelievable. These guys know they're corrupt!

Threats would come next. Would they use physical force to beat a man, with cuffs behind his back? Tom searched his mind for other tactics, but lack of sleep, water, and food made thinking all the more difficult.

Briggs said, "Ye know, I will say this about ye. Ye are way tae smart tae be hangin' around a foolish cryptozoologist."

"He didn't deserve to have his leg blown off." The moment he said it, Tom knew he had overreacted. It had to be the lack of sleep.

"We agree," Briggs said. "Which brings us tae why ye're here."

"What do you mean?"

"Tis obvious, isn't it," Briggs said. "We know about yer arrest fur battery in America. Now we have ye fur more. Ye're accused o' stealing a boat, destruction of property, and now attempted murder…"

"What!" Tom stood up, his arms flinching behind his back. "Who did I try to kill? Him?" Tom nodded to the deceased albino on the floor.

"Th' accusation fur actual murder comes later, if ye don' do wha' we say," Vaas said. "Fur now, ye're wanted fur tryin' tae blow up Sean Paterson?"

"You're both maniacs, you know that?"

Vaas said, "Th' owner o' th' boat reported it stolen yesterday mornin'. We believe yer plan was tae dispose o' Mr. Paterson so tha' ye could make advances t'wards his daughter." Vaas grinned as he said it.

Tom sat down. "You're trying to blackmail me, aren't you?"

Briggs and Vaas grinned.

"Alright then. What is it you want?"

"Mr. Wayne, we believe ye know somethin'," Briggs said. "We don' know how, but we believe in yer short time here ye've discovered wha' it is under th' surface o' th' Loch."

Tom held his breath. Briggs had given him a hint. They wanted information.

"I know quite a lot about what's happening in this town of yours. More than you'd like me to know," Tom said.

Briggs stood up from his chair. He paced in and out of the light as he spoke, stepping around the albino. "I must say, we've all gotten off on th' wrong foot." Briggs lifted his leg and pressed the sole of his shoe on the albino's ragged coat. The stiff body rocked as Briggs pushed down with his heel. "Perhaps yer experience in Thurwick hasn' been e'erything ye thought it would be. Has it?"

Tom flinched. Then he caught himself.

Don't show emotion.

But it was too late.

"That's wha' I thought," Briggs said, taking his foot off the body. "And that's na' wha' we want fur our guests, especially those who come from across th' Atlantic." Briggs raised his voice. "Howe'er, we were thinkin' about wha' we could do in this situation. Why don' ye help us locate th' creature, and then all will be forgiven."

"Forgiven?" Tom said, nodding to the dead albino. "Is that the same deal you made to him?" He turned to Vaas. "You told me you didn't know him."

"We know e'erything tha' happens in Thurwick." Vaas leaned from his chair over the albino. "Poor lad. Drug addict, he was. Believed a lot o' things. Started his own cult. We thought we could help him. Bu' he didn' do wha' we wanted, so he was o' na use tae us."

"So you shot him?"

"Aye."

"What about his friends?"

"They are na longer a concern."

"So is that your plan for me?"

Vaas pulled a small pistol from his coat pocket and set it on the table. "Yer choice, lad."

The gun barrel pointed at Tom. His nerves triggered, but he commanded his muscles to stay still. It was a battle of wits. Did they think he was the only one with the information? If so, he had to take a chance. "Here's an idea, why don't you two go take a long walk off Ewan Coffee's yacht, and don't forget to waive goodbye before you hit the water!"

"There's na doubt ye're resourceful," Briggs said, not skipping a beat. "We could use a man like ye tae help us wi' our mission. Show us how ye brought th' monster tae th' surface, and we'll be glad tae let ye go."

"You son of a…"

"Don' cause an accident." Vaas said.

"I'm not afraid of you."

"We can see tha'. But yer friend Paterson, he's quite vulnerable now, isn' he?"

Tom didn't answer.

"Accidents happen all th' time in hospitals. It would be a shame if somethin' happened tae yer friend before he recovered from his injuries."

"So this is blackmail."

Vaas picked up his pistol. "Fur those o' us who play chess, laddie, we call it checkmate."

"Go to hell."

"Ye're wasting chances, lad." Vaas cocked the pistol, making it click. "Think it through."

Briggs stood with his arms crossed by the reflecting window. He was a person who would do anything to maintain power.

Tom shifted, half attempting to get a hand out of the cuffs. He wanted to reach over the table and punch Vaas in the face, but he had to maintain his wits. Tom pursed his lips, and remained silent.

Briggs continued, "Th' Loch Ness monster has been a phenomenon in our area fur centuries. I'm sure ye've learned much about it since ye've been here. But th' creature has eluded us. E'en Sean Paterson's efforts yielded nothin' fur thirty years, that is, until ye showed up. At first, we thought ye were just a ploy tae get him more attention. But now we can solve this mystery, and tha' would be good na' only fur Thurwick or th' Highlands in Scotland, but th' entire world. Imagine th' magnitude o' a discovery like tha', tha' th' past is still alive in th' present, and man is still connected tae th' creatures from two hundred million years ago. Imagine wha' it would do tae our perspective o' th' world, how we can dominate it, and use its resources. Imagine wha' it would do fur..." Briggs returned to his chair. "Well, I'm sure ye can imagine."

"I can imagine your goal is to catch the monster for your own benefit. You want the historical recognition that comes with finding it, and you'll use that to advance your power agenda," Tom said.

"And just wha' do ye know about power? Ye're in no position tae accuse anyone o' anythin'." Briggs raised his voice.

A vessel pulsed in Briggs's temple, emphasized by the low light from the lamp above. Tom knew he had hit on a sore spot.

Briggs calmed himself. "Lad, we'll ne'er be friends. But in my line o' work, I have learned I still can work wi' people I don' get along wi'. Isn't tha' th' character o' a man, tae achieve a goal fur th' common good, e'en if they work wi' people they don' understand?"

"It's a lot easier when you have a gun, isn't it."

"Aye. Tis insurance. But all th' same..." Briggs grinned.

Tom didn't know why, but even with his aches and soreness and hunger and thirst, he felt an urge to find the Loch Ness monster. In his weakened state, the curse of the old barn remained inside him. The obsession would never leave him until both the creature was found and the curse lifted, or until his soul left his body.

"We have a plan," Briggs continued. "Ewan Coffee's boat is ready tae leave th' dock. It has e'ery technology ye could imagine tae find th' Loch Ness monster. Th' only thing missing is th' information ye have. Together, I'm sure ye'll be successful. We'll feed ye and allow ye tae rest on th' boat. Then Alex, Ewan, and ye can do wha' ye need tae do tae find th' monster, capture it, and bring it back tae Thurwick."

"Do I have a choice?"

"E'eryone has a choice," Briggs said. "Th' question is whether or na' they are also willin' tae face th' consequences."

Tom considered Briggs's offer. With his hands behind his back, he had no physical way to escape. If he refused, they could walk out the door and leave him. No one would ever find him. Already one day without water, he'd be dead in about thirty-six to forty-eight hours.

The advantage he had was the information. He had something they wanted. What's better, they didn't appear to suspect the song, or the priests. He could use that information however he wanted.

Vaas sat like a chess player who was used to competing against Kasparov. The man was cunning. He knew pressure and psychology. Tom believed he would also use physical force at some point.

Could Tom beat him in a hand-to-hand fight? One thing's for certain, Vaas wouldn't play fair. He had to be ready for that.

"Food, water, rest, and you'll un-cuff my hands," Tom said.

Vaas said, "Ye have na negotiatin' power."

Briggs interrupted him. "We can talk abou' all o' tha' on th' way tae th' boat. Fur now, wha' do ye say we get goin'?"

Tom stood, his cuffs still locking his hands. His shoulders were tensed, stiff, and sore.

Briggs and Vaas stood from their chairs, and they motioned for him to exit the small dimly lit room into the dark hallway outside. Tom stopped before he left the room. The albino formed a dark mass on the floor. The small cup of water sat on the table. Not a drop of it had been sipped.

Briggs and Vaas had made no effort to remove his cuffs or to help him to drink the water.

I'm going from one prison to another. How will I make it out of this alive?

CHAPTER 46

The shiny SUV pulled up to the dock. Still handcuffed, Tom climbed out of the back seat. Vaas came up close and flashed his pistol, pointing it at Tom's mid-section. "Say anythin' until ye get on tha' boat, lad, and I'll pull this trigger," he whispered.

Tom stayed silent. Would it matter if he did yell for help? There was no local law enforcement. The only authority was under the power of the man pointing the gun at him. If Tom yelled, no one would come to help. If they shot him, they'd sweep him under the rug. His fear was, after disposing of him, they'd next go after Marella and Sean. Tom had to stay alive so Briggs and Vaas would deal with him and not with them.

Briggs stepped out of the car and walked toward the dock. The uniformed men pushed Tom along a wooden walkway. The walkway turned to the right towards Ewan Coffee's large yacht. The yacht floated like a large iceberg. In the back right corner stood the harpoon gun, its metallic sheen glinting in the sunlight.

Vaas pushed Tom toward the boat, the pistol pressing against Tom's back. They came to a rope ladder that hung over the side of the yacht. Tom said, "Handcuffs?"

"Damn it, turn around," Vaas said.

Tom turned. He was face to face with Briggs.

"So, do you plan to harpoon the monster yourself?" Tom said.

"Oh, I'm na' goin'. I understand power. Power is getting others tae do things fur ye, but then ye find th' way tae keep th' credit. Alex and Ewan will take care o' things just as I need them tae."

Tom's hands came free. He brought his hands together in front, rubbing them together. Relief entered his arms and shoulders.

"Don' try anythin'," Vaas said.

Tom raised his hands. He knew the pistol was still pointed at him. He nodded to the deck. "Food and water in the boat?"

"Aye," Briggs said. "Ye help us wi' wha' we need, and Alex will make sure ye are rewarded."

"I help you, and you'll stay away from my friends?"

"Aye. Just make sure ye keep yer end o' th' bargain."

Tom didn't believe a word Briggs said. But he did know he had to get on board the boat. He stepped toward the ladder. The sun reflected off the boat, and Tom squinted in the light.

He climbed the ladder. His joints hurt. He felt his lips as they cracked. His wrists ached. His arches under his feet gave way to pain. But he persisted. He thought of the promise he made.

He would finish this.

When he reached the edge of the yacht, a hand came down. He grabbed it. A man wearing a white captain's outfit pulled him up. "Aye, there ye are," he said. "I'm Ewan Coffee. Welcome aboard my beauty." He spoke cheerfully at Tom, as though the man had no idea of the sufferings he had undergone the past two weeks. Nor did he care. Ewan acted like a spoiled kid, showing off his things without any regard for his company. *Too bad*, Tom thought. *He could be likeable if he wasn't so arrogant.*

"I hear ye're going tae help us catch Th' Big One," Coffee said. He laughed as he said it. "I've heard ye've seen it yerself, is tha' right?"

Tom said, "Where's the food that was promised?"

"Food? Is tha' what they told ye?" Coffee laughed again, shaking his head. "Once we harpoon Nessie, how abou' we cut off a dinosaur steak fur ye?"

"Do you at least have water?"

Coffee pointed to a small cooler by a stack of ropes. "In there."

Tom reached down and opened the lid. There were bottles of water and glass bottles of beer. He pulled out a plastic water bottle and shut the lid. He tried to gauge the length of the ropes stacked near the edge of the boat.

Thirty, forty feet maybe?

Don't stare, he thought. *Keep a mental note, and go sit down.*

Vaas climbed up and over the side. He pointed his pistol at Tom and walked over to him. "We're goin' tae have some rules on this ship," Vaas said.

Coffee went inside the ship's control room. An engine motor hummed. The boat moved forward. Tom said a silent goodbye to

Thurwick as the yacht drifted from the shoreline. Tom turned to Vaas and raised his bottle of water in sarcasm. "To success."

Vaas frowned, and put the pistol away. Then he sat down across from Tom.

Coffee shouted from his steering wheel. "So, where do we go, lad?"

"Nothin' funny," said Vaas.

Tom hesitated, then said, "To the church. Saint Michael's Catholic Church." He shouted over the motor so Coffee could hear.

Coffee spun the ship's wheel, and Tom felt the boat shift its weight as it changed direction. It had taken Sean thirty minutes to row to the spot. The yacht's engine would get them there in less than half that time. Tom figured he had less than ten minutes to come up with a plan.

All he could think of was to pretend like he had one.

CHAPTER 47

Tom took a sip of his water, keeping his eyes locked on Alex Vaas who stretched his arms over the railing of the yacht. The glare from the sun reflected on the boat, but Tom tried to act cool, like he had been on a yacht every day of his life.

Vaas took his eyes off of Tom for a moment, and then he stood up. He took a few steps in Tom's direction, then without any warning punched Tom across the face. Tom fell off his seat and onto the deck, his water bottle spinning near the cooler and the ropes.

Vaas stood over Tom, smiling. "As I was sayin', we have some rules on this yacht." He kicked Tom in the ribs, and Tom felt like he would throw up as the air was kicked out of him. "Th' rules are simple. Give us wha' we want, and we let ye die quickly,"

Tom gasped for air as he rolled on the deck.

"Now, tell us how ye brough' th' monster tae th' surface."

Tom squinted at the shadow of Vaas, the sun beaming behind his adversary. "Go to hell."

"Laddie. We can do this th' easy way, or th' hard way. I'd prefer th' hard way, personally. I get more enjoyment out o' it."

"I'd bet you do." Tom climbed to his knees and tried to stand up, but Vaas swung a hard right into his stomach, and Tom fell over.

"Ye'd be better off if ye stayed where ye were and told me wha' I want tae know. What's th' secret?" Vaas pointed his pistol at Tom's head. "Tell me, lad. What's th' secret?"

Tom had thought he'd be afraid in this situation, but he wasn't. He had never faced a weapon in all of his altercations before. This was a first. "I appreciate your love for violence," Tom said. "But if you off me, how're you going to find the secret?"

"Simple. I'll pay a visit tae yer girlfriend and her father."

"They don't know," Tom said. "I kept it hidden from them." Would Vaas believe his lie?

"Paterson was wi' ye on th' boat," Vaas said. "He knows."

"Okay, then. Take your chance. Kill me, and dump me in the water. You'd better hope you're right."

"Lad may have a point, Alex," Coffee said. He had been listening from the control room as he kept his hands on the ship's wheel. "Tis obvious he's been through so much yer scare tactics aren' gettin' tae him."

"Ye do yer job, and I'll do mine," Vaas said.

"Best be careful wha' ye say tae th' guy who writes yer checks," Coffee said.

Vaas grunted. He kicked Tom one more time as he put his pistol back in its holster.

Tom fell over and clutched his ribs. His water bottle rolled back and forth in the rocking of the yacht on the water. The bottle had left a puddle, and he crawled through it, his stained jeans getting wet again. He went to the cooler and opened it.

"Wha' th' hell do ye think ye're doin'?" Vaas demanded.

Tom pulled out a bottle of water and held it up, closing the lid to the cooler. He counted at least four beer bottles in the cooler before he shut the lid. "Replacing my drink," he said. "You promised, remember?"

Vaas returned to his seat and sat down. His brow tensed with anger.

Tom climbed into his seat. He stretched out his arms once again on the railing, just as he had done before Vaas hit him. Tom took a drink and kept his eyes on Vaas.

Vaas kept eye contact.

The two said nothing to each other, but Tom imagined Vaas had a history of violence. That was his thing. Vaas helped power people for his own benefit. Their protection allowed him to do evil things above the law. In fact, Vaas thought he was the law, except that the man steering the yacht was the one with the money. Vaas appeared bothered by that. Even on this boat, while Vaas tried to say there was no law, Coffee reminded Vaas there was.

There's always a hierarchy.

Tom spotted the predator inside Vaas's black pupils. Tom had never killed anyone before. He had always tried to get his way peacefully, though force would be an option if necessary. Each occurrence had ended far before they became too serious. Tom's encounters had never come to the point of death.

If there was a hierarchy on this boat, Tom was at the bottom of it. He might have to come to terms with all he'd have to do. Could he kill a man if it was necessary?

He didn't think so.

But Vaas might force him to change his mind.

CHAPTER 48

Tom felt the cool breeze against his hair as the yacht shipped over to where he and Sean had found the monster. It was the first time he felt good, even though he was hungry, battered, and bruised.

As Vaas watched him like a hawk, Tom developed a plan in his mind. It was simple. They believed he had a secret, and he did. What they didn't know was what it was. He could stall them by lying. But he wasn't a very good liar. How many lies would they go for until they lost their patience? That was the question. Vaas appeared too ready to pull the trigger if not for Coffee.

And what was Coffee's motivation? Did he want to keep Vaas from shooting Tom out of the goodness of his heart? Tom doubted that. There was something in it for Coffee. Why else would he loan his boat on an expedition to harpoon a prehistoric monster. *It might be ego,* Tom thought. *Then again, who knows?* Vaas gave the impression he wanted to kill Tom a moment ago. Coffee stopped him. Was it to keep blood from staining the deck of his yacht? If that was the reason, Tom decided he had to go with it.

Tom knew he needed to come up with other ideas. What could pass as a call to get the Loch Ness monster to surface? Heck, they'd never believe the truth, let alone any lie he made up. If he told them to play "Veni, Veni, Emmanuel", they'd shoot him and throw him over anyway.

Tom shook his head. Maybe that was it. The truth was so outlandish, he'd have to tell them something that would appeal to their reason, something they might believe, but something they'd need Tom to do, to help, so that they'd keep him alive.

But what could that be?

The boat proceeded westward. Saint Michael's Church was approaching on the yacht's left. It stood elegantly in the sunlight, its dark cross at its pinnacle decorating a blue sky. The rectory next to the church was quiet. The windows appeared dark. *Would any of the priests observe through the windows?* What happened to Caleb? Had he waited for him at the dock the night before and, sensing trouble, informed the priests? Was he somewhere able to help?

If Tom struggled with Vaas on the deck of the boat, could the priests call the authorities for assistance?

No, that wouldn't work. The authorities are bought by Coffee and Briggs.

The sky above was bright blue behind rapidly moving clouds. Was there a God? If there was, Tom would welcome some divine help right about now.

"So what's th' secret?"

Tom flinched at Vaas's question, hesitating.

"What's th' secret?" Vaas said again, this time more forcefully while jabbing the pistol pointed at Tom's chest.

"Don't you remember?" Tom said. "Paterson said it at the Council meeting. He used steaks and pork, and he put several of them over the side at one time. That's what he did."

"That's na' wha' ye did when ye brough' him up before th' boat blew up."

"So, you watched us? Is that what you did before you blew us up?"

Vaas didn't flinch. "I wouldn' be so crass if I were ye. That's a lovely girl ye've got yer heart set on. It would be a shame if somethin' would happen tae her while ye weren' on th' mainland tae protect her."

Tom felt a twinge of anger, but he forced himself not to react. Would Vaas make a phone call to one of his cronies and send them to threaten Marella? *Yes,* Tom thought. *Vaas was the kind of man who would do that.* "So, what kind of an answer do you want," Tom said.

"I wan' th' truth," Vaas said.

"Okay. But you won't believe the truth."

"Try me."

"We drank Guinness, and we sang songs."

"I'm abou' done wi' yer games." Vaas pointed the pistol at Tom's head.

"It's the truth. You saw us. We drank Guinness, and we sang religious songs because we were outside of Saint Michael's Catholic Church. In fact, there it is." Tom nodded his head to the building on the port side of the yacht. "You wanted the answer, and there it is."

Vaas paused. "Wha' songs?"

Tom said nothing.

"Might as well tell me, lad."

Tom grinned, daring Vaas to pull the trigger.

CHAPTER 49

Vaas stood up, this time placing the pistol inches from Tom's head. Tom sat back, acting calm, though inside his heart was like pistons going off in a racecar.

"I don't know. A bunch of them. Then they showed up. Maybe they knew it was us and they thought we had steak for them," Tom said.

Vaas was getting impatient.

Tom thought he'd better send Vaas down a path or else he'd lose his temper. "I have an idea. Maybe you could download several songs. I'm sure this yacht has speakers."

"I've go' my phone. I can download several songs," Coffee said. He had overheard them from the ship's control room.

"You have a speaker?" Tom asked. The sound of the motor hummed beneath them.

"Aye!" Coffee shouted back.

Vaas grunted. He didn't like the idea of religious songs playing when he was contemplating murder. Tom chuckled softly at the irony.

"Which songs!" Vaas shouted.

"Coffee, you able to search for Gospel songs?" Tom asked. Tom liked talking directly with Coffee, if only to cut Vaas out of the conversation and make him angry.

"Aye," Coffee said. He shut down the motor, and he maneuvered out of the control room and around the side of the boat where he dropped the anchor. The chain fell for several moments until the anchor rested on the Loch's floor bed seven hundred feet below the surface. Coffee approached Tom. Vaas stepped away, putting the pistol back in its holster. "I've go' my iPhone up," Coffee said. "Any artist in particular?"

Tom's mind worked. He tried to remember the other songs he and Sean Paterson sang, but he couldn't recall hem. It didn't matter. So long as they didn't download "Veni, Veni, Emmanuel" he could stall them. "Try something in Gospel," Tom said.

Coffee pressed several buttons on his phone. As he was doing it, Tom said, "You know, last time we brought the Loch Ness monster to the surface, we were also drinking Guinness."

"Don' e'en think abou' it," Vaas said.

"What? I'm just telling you what we did. You were watching us. If you want to do things the same as we did the other night, that's what we did."

Coffee pressed more buttons. "I wouldn' mind one myself," he said. "Okay, lad. I've go' Gospel. Wha' songs?"

Tom had to play his hand. "We had been drinking for some time. Read a few off to me and I'll let you know if any sound familiar."

"This is a waste o' time," Vaas said. "I should just pay a visit tae yer friends…"

"How about that beer?" Tom said to Coffee, interrupting.

"Check th' cooler," Coffee said.

Tom got up. Would Vaas stop him? To his surprise, he didn't. Tom reached into the cooler and pulled out two bottles. He tossed one to Coffee and another to Vaas.

Vaas caught it, fumbling his pistol.

Tom grabbed a third beer and broke it over the railing. Before Vaas gathered himself, Tom rushed, broken beer bottle in hand. A shot fired, but Tom lunged. He swung with his broken beer bottle. He felt a punch in the side. His broken glass missed its target. He fell onto the deck. Coffee and Vaas stood over him.

Vaas pointed the pistol at Tom's head.

"I may be th' money behind this operation, bu' tha' doesn' mean I'm foolish." Coffee turned to Vaas. "Looks like ye grazed his ribs."

Blood spilled on the deck. His side had been grazed by the bullet, and it bled out onto his shirt.

"Let's end him now and throw him o'er th' side," Vaas said. "We can get th' information another way."

"Na. I've seen this before in negotiations. He's tired, and he's runnin' out o' things tae say. We know there's a trick, bu' I believe he's givin' us decoys until he's got nothin' left but tae tell us th' real thin'," Coffee said. He picked up his phone. "Gospel music, right? We knew ye were singing. Wha' was it, lad? Ye don' wan' tae make my friend here more impatient than he already is."

Tom lay on his side, glaring at the two of them. They were on to him. They were also a lot smarter than he had hoped. He closed his eyes, knowing if he told them something other than the truth,

Vaas would pull the trigger and next go after Sean and Marella. He had to think of something.

"'Veni, Veni, Emmanuel'," Tom said. "That's the song. 'Veni, Veni, Emmanuel'." He opened his eyes.

"We don' need him anymore," Vaas said.

"We don' know tha'," Coffee said. "We can play it o'er th' speaker. If it works, we shoot th' lad and he dies quickly. If it doesn't, he goes o'er th' side and drowns."

"What's th' point o' keepin' him?"

"Tis possible there may be one or two more things he hasn' told us. We've got th' le'erage, and he's becomin' weak. If there's another item or two, we'll get them out o' him."

Vaas pointed the gun at Tom. "How about it, lad? Anything else ye want tae tell us,"

Tom remained silent. He shut his eyes.

"Tie him up," Coffee said. "Then we'll wait."

Vaas grabbed Tom by the collar and lifted him. Tom's legs were tired as he tried to stand. Vaas shoved him to the railing and took out his handcuffs. He put them on Tom's hands around his back. Tom stood next to the railing, and Vaas grabbed Tom and shoved his torso over the railing, holding him up by the collar. "Ye see tha' water down there, lad," Vaas said. "That's o'er two hundred meters deep. If ye fell down there and sank, na one would e'er find ye."

Tom said nothing. He was beyond fear. He questioned his life's meaning, and whether he would survive, or if he should come to accept death.

Vaas jerked Tom back up and threw him down on the hard seat. Tom lay on the seat on his side with his hands cuffed behind his back. Then he shifted his weight so that he sat upright.

Coffee said, "I've go' it downloaded. Now I just need tae connect it tae th' speakers."

Vaas took out his pistol again, pointing it at Tom's head. "Lad, ye'd better hope this works."

"What does it matter? You'll kill me anyway."

"Aye. Bu' one will involve a lo' more suffering than th' other."

CHAPTER 50

"Veni, Veni, Emmanuel" played over the yacht's speakers. Tom heard it, and he felt calm from the tone of the music. He didn't understand the words, as they were all in Latin, but he imagined in his head he was a part of the prayer, seeking divine assistance. The blue sky above him was majestic, rare for this time of year in Scotland. The sun was still high, with several hours to go before sunset.

Before, the monster had come out at night. *Would he come during the daylight?*

He remembered Father Gibson's words. "E'ery time," he had said. Every time the song was played, the monster surfaced. *Did the priests ever sing during the day?*

Tom cleared his mind. He needed another plan. The bottle hadn't worked. What could he do? He examined the deck. *Could he somehow blow up the yacht?* He didn't know how. He was too unfamiliar with yachts to know where the gas tank was. Maybe there was a flare gun somewhere. If he got his hands on one of those, could he shoot a flare into the gas tank? If he blew Vaas,

Coffee, and himself up, at least Marella would be safe. Would the curse be broken?

Who knows?

"How long did it take," Coffee said.

Tom said, "Don't remember."

"Tell him," Vaas demanded.

"I said I don't remember. The boat blew up underneath me right after, remember?" Tom's body ached, and he felt the pain in his side where the bullet had gone through him. His shirt had a hole in it, and his skin stung. Blood stained his shirt.

A lot of blood.

Vaas laughed. "Don' worry lad. Ye don' have much longer now." The music played. Each time the song ended, it returned to the beginning. In the distance stood the Church and the cross. He couldn't give up. Even though his hands were cuffed, there had to be a way. He scanned the deck. There were several locked compartment doors. Emergency flares had to be on the deck. They wouldn't be down below.

An idea came to him.

The ship's control room! That's where they had to be. It was somewhere over there.

He observed the ship's wheel. Coffee wasn't paying any attention to it as the yacht was sitting quietly, anchored to the floor of the Loch. There was a radio by the wheel. But who could he call? The two man police department? They'd be useless.

He knew he needed to find a compartment that contained a flare gun. He scanned the yacht for any sign of a compartment, and he found one, a small crease in the wall by the ship's wheel inside the control room. It was large enough. Maybe there would be a first aid bag in there as well.

Tom said, "You know, I'm bleeding pretty good here from that bullet. Do you have a first aid kit around where I could patch this thing up?"

Vaas said, "Don' worry. Patchin' ye up won' do ye any good."

Coffee said, "Afraid he's right, lad. I say ye've go' fifteen minutes. If yer friends don' surface by then, we won' have any more use fur ye."

Tom said a quiet prayer. The music relaxed him. Even under duress he was surprised he continued to have his wits.

"You mind if I at least look?"

"Ye're goin' tae sit righ' there," Vaas said. "Ye've had yer chance." Vaas stood up and walked over to Tom. "Bu', just fur th' hell o' it…"

Vaas raised his pistol and swung it at Tom's face, hitting him above the temple. Tom felt the blow and fell over. His head rang.

What the hell's wrong with this guy?

Tom raised his eyes at Vaas. Anger seethed inside him. He didn't know how, but so long as he was alive, he'd continue to find a way to survive.

CHAPTER 51

A few minutes passed. Tom gathered himself while he lied horizontally on the deck. Slowly, he clamored on his knees, and found the strength to sit on the seat. Vaas huffed, shaking his head. "Lad's go' some guts," Coffee said.

"So, what's the plan?" Tom said. "Why do you two even care about the Loch Ness monster? What's in it for you?"

Coffee and Vaas exchanged eye contact.

Vaas nodded.

Coffee said, "Tis simple. We're takin' Briggs tae th' Highland Council, and then th' Parliament. He's go' connections and th' willingness tae pass laws tae benefit us. If we get him up th' food chain, he'll vote tae eliminate our competition. My businesses will be able tae raise our prices, and we'll make more money."

"So, that's it? You're willing to kill to increase your power?"

"Tis na' th' foremost time," Vaas said smiling.

"Like the albino?"

Vaas grinned.

"You enjoy killing, don't you?"

"I do wha' has tae be done."

"He's our muscle," Coffee said. "I'm sure ye've figured tha' out by now. In order tae keep power, ye've got tae have someone willing tae do th' things behind th' scenes. Ye know, those things people wouldn' expect ye tae do."

Tom shook his head. "You're nothing but a Scottish mafia. You're all nothing but a crooked cartel, aren't you?" Tom wriggled his hands in his cuffs, trying to get his wrists out of their clasp. His hands couldn't wriggle free, and his wrists stung from the cuts.

"When yer friends surface," Coffee continued, "we'll catch one. Alive, maybe. Dead works though, tae. We have th' harpoon, and when it latches on, we'll drag it tae th' dock. Take a bunch o' pictures. Show th' world tha' it exists. And th' three o' us ge' credit."

"Minus one American," Vaas interrupted. "When he said 'three o' us,' he's talkin' abou' Briggs, Ewan, and me."

"I gathered that," Tom said.

"Bu' ye'll be a part o' th' story," Coffee said. "Tae bad ye, our poor American friend, were tae excited at th' sight o' th' Loch Ness monster. Ye leaned o'er th' railin' and fell o'er, only tae be devoured by th' prehistoric beast. That's why we had tae harpoon it. We tried tae keep it from killing ye, only ye were tae clumsy, and ye fell tae yer death."

"And that's how you're going to get away with this," Tom said. "You'll admit that I'm here, but that I came voluntarily. And you'll allow me to be a part of the story, but the locals will enjoy the fact that the American fell to his death. Is that it?"

"Pretty much," Vaas said. He grinned, holding the pistol. He scratched his red beard. "Ye'll go a clumsy hero, bu' Briggs gets th' credit fur bein' th' man in charge when th' monster is caugh'. He'll go high in politics, and we'll amass our fortunes t'gether."

"So what are they going to believe when they find my body and the cuffs are still on?"

"Won' matter. We run th' police aroun' here. Whate'er they report will be whate'er we tell them tae report."

"So much for honesty in government."

"Tis th' way o' th' world," Coffee said. "Good thing ye're learning it before 'tis tae late." Then Coffee laughed and leaned on the ships wheel. "Oh, that's right. '*Tis* tae late fur ye, isn't it?" He laughed some more. Vaas smirked, and aimed the barrel of the pistol at Tom.

Tom ran out of ideas. He had his hands cuffed, and he couldn't get a weapon. He couldn't go anywhere while Vaas was watching him. Coffee had his ship under control. And on the mainland Briggs handled the authorities. Everything was controlled by a system, one in which Tom had no influence.

Saint Michael's Church rested on the shoreline, its stone walls like a fortress under the blue sky. Tom wished he had spent more time inside…

"Wha' th' hell was tha'?" Coffee said. Tom had heard it, too. It was a sound below the yacht. It was a sound that caused the hairs on Tom's neck to stiffen.

Vaas's eyes focused toward the sound and away from Tom. His pistol lowered. He hesitated getting up, but the noise was so unusual his curiosity got the better of him. He stood and joined

Coffee. Vaas and Coffee leaned over the edge of the rail, mesmerized by the sound.

"Do ye smell somethin'?" Coffee said.

"Aye," Vaas said.

No more waiting. I have to act now!

CHAPTER 52

Tom planned his moves while Vaas and Coffee leaned over the side. They had their attention on the water, mesmerized at the prospect of seeing a prehistoric creature. Tom tiptoed past them to the control room. Coffee's phone rested next to the ship's wheel. It was hooked by a wire to the speaker system. With his feet, he kicked the wire off the phone. The music stopped. Coffee and Vaas didn't notice him. Both were so curious about the creature in the water that they paid no attention to Tom.

Tom bent down to find a weapon. Something.

Anything!

He pulled on the door to the control console, but it was stuck.

Then Vaas said, "Wait. Where'd he go?" Vaas pointed at him.

Tom hurried and pushed the phone on the top of his foot. Then, with one solid kick, he flung Coffee's phone into the air. The three of them watched as it disappeared over the edge and splashed into the dark waters.

"Ye son o' a bi'!" Coffee yelled. They rushed over to him, Vaas pointing the gun.

There was a loud roar from over the edge. Vaas stopped. As he pointed the pistol, he leaned over the railing.

Tom knew he had to make his escape. He jumped over the wheel's desk to the other side of the control room. While he was in the air, he heard a gunshot. He felt a bullet whizz past his head.

Vaas had missed.

Tom landed with a thud on the other side of the desk and fell on his side. It was a deeper fall than he thought it would be, and he felt his back twinge. He hurried to his feet and scuttled away, worried that they'd follow.

"Damn laddie," he heard from behind the wheel. Another roar bellowed from the port side of the boat. Tom's urge to look upon the creature grew stronger, but he knew if he did so he'd be dead. He had to find a way to escape.

"Look!" he heard. It sounded like Coffee. "Wha' is tha' thin'? Tis huge!"

"We need tae get tae work," Vaas said.

"Th' lad or th' monster?"

"Get th' monster. Th' lad isn' goin' anywhere."

Tom ran away from the voices to the ship's bow. He had to find a way to get more time. He cursed that he hadn't been able to get the flare gun. He searched around the bow. His eyes scanned right and left.

Nothing.

With his hands cuffed behind him he was completely helpless.

"Quick. Throw th' ropes o'er!" Vaas said.

"I'm workin' on it," Coffee yelled.

They sound frantic!

"Where th' hell are they!" Vaas's voice rose to the point of screaming.

"Damn it. They're goin' below th' surface!"

"Brin' them back up!" Vaas yelled over the railing. "Where's tha' damned laddie?"

With the creatures below, Vaas would come for him. Suddenly, a bullet hit the bow at his feet. Tom shuddered.

"Ye take one more step and I'll take ye out," Vaas said. He was pointing the pistol as he stood opposite the ships wheel inside the control room.

Tom froze.

Vaas swung his legs over the desk, and he slid down onto the bow. When he landed, he raised the pistol at Tom. "Come here, laddie."

Tom stood still.

"Time's up."

Tom didn't move.

"Alrigh', have it yer way." Vaas approached Tom. When he got close, he leaned forward and punched Tom in the stomach.

Tom doubled over. The wind had been knocked out of him.

"What's tha' song again, lad? We need tae know."

Tom hunched over for several moments. He did not speak.

"I'm getting' impatient."

Tom raised himself to his knees, and then stood up and faced Vaas. "Just pull the trigger."

"Lad. If I'd wanted tae kill ye, ye'd be dead already. Tell me th' song and I'll think abou' lettin' ye live."

"You're a liar. You'll kill me anyway."

Vaas grabbed Tom by the collar. He dragged him back around past the control room and he threw Tom down onto his seat. Coffee was working to get the ropes ready to capture the monster. "Ewan, do ye remember tha' song's name?"

"Vedi Vedi Vici, I think." Coffee said.

"'Veni, Veni, Emmanuel'," Tom said. "Now go ahead and pull the trigger."

Vaas grinned. "Ye know, in th' end, I always ge' wha' I want." He lifted his phone and pressed buttons.

Tom was too tired to move. He chose to sit, realizing it might be his last moment of daylight.

"Ah, found it," Vaas said. "Where do I plug in th' speakers?"

Coffee said, "O'er in th' control room by th' wheel. Should be a white wire somewhere on th' floor."

Vaas said to Tom, "Ye move, and I'll shoot. Bu' ye already know tha', don' ye?" He got up and went to the ship's wheel, where he kneeled down and picked up the white wire on the floor. In a few moments he had "Veni, Veni, Emmanuel" playing on the speakers as they had before.

"Think they'll come back?" Coffee stood over Tom.

"To hell with both of you," Tom said.

"Maybe they'll like th' way ye taste." Coffee laughed. "Actually, I'm surprised they didn' already make a meal out o' ye th' other night."

Tom glared at Coffee. If I had my hands free I'd…

"Lad, ye look like ye're gettin' quite upset," Coffee said. He rested his hands on his hips, arrogant and confident. "Oh, that's righ'. Ye didn' know we planted a bomb on McGavin's boat. Did

McGavin know, ye ask? Aye, he was a part o' it. He was goin' tae sell th' boat, but when we told him he would ge' a large insurance claim from Briggs' insurance company, he agreed. He'd pocket far more money tha' way. Once he reported th' accident, all th' authorities had tae do was confirm negligence on yer part. Then he'd ge' a sizeable check." Coffee laughed. "I though' it was a great idea, bu' Briggs gets th' credit fur tha' one."

"Veni, Veni, Emmanuel" played over the speakers. "Winnin' always makes me feel good," Vaas said.

"Shouldn' be long now," Coffee said. He left Tom and worked on the ropes.

"Is th' harpoon gun ready?"

"Go double check. I'll finish these, and when something comes up in th' water, I'll le' ye know."

"Canno' wait tae see th' blood in th' water once I harpoon th' bastard!" Vaas walked past Tom. He sneered at him, taunting him with his soon-to-be victory.

Tom grew furious. His insides swelled with rage. He tried to stay calm and think tactically, but what was the point? Vaas already had the song playing over the speakers. He'd play it until the monsters resurfaced.

What the hell!

He flung his leg out and kicked Coffee in the rear. Coffee stumbled, and then lost his balance.

"Aaaghh!" Coffee yelled as he and the ropes fell over the side of the boat. He reached out with one hand and caught himself from falling into the water. He hung over the side. "Pull me up!"

Tom stood up and ran to the aft of the boat.

Vaas pulled out his pistol but hesitated, turning first to Tom and then to Coffee.

Tom ran.

He expected a shot in the back.

Then he heard Vaas swear behind him.

Did Vaas Misfire? Or maybe he was out of bullets?

Tom didn't wait to find out. He saw a door, and he rammed into it with his shoulder. The impact made a blunt "thwang" sound. It didn't open. Tom felt pain in his shoulder from the impact.

Then he went to the railing. There wasn't anywhere to go. He turned around. Vaas was helping Coffee up over the rail and onto the deck.

Tom leaned over the side. The blue water splashed against the side of the yacht. Then something moved under the surface, and quickly disappeared.

Nessie. It had to be!

A roar rose from the depths. It sounded so ancient Tom couldn't make sense of it. It didn't sound like any creature he had ever heard. His hairs on his arms tingled.

He noticed something move to his right. *Was that movement? A second one?*

It was like a serpent in the water. Then a large mound rose from below the surface. Streams of water ran down its ridged back before it disappeared below the surface. It moved so quickly, so stealthily. In half a second, it was gone. *No wonder it had stayed hidden all this time.*

"He's back!" Coffee frantically worked the nets again. "Tis our lucky day, tae. There's more than one!"

Vaas let out a grunt and put his pistol back in his holster. "Dammi'. Stay on th' creatures. Get one o' them. Don' le' them ge' away!" He moved over to the harpoon gun which was still connected to its stand. He struggled pointing it at the monsters. "Hey, how do I work this thin'?"

Tom recognized that Vaas's attention had focused on the creatures.

He decided he had a plan.

"What the hell," Tom said. "What have I got to lose?"

CHAPTER 53

Coffee tried to untangle the nets. "Th' ropes won' separate!" he shouted.

Vaas yelled back, "Hurry!"

"Those creatures are makin' me nervous!"

"No time fur tha'!"

Tom watched from the aft of the boat as Coffee failed to work the nets in the calm purposeful way they had planned. The nets appeared cumbersome, and Coffee had trouble lifting them. They were made of thick rope designed for deep sea whaling. Coffee's inexperience showed.

"Damned thing's tangled," Coffee said.

Vaas worked the harpoon gun. It remained connected to its stand. "Can I disconnect this thin'?"

"Aye. Bu' if ye're goin' tae fire it, make sure we've go' a rope connected." Coffee returned to the netting.

"Veni, Veni, Emmanuel" played over the speakers.

A prehistoric roar echoed from the depths below. The sound made Tom shudder. Vaas and Coffee glanced at each other, shaken and confused.

"Damn, wha' th' hell is tha' thin'?" Coffee said.

"Shut up and just find a way tae catch it," Vaas said.

"Smells like rottin' fish!"

Vaas didn't respond. He ran to Coffee and helped with the netting. "Get these nets workin', and do it now. We don' have any time tae waste. Catch th' creature. Damned harpoon is on th' wrong side o' th' boat!"

The two worked furiously on the ropes. Tom was amazed that they ignored him, especially after he had been a thorn in their side for so long. It gave him another idea. His hands were still behind him. Could he ram one of them? If they stay close to the railing, he could take one of them out. He might go over the side, but if he took one of them with him...

"There's a third one!" Coffee said. He pointed at the water.

Tom peered over the railing. A darker, larger ridgeback broke the surface of the water. Tom's eyes widened at its size, and its speed. The water broke on either side of its ridge, much the way he remembered the water did around the dorsal fin in the movie "Jaws". It turned quickly, went below the surface, then it appeared several yards closer to the yacht in the blink of an eye.

"They move tae fast," Coffee said.

"Damn it. Get one tae come o'er here!" Vaas yelled. He opened his end of the net, and he walked away from Coffee, stretching the net out. The net had a length of thirty feet. The two of them held their corners. Coffee struggled. He didn't appear strong enough for the weight of the ropes. If Tom would ram one of them, he'd go for Coffee first. Then, Vaas would be left alone to fend for himself.

"Come on, Nessie. Come tae th' boat!" Coffee said. He lifted the net high, but his arms were not strong enough to keep it up but for a moment.

"This isn' goin' tae work," Vaas said. "We need tae harpoon one foremost tae latch ontae it. Then we drag it o'er wi' th' rope tae throw th' net on it."

"Okay." Coffee turned, just in time to see Tom running at him with his head and shoulder down.

Tom let out a battle cry, as though he'd send Coffee down to the depths of hell.

Coffee, holding the net, stepped backward two steps. He still held the net.

Tom, having closed his eyes for the impact, ran head-first into the netting, his momentum carrying him over the railing. He found himself caught in the rope. He swung back and his body rammed against the side of the yacht.

"That's it," Vaas said. "Lift him up. I've had it wi' this lad. We don' need him anymore, and tis time we ge' rid o' him."

Tom felt the net being pulled. He kicked his legs with his hands still cuffed behind him, but he got more entangled.

They brought him up over the railing, and dropped him onto the deck. Vaas kicked him while Tom wriggled to free himself.

"Where th' hell's my gun," Vaas said. He stopped kicking Tom and reached for his pistol. He pulled it out and pulled the trigger. It clicked. "Damn it. I didn' reload."

Coffee stood, watching.

Tom saw his moment, and he wriggled free from the netting. Without stumbling, he climbed to a knee and lifted himself. He ran to the yacht's starboard side.

Coffee gave chase.

Straight ahead, the walls of Saint Michael's Church loomed in the distance. Tom ran, knowing Coffee chased him in pursuit. He sprinted to the railing. When he got to within a few feet, he leaped, trying to get his right foot on the railing.

His foot landed on it.

He tried to jump, but he slipped instead.

His feet flew high into the air, and Tom fell backwards over the railing and alongside the hull of the yacht. The air breezed past him. He saw the gray clouds and the bright sun and the white side of the yacht and the blue water and the church and the clouds again as he spun in the air.

With a slap, Tom landed on his back into the water. It stung his torso and he couldn't breathe.

He gasped for air.

Then he sucked water into his lungs as he sank below the surface.

CHAPTER 54

Tom kicked his legs in the water, but they were slowed by the currents. He opened his eyes. The water was murky, but a light penetrated it. First it was there, and then it wasn't, and then it was again. Tom's eyes stung. He tried to swim to the light, but the currents disoriented him. A fish swam near him. His lungs tried to cough. Death ran through his thoughts.

He was about ten feet below the water. He kicked and wriggled, just to get air. He felt water displacement. He shifted to his right as the water pushed him. Something large sped behind him. He let out a scream. The water was too dark. He caught the movement of a large shape. It terrified him. Then another force pushed water behind him, forcing him forward. The large shape disappeared. He kicked towards the light, his air running out.

His head popped out of the water. He gasped for air, and kicked harder. His shoes weren't helping, so he kicked hard, and then with one foot he pushed off one of his shoes. He did it again, and the other shoe dropped off his feet. He found more power in his feet, but his socks felt strange as they moved in the water.

Another large push of water went past him. He yelled. Fear gripped. He imagined the monsters would eat him. He remembered the replica plesiosaur from the museum, how those teeth bore down at his head when he turned the corner.

Oh my God. Three of them are in here with me!

He shifted onto his back, and he kicked. He swam away from the yacht. He didn't want to be eaten. That wasn't how he was supposed to go.

God, don't let the bad guys win!

He kicked, his head facing the sky. His hands were still cuffed behind his back. He struggled to keep afloat. Coffee's yacht floated in the water beyond Tom's feet. Coffee and Vaas worked on the deck, yelling. Tom suspected they weren't as coordinated as they had planned.

The boat floated in the distance. Vaas went to the side of the yacht and pointed at him. The two yelled at each other. Coffee wanted to get the monster, but Vaas appeared more concerned that Tom was getting away.

Tom got into a rhythm. He kicked and arched his back, breathing air and moving further from the yacht.

He heard something. *Was that a motor?* Coffee's yacht was drifting further away. Vaas pointed at Tom, waiving his pistol.

He's going to shoot!

An arm appeared inches from his face. It was right above him. He yelled, surprised it was on top of him. It reached down and grabbed him by the shirt.

"I swear, ye've go' more lives than an alley cat," said a voice. Tom was lifted out of the water and into a boat. It was a small one, but sleek. He saw whose arm it was.

"Thank God," Tom said.

It was Caleb.

CHAPTER 55

"How'd you know to find me," Tom said. He rested on the floor of the boat. It was a speed boat, with lots of technical devices.

"Stay down!" Caleb said.

A shot rang from the yacht. The bullet whizzed past them.

Caleb turned on the motor and sped away from the yacht, out of range of Vass's pistol. When they were several hundred yards away, Caleb stopped the boat.

"Father Gibson's been watchin' from o'er at th' Church," Caleb said. "When ye weren' at th' dock last night, I suspected somethin' happened. What'd they do, kidnap ye?"

"Pretty much," Tom said.

Caleb pulled out a set of wire cutters. "I don' have a key, bu' this will at least ge' yer hands free. Stand up and turn around." Tom did so, and he heard the break of his cuffs. His arms were suddenly able to move. His shoulders had been stiff from being in that position for so long. He moved his arms in circles a few times to get the blood flowing. "Now give me yer wrists. Let's ge' these things off ye."

Caleb was freed Tom's wrists. Coffee's yacht floated several hundred yards away from them. The small images of Coffee and Vaas were trying to get the harpoon gun disconnected.

"The monsters are over there," Tom said. "Three of them."

Caleb said, "Aye. Father Gibson said he though' there was more than one." The cutter broke Tom's metal cuffs, and they fell to the floor in a metallic clang. Tom picked them up and threw them at the yacht. They landed in the water, causing a small splash, and they sank below the surface. Caleb sat in the captain's chair. "What do ye wan' tae do?"

"You're leaving it all up to me?" Tom laughed. "I came here to finish this. I'm not going to let them get away with this. We have to stop them. Not sure how, but we have to stop them."

"Do they have any weapons?"

"Yeah. Vaas has a hand gun. And there's a harpoon gun on the yacht. How about us? Do we have any weapons?"

"I've go' a flare gun in tha' compartment. Two shots, one fur each o' them."

"That's not much."

"Tell me abou' it. When we get on board, wha' do we wan' tae do?"

"Get them off that boat. Tie them up? I don't know. Something. Anything. I asked Marella to contact the US Embassy. I hope they show up."

"Tha' would be good, bu' there's na tellin' if they'll show up in time."

"It's up to us, then. No time like the present. Let's go save some dinosaurs!"

CHAPTER 56

Caleb's hair blew in the wind as he pressed on the gas and steered the boat back toward the yacht. Tom was surprised at how the boat picked up speed. The air rushed past him, blowing his hair. The yacht loomed large ahead.

A figure appeared over the yacht's railing. It was Vaas. He stood still, and raised his arms.

Tom and Caleb heard a metallic clink muffled by the sound of the motor. "What was that?" Tom asked.

"He's shootin' at us!" Caleb said. "Duck, and hang on!" He pressed the gas full throttle. The boat flew over the water. Vaas aimed and shot at Caleb and Tom.

Clink!

Clink!

Tom ducked down. He heard glass shatter. Caleb's head rocked violently amidst shards of glass, and then fell forward. His shoulders pressed against the throttle. The motor's engine grew louder. Caleb had been shot dead. The metallic clinks continued to his the boat.

Tom peered over the dashboard. Caleb's boat approached the yacht at an incredible speed. He knew he had to get out. He stood atop his char.

Clink!

Clink!

Vaas was shooting with better accuracy as Tom neared the yacht. Tom heard more glass shatter. He put his wet feet on the edge of the boat. He felt clumsy as he tried to balance. He leaned forward. He lunged into the Loch, ten feet from the yacht. His legs whipped sideways as the force of impact slapped his body into the water.

He heard a loud crash, and an explosion. His head popped out of the water just as yellow and orange flames blew out of the yacht. Heat touched his wet skin. He tried to swim, but suddenly felt a current. It pulled him toward the yacht. He tried to swim the opposite way, but it was too strong. The boat's impact made a gaping hole in the hull of the yacht. As the cold water rushed in, it sucked Tom into the hull. The sun disappeared as the currents of the water pulled Tom inside the yacht's hull.

When he was inside, he gathered himself. He examined Caleb's boat, smashed and broken in pieces inside the hull of the yacht. He scanned the area to determine where he was. Several metallic gears and pipes reflected the light from the flames. Tom determined he was inside the yacht's engine room.

The current continued to push water inside the hull. *This ship is going down fast*! As Tom tried to steady himself, he remembered the compartment in Caleb's boat. *Flare guns!* The compartment door was cracked open. He opened the broken door.

Then he heard the voices coming from above. There was a door that opened, and light appeared. The light uncovered a stairwell. Tom knew he had to act. He found a bag inside the compartment. Without opening it, he grabbed the bag and pulled it out of the boat.

"Damn it! Damn it!" Coffee came rushing down. "They go' us. This ship is goin' down. Na way can we repair tha' hole. We've go' tae abandon ship."

Vaas said, "We aren' goin' anywhere until we capture one o' those creatures."

"Bu' we're goin' down."

"Ye radio Briggs fur help. He'll send another boat. In th' meantime, we've go' tae harpoon one o' these beasts. I don' care if we catch one and it goes down wi' this damned ship, we're na' goin' tae fail at our mission!" Vaas's voice was becoming unstable.

"Wha' happened tae th' two o' them?"

Vaas flashed a light. The light hit Caleb's hair. Caleb's body was slumped in his chair. "That's th' one I got. Th' American must have drowned in th' Loch. I don' think he survived." Vaas turned off the flashlight. "Come on. We've go' work tae do."

Tom hid in a dark crack. Water filled the hole. Flames danced and spurted around Tom. He smelled fuel. He had to leave the area, but he needed them to leave first.

Then Coffee and Vaas climbed up the stairs. Tom watched them from the shadows. When the two of them departed the room, they left the door ajar.

A way out!

The rising water forced him to keep his head up. He knew if they had hung around a few more seconds, his head would have been in view. He swam over to the shadows and opened the bag. There was a first aid kit, a radio, and a flare gun. He held it up and examined it. He made sure it was ready. "Two shots," Tom said.

Caleb's boat took on its own water, and lowered into the torrent of flooding water. Caleb's body was drifting in the rising water. Caleb's head sank under the current. Tom felt sadness. *Caleb had been a help to him before anyone else,* he thought. Tom had to survive, if only to testify to Caleb's heroism.

Caleb's death had to be known.

And those who caused it would have to pay.

Tom swam to the stairs. Cold water rushed between his toes. His toes cramped, locking together. He knew he hadn't had much to drink in the past twenty-four hours. He put his hands below the water and massaged them, trying not to let out a sound. The cramp went away.

He found the stairs. Above him, the door was still open. The ship was leaning to the port side as it sank into the water. The stairs were off kilter as they protruded out of the rising water. Tom held the flare gun in his hands, and his socks made squishing sounds as he took the steps up to the door and leaned against the angled wall.

* * *

"Get him!" he heard. Tom crouched on the stairs and listened. He expected a shadow to come at him through the doorway, but he heard a loud roar instead. It came from the port side, and it echoed through the hull and into the room where he was. "He's caught. I told ye we didn' need th' harpoon." The voice was Coffee's. Tom took a step, his legs now out of the water. He heard the water drain from his jeans and land on the steps, and Tom was nervous the two of them heard him through the doorway.

"Tighten it, damn it!" Vaas was barking orders. "Don' le' him ge' away!"

Another roar bellowed, and then a second. *The creatures are loud,* Tom thought. *They sound angry!*

Tom continued up to the top of the stairs. He heard "Veni, Veni, Emmanuel", which was still playing on Vaas's phone over the yacht speakers. Tom reached the doorway, his eyes adjusting to the light. Coffee was tugging at the rope. Coffee and Vaas had pulled on the ropes until it appeared that whatever they had caught was wrapped inside the heavy netting.

Time was disappearing. Tom knew he had to act now if he was going to save the Loch Ness monster.

CHAPTER 57

"I think we've go' him. Hold him while I go tell Briggs tae ge' some help," Vaas said. He left Coffee alone and walked out of sight. Tom presumed he had gone to his phone inside the control room.

This was his chance. He crept through the door into the light. Coffee was entranced with the creature over the edge, not paying attention to anything around him. Tom felt the deck flooring through his wet socks. He approached with stealth. He hoped his dripping clothes wouldn't attract attention as he moved toward him. He clasped the flare gun in his hand, double checking it to make sure it was ready to fire.

Two shots!

He came within a yard of Coffee. Coffee hadn't noticed him. Vaas was by the ship's wheel, working the phone and dialing a number. He was focused on his phone.

Tom only had a moment.

Tom reached out and tapped Coffee on the shoulder. Coffee, smiling at his capture, turned around expecting to boast to Vaas.

Only it wasn't Vaas. It was Tom. Coffee frowned.

Tom didn't give him a chance to react. He had the gun pointed at his torso and he fired. A hot red streak shot from the gun and hit Coffee squarely in the chest.

Flames spurted from the projectile, lighting his shirt on fire. Coffee flew backward against the railing.

He screamed. It was a scream of a man in severe pain. He writhed on the deck floor. A red and orange burst of fire poured from his chest. His white clothes caught fire and the fire enveloped Coffee while the red and orange flare spewed out of him. The screams grew louder.

Tom heard a shot behind him, and he felt something like a hammer hit him in the arm.

Vaas! I'm hit!

Tom stumbled but gathered himself and ran. His arm was numb. He found the open door to the engine room where the water was rushing in, and he dove inside as another bullet whizzed and clinked against the wall. Tom flew through the air, and landed head first into the onrushing water. He held his breath and swam several strokes underneath the water, searching for a place to hide. He heard gun shots above him and he saw dark lines of bubbles as bullets penetrated the water. He swam to the bottom of the engine room, hiding in the shadows.

He swam to a dark corner. He surfaced under the shadows and he raised his head to get air. He tried not to make any noise. The sound of the water filling the yacht echoed inside the room. The doorway was open, and Vaas was no longer standing in the light. The air was rushing in as the yacht was sinking lower.

He had to find a way to get Vaas.

The monster was now captured by the net, and it would only be a moment before Vaas had found a way to harpoon it. But with Coffee now dead or dying, there would be no telling what Vaas would do.

He swam. Vaas's shadow was guarding the doorway. "Ye can stay in there, lad. I don' care if this boat drags ye down tae th' depths o' hell!" He slammed the door, and the room went dark.

Another roar echoed from outside the boat. It was the plesiosaur, and it was trapped in the net against the yacht's hull. Tom felt the animal's anger, and its power.

Another roar echoed.

Tom remembered there were three of them. He had to get out. The gasoline smelled stronger in the engine room. There were small flames dancing on the surface of the water.

He had an idea.

He studied to the water where the gasoline was coming out of the boat. He climbed up on the stairs. He pointed the flare gun at the water, and he pulled the trigger.

A reddish orange streak flew into the water, and the entire room was lit with an inferno.

A large explosion went off. Tom was knocked back into the wall. The entire boat rocked. More of the exterior where Caleb's boat had crashed had been blown off.

Flames engulfed the water, and the entire engine room caught fire.

Smoke filled the room. He went to the door. It was locked. Tom tested it, and he found its structure wasn't very solid. He backed up, and he threw his shoulder into the door.

It budged.

He took some steps back from the door, and he charged. He put all his weight into the door, and it broke from the hinges. Tom fell through the doorway into the sunlight. Smoke followed with him.

He moved to a crouched position and held the empty flare gun with both hands, expecting Vaas. But Vaas wasn't around. The netting was being tugged by the creature. He scanned the area, pointing his flare gun. He had no shots left, but he didn't know whether Vaas would know that or not.

Coffee's body lay in flames on the deck. He was motionless. His shirt had caught fire and charred his face and torso. They were black under the sunlight.

The smell of rotting fish and charred flesh permeated the air.

The monster's breath!

The yacht shifted violently as it sank into the water. Tom's wet socks caused him to slip. The deck had leaned farther now. Tom removed his socks and threw them over the edge into the water, exposing his bare feet. He pressed his cramping toes into the grips where he maintained his balance.

He peered around the edge of a small wall. Vaas was not there. He noticed, though, that "Veni, Veni, Emmanuel" was no longer playing on the speakers. Was Vaas trying to get off the boat? Was there an escape raft somewhere?

That was it! Vaas was planning his escape.

Tom stood up. He surveyed the boat. A roar by the monster in the net echoed from the water. It was so mysterious, so ancient, so powerful, so prehistoric. Every time Tom heard it, he felt a connection to the earth's four billion year old history. It was impossible for him not to stop in his tracks.

He heard something behind him. He blinked just as Vaas's fist swung down upon him.

He tried to move, but the fist caught him in the forehead. Tom flew back. He landed with a thud on the hard deck behind him. The floor underneath him was now at a twenty-five degree angle because of the sinking yacht. Vaas was standing just downhill from Tom.

Vaas raised his pistol. "I'm goin' tae enjoy pullin' this trigger, lad."

Tom shut his eyes, waiting for the loud gunshot, expecting the end.

CHAPTER 58

Without warning, the boat's deck exploded. Pieces of the boat flew in all directions. Fuel and fire exploded from the engine room, scorching anything it their path. Tom flew backwards. Vaas had stumbled, being knocked down the angled floor to the cold water below.

This was his chance. With ringing in his ears, he stood up and rushed Vaas. He leaped upon him, knocking him into the railing that was just below the surface of the water.

Vaas tried to point the gun, but he fell upon his shoulder, unable to bring it up. He pulled the trigger, and a bullet flew into the air.

Tom punched at Vaas viciously. Kneeling over his adversary, he brought his fists down upon Vaas over and over again, straining with each swing of his arm.

Vaas brought his elbows up to protect his face and body, but Tom's rage got the better of him. Vaas dropped his gun and it splashed on the flooding deck floor and rested just under the water's surface.

Tom punched over and over and over again.

The boat lurched, and the deck beneath Tom sank, then rose, then fell hard with a splash into the water. The yacht was nearly submerged. The heat from the fire burned his skin. The unsteady movements of the sinking yacht made Tom hesitate. Vaas slowed his motions also. The gun was underwater resting on the railing. Vaas reached for it. Tom clenched his fist and struck Vaas in the ribs, and again in the face.

Vaas never grabbed the gun. He raised his arms to defend against Tom's blows.

Tom held nothing back. He unleashed a volley of punches with his fists.

Vaas made a move with his legs that twisted Tom's hurt ankle.

Tom winced, and Vaas regained control. He flung Tom back onto the deck and stood up. He went for the gun, but Tom kicked Vaas in the knee, and his knee buckled. Tom crouched and leaped for the gun. His hands touched it, but couldn't clasp it.

Vaas also reached for it.

Neither was able to handle the gun because of the efforts of the other, when Vaas accidentally pushed it over the railing and it sank into the deep darkness of the Loch.

Relieved the gun was gone, Tom smiled.

Then Vaas took a right elbow and swung it hard into Tom's head.

Tom fell backwards and landed on his rear. He saw stars and his head rang.

Vaas stood, angrily. He went to Tom and got on one knee, held him down with his left grip, and punched furious blows with a clenched right fist. Vaas's jabs were swift and strong, like they came from someone trained in hand to hand combat.

Tom blocked some of the blows, but too many were reaching him.

Vaas would try to beat him senseless before he drowned him.

The boat shifted, and the monster roared. Tom felt water as his legs sank below the surface. Tom knew he had to find a way to win, to escape, and to free the Nessie.

But Vaas was just too physically strong for him.

He didn't know what he could do. But he brought his knee up forcefully which hit Vaas in the thigh, tipping him off balance. Tom, his adrenaline rushing, stood up quickly. The deck was leaning now over forty-five degrees. He felt his toes dig into the surface of the deck, but it was getting too slippery. Ropes and machinery fell into the water. Smoke from the burning wood pumped into the skies. He heard the sound of distant sirens.

Vaas stood up.

Tom's eyes met Vaas's, and he vowed he would never give in to defeat.

CHAPTER 59

The starboard side of the yacht had risen high above the water as the yacht tipped over, leaving the port railing under the Loch's surface. Pieces of the burning yacht tumbled down the slanted deck into the water, splashing foam on the surface before they plunged to the depths below.

As the equipment fell, Tom had an idea in his mind. He climbed to the starboard railing which was still sticking out of the water at the top end of the deck. The ropes of the net were being tugged, and the large plesiosaur on the other side was tugging on the ropes. The boat, as it was mostly underwater, was rocking at the giant monster's efforts. The shifting made it difficult for Tom to stand and keep his balance, but it was hard for Vaas to keep his also. Tom climbed up high and he stole a glance of the Loch Ness monster.

And he saw it clearly in the daylight for the first time.

The monster was about thirty feet long. Its body was dark, almost black. No wonder it was so hard to find in the murky waters of Loch Ness. It was sleek and powerful, though. Its muscles bulged on either side of its ridgeline. Four massive fins moved back and forth. A long muscular neck protruded from its body, ending in a head with green eyes.

Its head snapped at the large ropes holding it to the yacht. It was trying to chew the ropes, and several sections of the rope had been cut. Its teeth were sharp. They flashed white as the creature chomped at the inch-thick ropes.

A smallish tail swung back and forth with each powerful stroke of its fins. The monster was incredibly stealthy, incredibly powerful, and incredibly amazing!

Then he saw the others.

Two more plesiosaurs swam around the third. *It was a family!* They were smaller than the one which was caught, but they had the same physique, the same attributes. Tom was amazed with the speed which they swam in the water. He had thought dinosaurs were slow moving, and any sea monster would be slow in the water.

Not so.

These were quick, able to navigate in the water with ease, turning on a dime despite their massive frame and elongated neck. They swam under and around the large one in the net, roaring and calling for it to escape.

The yacht descended into the water and tipped to the port side. The deck disappeared below the murky waters of the Loch. He would have to loosen the net, or else the monster would sink with the yacht and drown somewhere below the Loch's seven hundred foot depths.

Vaas grit his teeth. Sweat and blood dripped from his forehead as he seethed with every breath. He appeared tired, and physically beaten. Tom had delivered several significant blows. Vaas was twenty feet away from Tom, and he rested his left arm over the starboard railing as the ship shifted and creaked and burned. The monster roared again, and Tom's neck hairs stiffened. *It was so powerful,* he thought.

Tom said, "Let him go."

"He belongs tae Scotland," Vaas said.

"That doesn't mean you should kill it."

"He's ours tae do wi' as we please. He'll serve our purpose." Then Vaas scanned what was left of the boat. The harpoon gun glimmered in the sunlight, still in its stand. He made a move for it.

Tom had forgotten about the harpoon gun. He left the net and ran toward it. He felt his toes on the deck, and he tried not to slip. He held the railing to keep from falling into the water.

Vaas had reached the harpoon gun first. It was slightly in the water, but he was working to figure it out.

Tom leaped and landed on Vaas.

Vaas let go of the harpoon gun.

Tom noticed the harpoon was attached to a rope which was floating in the water.

Vaas struggled, and Tom grabbed the rope on the gun. He swung it down, and wrapped it around Vaas's mid-section. He held Vaas down with his left hand.

He remembered the bowline knot Sean Paterson had taught him on the tiny rowboat. He moved his right wrist instinctively and tied the bowline knot together in three quick moves. He pulled the rope taught as Vaas punched Tom in the ribs.

Tom got up while taking the blows. He reached for the trigger from the harpoon gun. Vaas punched Tom in the face, and Tom raised his arms to block the blows. Vaas tried to stand, and Tom shoved him. Vaas fell backward, regained himself, and charged. Tom reached for the harpoon gun again and aimed it high into the air above the Loch Ness monster.

He pulled the trigger.

A loud bang shot the metallic spear parallel along the surface of the water. Vaas was just about to reach Tom, when the rope went taught. It yanked Vaas off balance, and he stumbled over the starboard railing and slid down the hull into the water. He splashed into the Loch and put his head up out of the water to breathe.

Tom leaned over the railing. Vaas was only a few feet from the captured plesiosaur. Vaas swam back towards the yacht. Then the two free plesiosaurs moved towards him.

The monsters had found Vaas. Vaas's head swiveled from side to side as two muscular necks on either side of him raised their serpent-like heads out of the water. The heads hovered six feet above the waves, their massive bodies appearing like large shadows below the surface. Their bodies lowered, their necks stiffened.

Vaas yelled, "Ge' away from me!" Terror filled his voice. "Ge' away from me!"

The creatures didn't go away. Their heads raised high into the air, like asps about to strike. They studied Vaas as he splashed and yelled. They communicated with each other with slight gestures. Their lips curled showing teeth, and their nostrils flared as they took in Vaas's scent. Nearby, the captured plesiosaur writhed inside the net. It let out a loud roar.

Suddenly, the dark eyes of the two free plesiosaurs flashed, and then the monsters struck simultaneously. Their muscle-bound necks moved with lightning speed and precision, like a viper striking at its prey. Their rows upon rows of white teeth clamped down on Vaas's flesh.

One struck Vaas in the abdomen, while the other inserted its razor sharp teeth into Vaas skull, penetrating his eye socket.

Vaas let out a blood curdling scream. It was filled with both terror and pain. His arms flung, trying to beat the monsters. It had no effect. Water splashed red and white with foam and bubbles and blood.

The monsters pulled Vaas apart.

Vaas cried in agony as water entered his lungs. His legs kicked and splashed the surface of the water one final time.

Then he was still.

Vaas disappeared below the waves as the creatures pulled him under. A pool of blood spread ten feet wide along the surface of the water. Something floated to the top and bobbed up and down. It was Vaas's right arm, the one he had held the pistol with for so many hours. Tom dry heaved at the sight. Then he closed his eyes and breathed heavily.

The two free plesiosaurs did not return to the surface, but the third let out a roar, still captured in the net.

Then Tom heard sirens. Several boats sped toward him. Hot flames leapt from large pieces of the exploded yacht. The fuel on the water burned. Smoke rose high into the sky above the town of Thurwick.

The ship's deck cracked. Tom grimaced at Coffee's charred body. Coffee's body slid down the slanted deck, and then it splashed into the water. Coffee's body floated on the surface of the

Loch, his charred chest swaying below the surface of the murky water.

Tom didn't have much time. He had to free the creature, or else those in the boat would try to catch it.

He went to the net. The ropes were complicated. It appeared they were like knots. He found some of the knots, and he tried to untie them but they were too tight. The ropes were too bulky. They twisted and tugged with each jerk of the plesiosaur.

The monster roared again. He felt tension.

The boats were approaching too quickly. He heard someone over a loud speaker, but he couldn't make out the words from the rising air bubbles, the creaking yacht, and the burning flames. Smoke filled Tom's lungs. He sweated, pulling and tugging at the ropes. The deck was falling apart, and his right foot fell into the water. He was going to be swimming with the plesiosaurs soon.

Coffee's body was floating away, his nose and toes poking out of the surface of the water. Tom didn't want to end up like Vaas or Coffee, a meal for prehistoric animals. Still, Tom knew he had to rescue this one animal.

The creature tugged, flapping its mighty fins. The boat creaked as it tugged. The creature's prehistoric muscles bulged. Its head chomped at the ropes. The boat was disappearing below the water's surface. It was going down, and in another minute, he'd be swimming.

He pulled the ropes. There were no knives around. The ones he bought from the store were stolen when they had kidnapped him last night. He worked the knot, not giving up. His body sank further into the cold water of the Loch. The monster's head writhed, and let out a roar. The motors of the approaching boats echoed now above the sound of the flames.

Tom gave one last pull on an end-piece of rope. A knot slipped undone. The net gave way, and the plesiosaur disappeared with a mighty stroke of its fins, splashing gallons of water at Tom.

Tom clambered on top of the last remaining part of the yacht. The boat shifted violently, and Tom scrambled to find a safe place to float. A piece of wood. A flotation device. Anything to stay above water, so that the creatures didn't come up and tear off his leg.

His eyes surveyed the scene.

Where was Coffee's body?

Did they eat him?

The flames were too strong, and the last remaining piece of ship was burning. He had to jump into the water. He had no choice. He leaped feet first into the water and he treaded along the surface. He heard a roar from below the water. He breathed quickly, fearing that the monsters would surface and take off his leg. Within seconds, the last of the smoke disappeared as the final remains of the yacht dipped below the surface of the water.

Then the boat arrived. Men wearing the strange uniforms stood all along the deck. They each held rifles. The boat neared Tom, and one of the men grabbed him. They lifted him up over the side and, once on the deck, threw him down into the boat.

"Where's Vaas? Where's Coffee!" one of the men yelled. Tom expected to get bludgeoned with the gun. "What's tha'?" he said.

Tom heard it, too. Was that a motor? It sounded different, and it came from the air. Tom sat up. The men in the boat listened toward the sound.

Helicopters.

Several of them.

They were approaching the Loch over the town of Thurwick. They were coming fast, their noses dipped.

They were military helicopters.

Tom stood. More boats came from the direction of the dock. They had several men on them. However, the boats stopped, and their passengers watched the approaching helicopters. *Who were they?*

Then one hovered over Tom and the men. The wind from the blades blew on the boat, unsettling all the men with guns. A painting of a flag was on the side of the helicopter. It was the insignia of the Royal Army. A man pointed a loud speaker at the boat. "Lower yer weapons. This is th' Royal Army. Ye are all holding illegal firearms. We demand ye hand o'er Tom Wayne immediately."

Marella did it. She came through. She reached the U. S. Embassy!

The uniformed men watched the helicopter. Then, one by one, they lowered their guns.

CHAPTER 60

Tom limped through the hospital doors carrying a bright bouquet of flowers. His other arm remained in its sling, healing from the gunshot wound that happened four days ago on Coffee's yacht. He had seen enough of this small hospital the last four days. He had made friends with much of the staff while he had been in and out receiving care for his own injuries. Mostly, he wanted to make sure Sean was recovering.

"Hi, Erin," Sean said to the front receptionist. "Am I okay to go back?"

"He's awake. Ye know where tae go," she said.

"Marella make it here yet?"

"Na th' now."

Tom nodded and made his way down the hallway to Sean's room, his ankle and feet still stiff and sore. He approached the door and knocked.

"Aye. Come in!" Sean said through the door.

Tom opened it. Sean was sitting up in the hospital bed, holding a prosthetic. The bandage over Sean's knee, and the rest of the leg missing, made Tom shudder. Tom had told himself he'd get over that feeling eventually, but it hadn't happened yet.

Sean noticed the flowers. "My daughter's na' here ye'."

"Actually, these are for you."

"Don' be a fool, lad. Ye know I don' need them."

"I'll just put them over here." He went to the nearby table and placed the flowers onto it. "How are you?"

Sean rested the prosthetic in his lap. "Leg hurts. So does my foot, e'en though 'tis na' there anymore."

"Morphine wore off?"

"Aye."

"It did a number on you yesterday."

"Aye. It did. I told th' doctors tae stop it. Time I get tae healing properly."

"Is that thing going to work for you?" Tom nodded at the prosthetic.

"Na' sure. What's wi' this design?"

"What do you mean?"

"Whoe'er made this ne'er lost a limb."

"Can I get you anything?"

"Na. But ye can tell me wha' happened."

"There was a lot that happened."

"Look at me, lad. I'm na' goin' anywhere."

Tom chuckled, and then he caught himself when Sean's expression didn't change. "They arrested Briggs."

"They did? On wha' charges."

"A bunch. Kidnapping, insurance fraud, accomplice to murder, and attempted murder."

Sean shook his head. "Wha' abou' McGregor?"

"Also arrested. Same charges except kidnapping."

"I'm sure Coffee will pay fur th' lawyers tae ge' them off."

"No he won't. Coffee's dead."

"Dead? Are ye sure?"

Tom closed his eyes and pictured the charred body that sank below the waters. Tom tried to get over that he was the one that pulled the flare gun's trigger that cost a man his life. "Yeah. I'm sure."

"How?"

"Can't say right now. Please trust me on this. Too many people asking questions, and I want to make sure you stay safe."

"Who's askin' questions?"

"Government officials. Lawyers. Police. Reporters. Everybody."

"Wha' are ye tellin' them?"

"The truth. They killed the albino. Then they kidnapped me in order to find the Loch Ness monster. Vaas told me they blew up McGregor's boat for the insurance, and to keep you and me from finding the monster."

"Wha' happened tae Vaas?"

"You don't want to know."

"What'd ye tell them abou' th' monster?"

"That we believe the monster exists, but we have no proof of it."

Sean leaned his head back on his white hospital pillow and shut his eyes. "I don' care if I e'er go on th' Loch again."

Tom nodded. "Me too."

Sean opened his eyes. "Ye didn' tell them th' secret, did ye?"

"What secret?" Tom said, managing a slight smile.

"Ye know. The song…"

Tom winked, and then put his index finger to his closed lips.

"Go' it," Sean said. He rested his head again. His face winced. Sean had to be feeling the pain from his leg. "Where's my daughter? Is she alrigh'?"

"She's fine. She's worried about you. She's on her way."

"Has she made up her mind if she's leavin' fur America?"

"Don't know. She hasn't told me."

"Did ye ask her?"

"I will," Tom said. "You know, she saved my life."

"Did she? How?"

"Called in for reinforcements."

"Reinforcements? My God, wha' happened while I was in here?"

Tom didn't answer. The images of the events the last few weeks kept running through his mind. He admitted that he, too, was trying to make sense of them. He also considered that, if he told Sean what had happened, Sean might become a target for the media and the lawyers. They would come and interview him anyway in a few days. Fortunately, the hospital had instructed the media to stay away until Sean was able to stand, which wouldn't be for some time.

The authorities, however, would usurp the hospital's instructions. Now that Sean was off his morphine, an investigator of some sort would show up. It could be a matter of hours.

At that moment, Sean's door opened. Marella walked in, holding a bouquet of flowers.

"My dear," Sean said. "How are ye?"

"Da'," Marella said. Her lips curved upwards while she held back tears.

"Don' cry. Tom and I were just talkin'."

"I brough' ye these."

Sean nodded to the table, where Tom's flowers rested. Marella placed her flowers next to Tom's.

Marella said, "Ye're na' goin' tae go out on th' water tae hunt fur th' monster any time soon."

"Don' care if I do," Sean said.

Marella paused. "Bu' Da', that's all ye've talked abou' fur thirty years."

"I've been ou' there tae much. Th' monster can take care o' itself."

Tom watched as Marella took in Sean's answer. She stood, disbelieving. Tom caught her eyes with his and nodded.

The curse is broken.

Tom had talked with her the other day about it, and he had wanted to convince her it was true. She, however, had said she wouldn't believe it unless she heard it from her father herself.

"Bu', don' ye wan' tae prove he exists?" Marella asked.

"I have all th' proof I need," Sean said. He pointed to his missing leg. "I know he's there, and that's good enough fur me."

"I don' believe it." Marella blinked, astonished.

"I will tell ye this, though. Lyin' here's given me an idea." Sean raised his prosthetic off his lap to show them. "The nurses gave me this thin'. Canno' believe they expect me tae wear it. Honestly, I could make a better one."

"Ye could?"

"Aye. In fact, would ye do me a favor and brin' me a notebook and a pen and pencil? I wan' tae draw some designs."

Tom stood up. "We'll be glad to. Actually, we have to get going anyway."

"Where are ye goin'?"

"We have to attend a funeral."

"A funeral? Whose?"

Before Tom answered, a nurse walked through the door, pushing a cart. "Mr. Paterson. Tis time fur yer food and medication."

Marella said, "Da'. We'll be back. Just do wha' th' nurses tell ye, and we'll brin' yer notebook tae write on."

Sean turned to the nurse. "Did yer cookin' improve since lest time?"

Tom and Marella left the room in time to hear the nurse say, "Mr. Paterson, ye haven' grown any less stubborn since ye've been here, that's fur certain."

Marella's green eyes shined at Tom as they walked down the hallway. Her eyes flashed a glimmer of hope as her lips curved into a slight smile. Then she reached down, clasped Tom's fingers in hers, and gently squeezed.

CHAPTER 61

Inside St. Michael's Catholic Church, Tom and Marella stood in a row near the front. Several strangers were in the pews next to them. They dressed in black, singing the words to a song Tom didn't know. Tom held one of the blue hymnal books in his hands, but he only mouthed the words to the song, embarrassed that Marella might hear his horrible singing voice.

Father Gibson had said the Mass, and halfway through Marella had whispered to Tom that the homily was wonderful, except Tom didn't know what a homily was. What he did know was that Father Gibson had said all kinds of interesting things about Caleb. About how, when Caleb was a youth, he had helped his neighbors retrieve their dog that was caught in an ocean current, swimming out in the water to bring him back. How he joined the navy when he was first eligible, and became decorated in battle. How after he retired from the military he opened a simple technology business, which he sold quietly to a German company for several million euros. How even with his success he lived simply, offering his time to serve the Church with the gifts God had given him.

Caleb had no children of his own, but he split his estate to an orphanage in Inverness, and to St. Michael's Catholic Church. Father Gibson declared Caleb's life was an example of faith, trusting in God despite the uncertainties of the future.

As Tom pretended to sing the lyrics to the music, Father Gibson processed to the back of the church. Mass was over. Tom and Marella filed out with the others to the back of the church, where Father Gibson talked with attendees and shook their hands.

Tom and Marella walked past Father Gibson. Tom nodded confidently at the priest, but that was it. They did not talk. Tom didn't know who would be watching. It was best, in his mind, to stay apart, and to keep the secret of the Loch Ness monster safe. Father Gibson exchanged nods with Tom, raised his hand gently as if to say, "Thanks," and then he talked with the other attendees.

Tom acknowledged the simple gesture with a wink and a slight smile. Then he led Marella to the doors.

"You know, I'm going to start going to church more often," Tom said.

"Ye don' know th' foremost thing abou' it," Marella said.

"That's the beauty of it. I can learn what I don't know. But I do get a good feeling here."

"Won' always be tha' way. Ye still have tae go when 'tis hard."

Tom nodded. "True. But I won't do it for me. I'll do it for Caleb." Tom reached down and took Marella's hand. "And I'll do it for you."

Marella didn't answer.

They stepped through the church doors into the open. The cool spring air hit Tom in the face, and Marella's hair blew in the breeze. Annabel's Bed and Breakfast was across the street. Tom limped next to Marella, and his arm was still in a sling, but he hid his aches as best he could. To their right, the sun was setting, painting the sky with yellow and red and orange and purple hues.

"Let's go this way." Tom led Marella toward the sunset. The two walked away from the crowd until they were alone. Tom felt Marella's warmth next to him. Her hair glistened like gold under the remaining sunlight. Her perfume smelled like roses.

"So, what are your plans?" Tom asked.

"My father needs me righ' now. I'm goin' tae stay," Marella said.

"You should. It's the right thing to do."

"When are ye goin' back?"

"To America? I'll need to hurry and figure that out."

"Ye don' have tae rush, ye know."

Tom grinned. He understood her hint.

Marella said, "I need tae tell ye, I'm sorry fur th' way I acted when ye arrived. I wouldn' have been able make it through all this withou' ye."

"No need to apologize. You were only doing what you thought was best."

"Bu' I..."

Tom gently put his finger to her lips, and he gave her a warm, calming smile. "It's okay," he said.

She nodded. Her green eyes sparkled under the fading light.

Tom held onto Marella's hand, and he squeezed. His eyes met hers. He hesitated, and then he decided to take a chance. He leaned in to kiss her. As he shut his eyes, and her lips met his under the Scottish Highland sunset, he knew for the first time that they were finally free.

THE END

ACKNOWLEDGEMENTS

There are many to thank for the creation of this novel. Since it is my debut novel, the people who helped me most either inspired me to push through when things got tough, or they educated me on technique and tactics in order to create the finished product.

To those who gave me the fuel of inspiration, I thank first those I have spoken with personally. Fellow authors Carolyn Aspenson, Karen White, Emily Giffin, David Frizzell, Linda Sands, Marsha Roush Cornelius, and Haywood Smith each contributed nuggets of wisdom either in person or through phone calls. With their encouragement, whether it was one word of hope or an hour conversation of strategy, they inspired me to push through.

For those who were not authors, but recognized some ability in me to write, especially Father Matthew and Father Patrick from St. Brendan's Catholic Church in Cumming, GA, I thank them. They set me on a path of study that has been invaluable. Their wisdom about story and human nature raises our spirits in ways that expose us to the deeper meanings of life.

For those authors who have written so much about writing, thank you. I've read about thirty books on the subject, and each of you contributed in some way to my growth. But I want to thank especially James Scott Bell, Robert McKee, Larry Brooks, and Rayne Hall. Yours were the books I referenced the most. This project would not be complete without your advice.

Finally thanks to technology. I researched Scottish government, buildings, roads, and culture to create the fictitious town of Thurwick. Why did I create a fictitious town instead of a real one? Because I know politics, and I wouldn't want to accuse real politicians of corruption, and then go to visit the town. That wouldn't be good. So, I created Thurwick with the help of online research. And, thanks to www.scotranslate.com. One of my beta readers told me, "Your Scottish people speak impeccable English." Yeah, that had to be changed, but I wouldn't have had a chance if I hadn't seen your research.

And thanks to my Beta Readers: David Frizzell, Marc Arrington, Kathy Morgan, Remco Brommet and his daughter Carina, Dottie Marlan, and Robert Rosner. Your comments helped me to strive to be a better writer, to know what I was good at, and to know where I needed work. Your time was invaluable to me, and I'll never forget it.

Finally, thank you to my wonderful wife, RaDonna, who has been so supportive of the time I've spent on this book. Your hope drives me forward!

And thank you to God, and his Son Jesus Christ, for sending me divine help when everything seemed so insurmountable. I know you laughed every time I told you my plans. There definitely is a God, and I'm not him!

ABOUT THE AUTHOR

Matt Kunz is all about the adventure. He has climbed mountains, competed for sports championships, ran for office, and helped lead a city. An Eagle Scout and former walk-on football player at the University of Notre Dame, he spent years contributing to his community as a city councilman and non-profit president in the city of Milton, GA. He learned several insights into team building and human nature during his exploits, many of which can be found inside his books. Whether you pick up a fiction or non-fiction book, you'll find yourself pulled inside the stories, joining with a cast of characters as they experience life's lessons through conflict and suspense. So, don't just sit there. Your journey awaits. Come along, and enjoy the adventure!

Follow Matt on Twitter @MattKunz59, and definitely **sign up for his email list** using the following link:

Sign Up for Matt Kunz's Newsletter
http://eepurl.com/cIyKYP

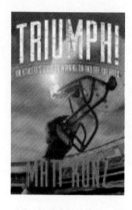 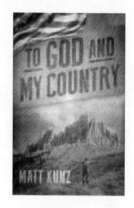

OTHER BOOKS BY MATT KUNZ

TRIUMPH: AN ATHLETE'S GUIDE TO WINNING ON AND OFF THE FIELD

BEFORE THE WHISTLE: FOOTBALL COACHING 101

TO GOD AND MY COUNTRY

Follow Matt on Twitter @MattKunz59, and definitely **sign up for his email list** using the following link:

Sign Up for Matt Kunz's Newsletter
http://eepurl.com/cIyKYP